The Misremembered Lighthouse

By

p.m.terrell

THE MISREMEMBERED LIGHTHOUSE

By p.m.terrell

Published by
Drake Valley Press, a Division of P.I.S.C.E.S. Books, LTD.
USA

Cover illustration inspired by Split Rock Lighthouse.

ISBN 978-1-935970-53-8 (Trade Paperback)
ISBN 978-1-935970-54-5 (eBook)

Author's website: www.pmterrell.com

What reviewers have said about p.m.terrell's historical books:

"Terrell introduces a new level of excellence to the historical novel. Using the mastery of an artist, Terrell paints colorful word pictures and descriptive phrases that are so exquisitely well-chosen that the reader is magnetically drawn into the plot, taking on a role as an active participant in the intrigue of the story." – Richard R. Blake, *Midwest Book Review*

"Truly well-written stories that grab your interest from page one, teaches you a lot of fascinating history, and keeps you from realizing the passage of time as you read. Totally engrossing." – author Maggie Thom

"P M Terrell's historical novels spring to life with vivid characters and descriptions. She is an artist, using words instead of paints to create her masterpieces. Her ability to merge fact and fiction makes reading about history an awesome adventure into the past." – Reviewer Sherry Fundin, *Fundinmental*

"I felt as if I had been to Ireland after I read this book [*April in the Back of Beyond*]. I got so engrossed I even went to my computer to read more about some of its history. Don't get me wrong; this is not a dry history book by any means. It's a story about its wars, its people and its beautiful scenery. It's one of those tales you just don't want to put down. The kind you keep looking at the clock thinking "just 15 more minutes" and pretty soon it's been a couple hours." – *Our Town Book Reviews*

Dedication

This book is dedicated to my grandchildren, Hayley and Hunter. The main character in this book and its companion, *April in the Back of Beyond*, is named after them.

And to Rob Stere, a brilliant world historian and academic. I am grateful for our numerous conversations that have inspired a multitude of historical backdrops, plots, and characters.

1

It felt disconcerting to return to America after a year in Ireland. Yet, here I was, trading the M6 for I-95, a white-knuckle driver who had grown unaccustomed to frenetic traffic after the leisure of Irish villages and quaint roads, most of which were only likely to be impeded by sheep and cattle. Honestly, I would rather be in Ireland right this very minute instead of fretting over aggressive drivers, curled in front of a cozy fireplace with a cuppa, enjoying the last vestiges of cool weather before the official start of spring. Nothing against America, as I'd been born and raised here, but now it felt too young and cheeky.

It hadn't been my idea to leave Ireland, but rather, the government's. My passport stamp expired after a year in the country, and I was required to go elsewhere for twelve months before I could return. I thought of moving across the North Channel to Scotland or further south to England or Wales. I'd toyed with Portugal, Spain, or Italy, which were actively soliciting ex-pats and remote workers like me. The truth was, I could live anywhere while I wrote my historical books.

But in the end, I returned to the States.

I did not return home, as that officially hadn't existed since I sold my condo and moved across the pond. Instead, after much soul-searching, I opted for the North Carolina coast. I wanted a place on the water to somehow feel closer to Ireland, in a home far from the intensity of traffic and people, a land filled with greenery, and a decent distance between me and my closest neighbor. Perhaps, not unlike many Irish immigrants of centuries past, I wanted to face east as if I could somehow still see her. Yes, Ireland was a woman—mercurial in temperament any day of the year, beautiful, wild, and beguiling. I might have left her behind, but I wanted to recreate here what I had experienced there.

It wasn't until I turned off the intense interstate and began navigating a winding road toward the Atlantic coast that my heart rate slowed and my breath deepened. It was close to noon before I passed through the last town, if one could call it that. It consisted of a single, deserted intersection, a few silos that might have been vacant for decades, judging from the unkempt landscape around them, and an isolated general store on a well-worn corner. It might have stood there for a hundred years, everything just as it appeared today. I made a mental note to return to the store after taking possession of my new home. I hoped they had enough to sustain me, as the next closest town was an hour behind me, and it hadn't appeared much larger.

Shortly after passing through, the road narrowed as it wound through farmland and swamps. Vultures soared overhead, their giant wingspans outstretched, searching for an animal that had met its demise.

April was hotter in North Carolina than in Ireland, and I lowered my window to breathe in an unusual aroma of water, salt, and soil. There was something else growing in the fields, plants I didn't recognize that spewed fragrant spores. When I came to the end of the road, it forked into two pockmarked dirt roads barely the width of a car. I turned to the right as my directions indicated.

Deep ditches appeared on either side, with barely a shoulder, had I needed one. My rented car lurched and tumbled over the uneven dirt. I glanced beyond the road to find myself surrounded by swampland. It reminded me of Ireland's ancient bogs, and for a brief moment, I felt some comfort. As I witnessed an alligator turning away from the road to slither into the water, the comfort disappeared, and in its place, I wondered if I had been crazy to rent this house sight unseen in the middle of nowhere. Realtors' pictures and descriptions could be misleading.

Eventually, the swamps parted to reveal a small, flat-topped hill, and upon that mound was my destination: a lighthouse. A chain link fence surrounded the knoll, its wide gate propped open. With relief, I saw the realtor's vehicle parked by the door and rolled my way up the incline to park beside her.

I raised my window lest an alligator or a snake find its way inside, and then I stepped outside, stretching my legs as I surveyed my new home.

In the center of the hill was a squat lighthouse, which now appeared unusually abbreviated for a structure of this nature. It seemed recently painted in an achromatic color that gleamed in the sun. Vibrant red trim at the top, around the windows, and about the base accentuated its unique shape. A more modern structure, around the size of a vestibule, was built at its base.

"What do you think?"

I whirled about to find an attractive woman with shoulder-length blond hair watching me intently.

"I'm Hayley Hunter," I said, extending my hand.

"Billie Keegan," she answered, shaking my hand. She squinted toward the top of the lighthouse. "I hope you enjoy heights," she added as though it were the size of an average lighthouse.

"We'll see, won't we?" I answered. I shielded my hand against the sun's brilliance to peer at the gallery, an open walk with scant railing. At least the railing appeared to be sturdy metal and not decaying wood.

"As I mentioned in my email," Billie was saying, "the lighthouse was originally built in 1770 to guide ships along a channel that used to exist through here. Sadly, it was only in use for about twenty years, as the channels shifted."

"You mentioned it had been abandoned?"

Billie nodded. "That's right. As you can see, it's a bit wild in these parts. I don't know if anybody even remembered it was back here—that is, until the mid-1900s when my uncle bought it as a vacation home. He's the one who renovated it—completely rebuilt it, actually. When he retired in his 70s, he moved here permanently."

"Just himself or his family, too?"

"Never married, so it was just him." She led the way to the alcove built onto the lighthouse. "This is a mud room," she said by way of explanation, passing a small bench and wall pegs as we quickly made our way through to the ground floor. An arched doorway revealed a round room around twenty feet in diameter. Uncovered windows peered out in all four directions. Beneath the windows was a row of polished mahogany cabinets broken only by a spiral staircase, what appeared to be a narrow closet door, and the doorway from which we'd entered. A kitchen island was tucked to one side, and I quickly registered a two-burner stove, oven, sink, and small refrigerator, all of which appeared vintage but decently maintained. Across from the island and in front of a window was a table for two. Tucked into another area was a small sofa and two chairs separated by a small table.

"There are three floors," Billie said, "including the lantern room at the top. As you can see, the ceilings are quite high, and the floors were thickened and reinforced during the rebuild."

"Concrete?" I asked.

She shrugged. "I'm not quite sure, but it's sturdy. It's withstood a host of hurricanes, which is more than I can say about a lot of structures around here." She began to climb the stairs. "The second floor is the bedroom."

As we stepped onto the landing, I spotted a four-poster bed, a tall wardrobe, and a dresser with a mirror. Like the floor below, cabinets encircled the room under uncovered windows. I stepped up to one and peered out. The hill upon which the lighthouse was built was surrounded by wetlands. A consistent canopy of cypress rose from the water. At their knees were reeds that gently bowed to the breeze that made its way across the flat topography. As far as the eye could see, there was nothing but the shimmer of water and a hundred shades of green and blue.

"Beautiful, isn't it?" Billie said as she stood beside me. "That's why there are no drapes on the windows," she added, half-pointing at the window. "There's nobody for several miles."

"It's completely isolated?" I felt myself frowning.

"Oh, it's safe," she hastily added. "There might be a few hunting shacks within a couple of miles."

"Hunting shacks? What do they hunt?"

"Ducks."

"Ah."

"But don't worry. Duck season isn't until October. You won't hear any shots to disturb you."

"So, if duck hunting doesn't start until October, the hunting shacks are empty?"

"Yes. But, as I said, you're perfectly safe." She gave a little half-laugh and stepped to a wall that curved outward from the rest of the room. "I think you'll like the bath. It's small but functional. The well was inspected this past week."

I followed her to a semi-hidden open doorway and peered inside. A claw-foot bathtub reclined in front of a window with a similar view to the one we just witnessed. I immediately envisioned myself enjoying a luxurious soak with a good book and a glass of wine. I stepped to the sink and turned the handle. "Is the water safe to drink?" I allowed some to pool into my palm.

"Absolutely. It won't be crystal clear; blackwater tends to run in these parts. But it's safe. And the contractor treated the well and bled the lines." With that, Billie crossed the room and ascended the spiral stairs to the next level.

I dutifully followed. As I neared the next room, a sudden draft wafted over me. It was unmistakable in the warmth of coastal spring, the cold air causing goosebumps along my exposed skin. I hesitated and peered upward. I spotted a window on the next floor and wondered whether they were properly sealed. I was just about to step onto the next stair when I felt a heavy hand on my shoulder. It bore down as if to stop me, and I hurled around, which was no easy feat with the hand squeezing against my shoulder.

No one was there.

The weight disappeared as suddenly as it had arrived. The draft was gone. I walked back down a few steps, as the spiral stairs were built so they seemed to disappear a few steps below wherever I stood. An odd feeling began to come over me, a sensation that I was not alone. I stood perfectly still. After a moment, it felt like a finger had gently wrapped itself around a strand of my hair.

I smoothed my hair back into place. "Do I need a humidifier here?" I called up to Billie.

As I climbed back to the third floor, I saw her peering down at me with an odd smile. "Maybe a dehumidifier," she chuckled.

I felt my face begin to warm. "It's just that the air— it felt very dry." I cleared my throat. "Maybe the dehumidifier is working too well?"

"There isn't one unless you choose to install it." She waved her hand to encompass the room as I reached the landing. "This is perfect for writing, don't you think?"

I caught my breath. In contrast to the floors below, this room had a continuous flow of windows. In the center was a mahogany pedestal with claw feet. Beneath the windows and encircling the room were more polished cabinets, broken only by the stairs and a door leading to the gallery. A generous ledge was above the cabinets, allowing me to choose the perfect spot for my laptop. "This is incredible," I said in a hoarse whisper.

"I thought you'd like it. When I found out who you were—I mean, the books that you write—I thought of this immediately."

I ran my hand along one of the ledges. "The wood here, it's—"

"Gorgeous, isn't it? Do you know anything about the previous owner?"

I shook my head. "Only that he died recently, and, like you said, he rebuilt the lighthouse where the original once stood. But it seems so new and fresh."

Billie pulled up a chair in front of one of the windows and motioned for me to join her. "His name was Harrison Ellsworth Cooper."

"I've heard that name…" I tried to jog my memory.

"In these parts, people just called him Harry. He was a quiet man, genteel, unassuming."

"You knew him well, then?"

Billie chuckled. "He was my uncle."

"Oh. Yes, you'd mentioned that."

"He was born in 1930 in upstate New York. He moved to New York City as a young man—"

"Of course," I interjected. "I remember reading about him now. He was a real estate tycoon."

"That's right. Real estate and later, investment strategies."

"How did he—I mean, this feels like a world away from New York City."

Billie peered wistfully out the window. "He and my father came here as teens in the 1950s. Duck hunting, you see. They enjoyed the outdoors. Nature." She smoothed her blouse. "Anyway, they both fell in love with the area. They happened upon the original structure, which, according to them, was so derelict they wouldn't dare venture inside. It was originally a wood structure; the stairs had caved in, and the roof was gone…"

"I assume the wetlands had also taken over it."

"Oddly, they hadn't come anywhere close to it. That's what intrigued them both. The top of this hill looked as though it had been recently mowed, though it hadn't. Not a single sapling grew on it. Anyway, Harry bought it. Twenty dollars, I think he said."

"Are you serious?"

"Twenty dollars, and the locals thought he was an idiot. But he kept coming back. He had the original lighthouse torn down and built this one. Wood was replaced with brick. As he grew wealthier, he was able to envision the interior in a way it could never have been before. That's all the mahogany you see." She ran her finger along the ledge. There wasn't a speck of dust on it.

"When Harry retired, he moved here permanently. That's when the kitchen and bath were put in."

I peered out the window. I pointed to the chain-link fence, bent by the winds, that encircled the bottom of the hill. "Is that the property line?"

"No. The property extends about a hundred acres in a circumference around the hill."

"Then, why—?"

"Harry had a dog, a white German shepherd."

"But the fence doesn't reach across the driveway, unless—?"

"The fence wasn't installed to keep the dog in. It's to keep the gators out." Billie took a breath. "Lola was just a pup when Harry adopted her. Even as an adult, she'd have been no match for a gator. The fence extends underground."

"And they won't just find the opening in the driveway?"

"They never have. There's a gate in any event; I opened it for your visit."

"Oh, yes, that's right. I noticed. And the vultures? They couldn't pluck a puppy off the lawn?"

"Vultures never will. They prefer carcasses. You want them around, actually. Anyway, that's a subject for another day." She stood, returned the chair, and moved into the center of the room. Standing, I noticed steel channels in the windows and iron grates covering the exteriors. I imagined the punishment this structure must receive in this hurricane-prone region.

Billie remained in the center, and when I turned around, she gestured to the lighthouse lamp resting atop the clawfoot pedestal. "The original would have burned whale oil," she said enthusiastically. "This one was to be powered by electricity."

"Was?"

She shook her head. "Harry didn't live to see it function."

"But—he passed away only recently?"

"About a month ago. No, it wasn't that. He had electricity run up here, but the light never worked. They could never figure out why." She glanced around as if she could spot the answer.

"That's odd." I strolled around the lamp, noting the components inside that would magnify the light to ships passing in the night. "Maybe it requires higher voltage?"

Billie shrugged. "I haven't the foggiest. But, it's not like ships are going to pass by here, huh?" She stepped to a doorway across from the stairs. "Come outside," she beckoned.

I turned abruptly and gasped. A portrait hung from a chain in front of one of the windows, placing the man's face just above eye level. "Is this Harry?"

Billie laughed. "Not hardly."

I stared into his face. It was an old portrait painted in dark colors. Only the bright Carolina skies and the determined sun managed to coax the details into the open. The man had dark hair and a black, closely manicured beard. His eyes also appeared black, the pupils nearly blending into the surrounding irises. There was something abnormal about his skin, what little I could see; he was almost too pale. Then my eyes fell on his shoulders. The red fabric, blue collar, and brass buttons were unmistakable. "He's a British soldier," I said flatly.

Billie remained in the doorway, unlikely to join my side. "Harry found the painting during renovation. He hung it here, and he didn't want it removed after his death."

"I wonder why. Is it an ancestor?"

"Absolutely not. We were Colonialists. We fought for independence."

"But he wanted it to remain here?"

Billie opened the door wider.

I forced myself out of my head and reluctantly moved to join her. The eyes seemed to follow me across the room. They were stern eyes. Determined. Focused. It was only when I stepped onto the gallery outside the lantern room that I was able to break the spell.

The gallery jutted out from the rest of the structure by about five feet. The firm flooring and metal railing dissipated any fear I might have had as I made my way completely around. The breeze I'd experienced on the ground was replaced at this height by a relentless wind that caused me to reach for my long brown hair and restrain it at my neck so that I could see. I suppose I couldn't view any more from this height as I had from the floor below, but the bouquet of salt on the inland winds mingled with the flora and fauna to transport me to another place and time. I could imagine a lighthouse keeper circling the lantern room, watching for ships laden with goods navigating inland from the Atlantic coast. Perhaps I should get a book on lantern signals, I thought impulsively.

"Once upon a time," Billie said mischievously, "this inlet was a wide and deep channel that led to the Cape Fear

River. That, in turn, led to a point near Wilmington. It was a bustling port during and after the Revolutionary War."

"But, why did the lighthouse only operate for twenty years?" I shook my head.

"Storms." With that, she returned to the lantern room. Reluctantly, I followed her. "So, is this what you had in mind?" she asked hopefully.

"Yes," I heard myself saying. "It's perfect for my writing. You're sure everything is in order? Electricity, water?"

"Even Wi-Fi, though I can't say how reliable it will be here. It comes fully furnished just as you see it. And, after a one-year lease, perhaps you'll even want to purchase it."

I forced myself to chuckle. It was lovely, but it wasn't Ireland, so let's get real. "We'll see."

"Come," she said, smiling. "I'll show you how to use all the appliances. The home even features solar panels on the cupola, allowing it to generate power independently. And," she continued as she started down the stairs, "I took the liberty of stocking the frig with a few items. But if I were you, I'd certainly consider a dog because it's so isolated. There's a shelter not too far of a drive from here…"

2

I'd fallen asleep on the ground floor sofa and awakened to a darkening sky. As I sat up, my phone slipped out of my pants pocket and landed on the hardwood floor with a thud. The screen lit up as I retrieved it, and I was surprised to discover several texts from Shay MacGregor. I wasn't one to sleep through the alerts. The last one asked me to phone or text as soon as I saw the message, regardless of the time.

I groaned as I checked the clock. My body was still on Irish time, and I was suffering jet lag I hadn't experienced when I'd left America for Europe a year prior. No doubt I'd wake up Shay, but I knew he'd be worried if he didn't hear from me.

I tried calling, but I discovered that my phone had no signal, and my texts remained undelivered. I was just about to give up when I decided to ascend to the top of the lighthouse.

The lantern room was lit up in a cozy orange and red glow. As I selected Shay's number, his face popped up on my phone screen. It was a picture I'd snapped on one of our forays into the Inishowen Peninsula. The sun was setting behind him just as it was with me now. He looked relaxed, his green eyes twinkling, his chestnut hair tussled by the Irish wind, his dark beard broken by a wide smile. The photograph brought back warm memories; after corresponding about my Irish ancestors, he'd agreed to meet me in his capacity as a university historian to lend research assistance for my latest book, which had recently been released. Suffice it to say that our relationship didn't remain entirely professional for long, and my heart ached that I hadn't been allowed to remain near him.

"Hayley?" His voice was thick with sleep. "So, you're alright, then? You had me quite the worried one."

"Did I wake you?" I asked, knowing full well I had.

His voice changed slightly, and I pictured him rising to rest on an elbow. "It's one o'clock in the morning, darling. Are you alright?"

"I'm fine. Sorry to wake you. It's evening here." I peered out the window at the horizon. The landscape didn't look real but rather like a comforting French impressionist painting. The reeds bowed in the evening breeze, and the water reflected its surroundings like stained glass. The terrain beneath the cypress trees was becoming dark and shadowy, their characteristic cypress knees appearing like miniature wood carvings peeking out of the water. Two seagulls crisscrossed paths as they searched for food below. I opened a window to allow the scent of the water to reach me.

"Are you settled in, then?"

"For today, yes."

"Talk to me about the lighthouse. Is it what you expected?"

I told him about each floor and the history of the place, as I knew his historian mind would appreciate the nuances of a squat lighthouse built upon the banks of a channel fated to reroute away from it. I explained that I didn't know much about its original construction, but I'd learned a bit about the man who restored it. As I glanced at the rich, dark wood around me, I appreciated Harry's attention to detail and the finer things in life. "And how are you?" I ended. "How is the conference going?"

"Ah. The conference. It's been quite interesting. You would enjoy it. There's a lad here with mountains of information from YDNA tests. They have the ability to define family trees in a way we've never experienced before."

"And what of your talks?"

"Mine have been well attended. There's quite a bit of interest in Irish history, so there is. We have a varied audience—even a couple from Canada."

We chatted a bit about his prepared lectures on ancient Irish history. I was pleased to learn there was so much interest. Shay MacGregor was a noted historian connected with the prestigious University of Galway. In our first meeting, he'd spoken of his Gallowglass ancestors, a mix of Scottish Highlanders and Vikings. Some even classified them as mercenaries to fight ancient wars between Irish factions. I could picture him on a captain's deck as though it were the 18th century, ordering those below him to guide the ship into port, his feet planted wide apart and his hands on his hips.

"And how are The Netherlands?" I asked.

"Beautiful, as always. The hotel is superb. It's right on the Amstel. I'm looking out the window now at boats moving past. They look peaceful in the moonlight. It would make for a romantic getaway." His voice turned silky.

"Then, let's put it on our bucket list," I said. I took a soft breath. "I think you'll find the lighthouse a great spot for a romantic getaway as well."

"I'm looking forward to seeing it, love, and experiencing it with you."

"Your plans haven't changed?"

"Not even banshees could stop me. I should be there within the week. I'll send you my arrival time."

"And you'll spend the summer?"

"Absolutely—apart from a conference in New York. It's what we discussed, is it not?"

I smiled, though I knew he couldn't see my face light up. "Yes. I've missed you."

He said something then, but my mind was shaken by a brilliant light that shone behind me. Whipping around, I discovered the lantern had turned on by itself. I nearly dropped the phone in my surprise, and I quickly described what had happened to Shay. "I don't understand it," I said, moving toward the switch by the open stairs. "Billie—the realtor—told me it had never worked." I flipped the switch, but it had no effect.

I moved around the room, searching for another switch. As I did, the light went out. "It's off now," I said shakily. "But I didn't turn it off."

"But you muddled with the wall switch, you said?"

"Yes, but…" My voice faded in my confusion.

"Sounds like a faulty connection to me."

I became aware of my heart pounding in my chest and a deep chill permeating the room. I closed the window, though the outside air felt balmy in contrast. "Yes," I managed to croak. "A faulty connection. That must be it."

"I'll sort it when I arrive. In the meantime, do be careful plugging things in, 'eh? Use things the Irish way and unplug them when they're not in use."

His suggestion brought to mind how I paid for electricity in advance and kept an eye on an indoor meter to monitor my usage. "I will," I said, "though the power here will take some getting used to. The lighthouse is self-sufficient with solar panels."

"Ah," he said. "That's grand, though perhaps a wee bit faulty, 'eh?"

I circled the lantern as we wrapped up our conversation. There were no visible wires, which meant the wiring must have been snaked through the hollow stand. My eyes swept toward the wall switch, where a plastic tube was expertly painted to blend in with the wall. I followed it as it reached the floor and became hidden underneath the polished floorboards. As we hung up, I flipped the switch twice more, but nothing happened; there appeared to be no bulbs except the lantern, and why should there be? The brilliant light was designed to be visible for miles, dwarfing any other light source that might have been present.

I backed up and felt something give way behind me. Alarmed, I spun around to find the painting swaying from the chain on which it hung. It was disconcerting, to say the least, as the portrait was life-size and his eyes were mere inches above mine. He seemed to look down on me, locking my eyes with his own.

"I don't know who you are," I said shakily, "but you shouldn't scare me like you do." I reached up and fumbled with the chain until I removed the portrait. It was heavier than I imagined, and it took both hands to slide it delicately to the floor. I turned it around to face the vestiges of the sunset. "There," I said, sounding more confident than I felt. "That's better. Now you can see the scenery. Did you once live here?"

As soon as I spoke, I realized I would run for the hills—a good three hours away as the crow flies—had I received an answer. With a final glance at the lantern, which now sat still and dark, I made my way down the spiral staircase to the bedroom a flight below.

~~~~~

I awakened shortly after one. I wondered briefly if it was instant karma for having awakened Shay before realizing that my body would likely remain on Irish time for a few days. The air had turned colder in the absence of the sun's warmth, and I snuggled under the light cotton sheets and summer blanket. I was surprised to see the skies from my bed, as I'd grown accustomed to small, cozy rooms with deep-set windows and tidy curtains. I felt exposed since more than half the walls consisted of uncovered windows, but the focus on myself faded quickly as I realized how brilliant the skies appeared.

I found myself staring at the seemingly countless stars twinkling in the night sky. There must not have been a cloud in the sky, and there was no artificial light pollution to interfere with nature's brilliance. I could visualize Vincent van Gogh gazing at skies identical to these, his easel beside an open window. The stars seemed like living, breathing beings, and I marveled at how they remained so fixed and luminous.

An intense flash turned the night sky into day for the briefest of moments, and I instinctively began to count from the lightning flash to the thunder, but I never heard the expected boom. It must be far away, I thought, snuggling myself deeper into the covers. I closed my eyes as I pictured a cozy lightning storm while I drifted back to sleep. I was in the safest of places, I realized. I envisioned a ship with tall masts making its way up a wide, deep channel in the dead of night, the lighthouse a beacon of safety, the keeper perhaps standing on the open gallery with a rain slicker and hood, pelted by the rain as he guided the ship safely through the water. He had a black beard, closely cropped, and wore a red suit under the dark coat.

Another flash of light occurred through the thinness of my eyelids, and I dutifully counted the seconds. Instead of thunder, another flash occurred, and I counted again.

Then my eyes flew open. I sat up in bed as the air seemed to swirl around me. It was as though a door or window had been opened in the lantern room, and the strength of a windswept storm was billowing down the stairs toward me. When the light flashed again, I counted wide-eyed. It was the same. They were all the same.

I bounded from the bed and dashed to the nearest window. It wasn't lightning that caused the night to turn to day. There wasn't a cloud in the sky. It was the lighthouse.

I backed away from the spiral staircase as though it were a snake in my room. It couldn't be. The logical part of my brain deduced a short in the electricity. Billie had said the lantern never worked. Perhaps, I told myself, it had never worked *properly*. Maybe the proximity to the elements had rusted a connection somewhere. That had to be it. Like Shay had said, there was a faulty connection.

Well, I owed it to myself and the lighthouse owner to ensure the lighthouse wasn't about to catch fire. Didn't I?

I struggled to calm my racing heart. Then I made my way to the landing and peered upward. From this angle, I could see the light rhythmically circling. At one point, it appeared as if something was interfering with the lantern's light, almost as if someone was standing in front of it, waving a blanket. Or a flag.

I stepped onto the first step, grateful for the solid wood beneath my feet. This was no shaky, hastily constructed spiral staircase. It had rails on both sides and polished mahogany steps so thick that they'd clearly been built to last. I remained on the outside nearest the wall as the inner section of each circling step narrowed. I could only see a few steps in front of me and a few steps behind, and I tried to calm my imagination as I encountered each curve.

The light abruptly died once my head became visible above the lantern room floor. Aha, I told myself. Perhaps I touched a loose hardwood strip, and it caused the connection to falter. Maybe I even stepped on the same spot the evening before. But as I entered the room, I knew that neither had occurred. I hadn't caused the light to begin flashing and rotating, and I hadn't caused it to cease.

I remained transfixed midway between the stairs and the lantern table, staring at it. I tried willing myself to awaken, though I knew I was not sleepwalking. My eyes moved from the confines of the room to the windows. The stars remained luminescent. There still wasn't a cloud in the sky.

It took some time for my heartbeat to return to normal. I told myself that certainly there was nothing here to hurt me. But perhaps I needed a few security cameras. Once I discovered where they could be sent, I could order them easily enough. Then, instead of wandering up and down the stairs in my bare feet, I could lie in the comfort of the bed and peer at a phone app while assuring myself that all was well. Cameras would require less upkeep than a dog.

At the thought, I missed Shay's gorgeous Irish Setter, Sadie. She would have navigated the stairs to the lantern room in the time it took me to reach the first landing. Her mere presence would have calmed and reassured me. For a fleeting moment, I thought of calling Shay and asking him to bring her. Then I remembered the awful, lengthy quarantine dogs often endured when they crossed the Atlantic, and I knew it wasn't practical. While he visited me, Sadie would remain with Shay's sister, Bella, and I would buy security cameras. I almost felt as though my thoughts had accomplished something significant.

I hugged myself in the chill of the night and turned to leave when something caught my eye. I turned slowly, almost inconspicuously.

The portrait hung in the window, the man facing inward to follow me with his dark, brooding eyes.

3

I felt rather silly in the bright light of day as I drove to the meager intersection I'd passed through the day before. I tried convincing myself that I'd only thought I'd removed the portrait, though a debate raged in my mind as I thought of the stubborn chain and the unexpected weight. But that had to be the answer, I argued, as a weighty portrait wasn't going to spin around and find its way back up the wall, now was it? It had also been perfectly level, which was unlikely if it had jumped back up there. No, there were only two explanations. Either I had imagined removing it, or I'd sleepwalked and hung it back up myself. There. Issue explained.

I parked my car in the vacant lot and wondered if the general store was even operational. The building resembled something out of a mid-century noir film. If the Bates Motel had an attached general store, this could be it. The door was on the corner and consisted of an old screen with enough holes to allow a cat in, and I wondered why they bothered with it. I stepped inside to discover a hefty door that was pulled back and held in place by a rock. A rather unpleasant mixture of odors reminded me of raw meat on the counter, musty shelves, and overripe produce. It was larger than it had appeared from the outside, with long, narrow rows and a register off to one side. I glanced upward to find that most of the sparsely hanging lights were turned off or burned out, which accounted for the gloom.

As I stepped toward the register to grab an old-fashioned wire basket with aged wood handles, I realized the sign over it read "Dikshita General Store and Post Office." Peering more closely, I discovered a minuscule bank of post office boxes behind the register. I felt excitement well up inside me.

Looking around, I came eye-to-eye with a man hovering behind a stack of boxes so tall that it had formed a wall. But, rather than his head atop his neck in a straight line, he appeared to be hiding behind the boxes. He stuck his head out sideways like the old pull-out tabs in children's books, so only his eyes, forehead, and top of his head were visible.

"Excuse me," I said. "May I rent a post office box from you?"

His head disappeared only to reappear a moment later as if to see whether I was still there.

I pointed to the wall of post office boxes. "Do you have an available one I can rent?" I said a little louder. I smiled pleasantly.

His head disappeared again.

"I've leased the lighthouse," I offered, speaking to the boxes. "I think they call it the Cooper Lighthouse? Harry Cooper's old home?"

The eyes reappeared.

"I can see you, you know."

They disappeared.

"I'm still here. I'm picking up a few items and need a post office box." After a moment, I sighed audibly.

The screen door banged behind me. "Oh, miss, can I help you?"

I turned to face a man with a wide, pleasant face and a mountain of hair. "Yes," I said, smiling. "I want to rent a post office box."

"Of course, of course." He hurried around to the other side of the counter. Spying the other man hiding behind the boxes, he said something to him that I couldn't quite catch. When he turned back to me, he appeared more than a little annoyed. "Please excuse him," he said, tilting his head. "I had a quick errand and left him in charge."

I didn't respond. He slid a piece of paper toward me and rustled through the counter until he found a pen. "I just need this filled out." As I started to write, he said, "So, you're not from around here."

"I'm renting Harry Cooper's old place." I hesitated. "This form needs my home address, but I don't know—"

"Don't bother with that. We all know Harry's Lighthouse."

"So—that's what it's called?"

He nodded. "Do you want to pay by the week or the month?"

"The full year, if I may." I reached into my wallet for a credit card.

"A year? In Harry's Lighthouse?"

"Yes. I've leased it for the year."

He looked at the credit card. "Maybe you'll want to pay for a month and see how it works out. The box, I mean."

"No, I'd just as soon know I have it for the full year. Unless you plan to be going somewhere?" I glanced around.

He chuckled a bit nervously. "I'm Argo Dikshita," he said. "My family has been here for more than two hundred years, so I doubt I'm going anywhere."

"Ah." I glanced at the sign above the register. "Is that the town's name, also?"

"If you can call it a town, yeah. And you are—" He glanced at the form I'd just completed.

"Hayley Hunter," I offered.

"The author?"

"I'm afraid so."

He reached under the counter and handed me a key. "You don't need to ask for your mail," he said pleasantly. "Especially if Beckett is in charge." He glanced at a spot as if he could peer through the boxes to the other side. "Just raise the counter at the end there and get your mail yourself. You have that box there. Number 10."

"You trust me to do that? Behind the register, I mean?"

"Everybody does it."

"I see. Well, thank you, Mister Dikshita."

"Argo."

"Argo. Can you write down the mailing address for me? I assume you take packages here?"

"FedEx, UPS, postal service, you name it."

"Excellent. I'm just going to pick up a few food items, too, while I'm here. I might stand here for a moment and order some security cameras to be delivered here, too, if you have Wi-Fi."

"Absolutely, we have Wi-Fi." He handed me half a dozen business cards, each with a different vocation. "We're the post office, tree removal, electrician, plumber—" he waved his hand "—and of course, the grocery and hardware store. In fact," he said excitedly, "I just got in some security cams. Want to see them?"

I hesitated, picturing a 1940s version covered in dust, but he produced them faster than I could react. To my surprise, they were exactly what I had in mind.

"I put the wireless in for Harry," Argo was saying. "These work on that system, and you don't even have to worry about a power failure—"

"Let me guess. You installed the solar panels."

"I did." He beamed. "It was Beckett there who crawled onto the cupola. But I wired everything. Even during hurricanes, the power at Harry's never went out. Not for a second. Can't say that about every place in these parts." He chuckled.

"Then, can you tell me about the electricity to the lantern room?"

His smile faded. "Are you having issues?"

"Billie told me the lantern didn't work, and I wondered…"

"Oh, the lantern will work. I checked it out on the floors below."

"Then, is there an electrical problem on that floor?"

He shifted from one foot to the other. The door opened, and a burly man called out a boisterous greeting. "Oh, Teddy," Argo said, "I have that bait you asked for—" With that, he was gone, rushing around the corner to attend to his other customer.

I inspected the security camera packaging. They were tabletop models, so they could be moved around as needed, or I could mount them. Tabletop would do, for now. I added two to my basket and picked up the paper with my new address. It read in neat block letters: Post Office Box 10, Dikshita, North Carolina, followed by the zip code. That was easy enough to remember. Then, I turned toward the groceries and began planning my meals.

In the end, it was Beckett who carried the bags out to my car. Surprisingly, he was a pleasant-looking young man. He was wiry with closely cropped blue-black hair and large brown eyes that reminded me of a doe. He was very careful when placing my bags, tying off the plastic handles so the contents wouldn't spill out, and testing to ensure nothing fell over on my drive home. I attempted to tip him, but he retreated. Perhaps he was mute, I thought. I smiled as pleasantly as I could as he backed his way through the door to the store.

4

I munched on a sandwich on the ground floor while I gazed out the window across the secluded swamps. Afterward, I made my way to the third floor. I set up my laptop in front of the window furthest from the portrait and paused while contemplating my surroundings. If I hadn't known better, I might have thought I was gazing at the bogs in Ireland.

I wondered at the Irish who left everything they knew to migrate to America. In search of a new life in a land they knew nothing about, the language and customs were often quite different and must have been jarring. Many immigrants would find their way to places similar to what they'd left behind. The Highlander Scots would migrate to the mountains, Scandinavians often moved to colder climates, and the Irish—well, the Irish would go in search of a livelihood, wherever that might take them.

It was, after all, why I was here. I would begin my genealogy work online, as I always did, and then I would hit the road to track down historians, archaeologists, and genealogists for on-site research. Just as I had left Ireland two days ago, my ancestors migrated generations earlier in search of new opportunities. While I had known America, having been born and raised here, and was returning to something familiar, they had been sailing into the unknown. And what had taken me a few hours in an airplane had taken them six weeks aboard a ship.

First, however, I had a job to do. I departed for the ground floor and returned with one of the cameras I'd purchased from the Dikshita General Store. I easily connected to Wi-Fi, silently thanking Harry for his attention to detail in restoring the old lighthouse. After some deliberation, I set the camera on the ledge opposite the spiral staircase. The wide-angle option allowed me to view almost the entire floor, including the mysterious portrait. I placed the second one on the kitchen counter on the ground floor, which had a good view of the door and nearly the entire floor.

Satisfied, I returned upstairs, opened my laptop, and connected that device to Wi-Fi. The signal was surprisingly good up here, and I reviewed the information I'd compiled thus far. In the 1720s, three of my ancestors left Ulster, where one had owned a fleet of ships, to settle in America. It was customary in those days for ocean vessels to transport passengers and cargo. It would be another 120 years before the Great Hunger, when the ships would be converted into famine ships, carrying scores of people crammed in like sardines, desperate to flee imminent starvation. Their journeys were quite literally ones of life and death.

My ancestors fared better than many. They landed in Pennsylvania, and after a time, they separated. While one brother remained in the Philadelphia area, another moved to New York, and a third to Virginia. It was the third one I was currently researching; he would move to the North Carolina Territory and eventually become involved in the American Revolution. The North Carolina Territory stretched from the Atlantic Ocean and encompassed North and South Carolina, Georgia, and Florida, and as far west as Tennessee and Mississippi. From 1712 to 1776, it was known as the Province of North Carolina or Albemarle Province. That meant when my ancestor fought in present-day Tennessee, the records would be housed in Raleigh, North Carolina.

I logged onto the Raleigh Archives. They had an impressive and extensive online data collection, including entire sections on the Revolutionary War, land holdings, and family records. I knew my ancestors had been granted land after the war in return for their contributions to fighting the British. One had received 4,800 acres, which led me to believe he had played an instrumental role. It didn't take long for me to locate the grants.

I realized things were a bit odd as I reviewed information handed down through the generations. They had fought for the King or Queen of England as far back as 1608. It was in that year that my ancestors migrated from Lowland Scotland to Ulster, in what was known as the Plantation Era. In return for fighting for King James in O'Doherty's Rebellion, one ancestor was granted a thousand acres at the base of the Inishowen Peninsula. In 1641, his son would defend Derry during the siege inflicted by the Jacobites and receive 1,500 acres in County Tyrone. Then, in 1689, his grandchildren would fight for the king again at Derry, now renamed Londonderry —a name never accepted by the native Irish, even today.

They had been loyal subjects of the Crown. Yet, they had turned on England in the 18th century and fought against her. One ancestor would receive 640 acres along Gooses Creek; another would be granted 640 acres along the Cumberland River, and a third ancestor 640 acres at Cedar Creek. Two more were granted 640 acres each, but I didn't have the locations. That meant these men might have been privates; for each month they served, they received 7.6 acres in place of money. Money was scarce, but land was plentiful. If they served for the entire war, a total of 84 months, they were eligible for 640 acres. If they served as a major during the whole time, they received more than 57 acres per month, totaling 4,800 acres, which accounted for one very illustrious ancestor. By all accounts, my family had joined the rebellion early, turning on the same Crown that had granted them thousands of acres in their ancestral land.

I leaned back in my chair. Only 78 years later, their grandchildren would face a similar choice. Some would join another rebellion against their new country and fight on behalf of the newly formed Confederate States of America. Others would remain loyal to the United States, pitting brother against brother and father against son.

I realized that the afternoon had flown by while I was immersed in the digital archives. Though the sun set behind the lighthouse to the west, the brilliant reds and oranges were reflected in the window panes. From this vantage point, I could see across the tops of the trees to the horizon far beyond. As the skies morphed from the serene blue of daylight to the mysterious deep indigo of twilight, the landscape became heavier and haunting. The shadows grew deep, so the canopies of trees became intertwined in one dark ink-stroke, and the swamps beneath them transformed into black pools.

Though the windows were closed, I felt a drafty chill in the air. My eyes instinctively pivoted to the portrait. It remained perfectly still as the air swirled around me like a growing storm. I stood, closing my laptop and cutting off the last of the artificial light. I was left with the faintest twinkling of stars and a muted glow from a moon struggling to be relevant behind fast-moving clouds. I hugged myself against the cold as I made my way around the room. Finally, the chill became too much, and I retreated downstairs to my bedroom.

5

A chime penetrated my dreams. I had been standing on the gallery atop a lighthouse, but it wasn't the same one that I now leased. It was made entirely of wood and released an earthy and comforting aroma. At first, I thought the chime was part of my dreams. But as I stirred, I realized the sound came from my mobile phone. Groggily, I reached for the phone to discover a series of alerts indicating that one of my cameras had detected activity.

I bolted upright and tapped on the latest alert. I found myself staring at the lantern room. The security camera encompassed nearly the entire circular room, save for the wall behind it. My eyes skimmed the walls, alighting briefly on each window. The moon was high and full, and for a moment, I thought the camera might have picked up the glow or perhaps even something flying against the window. But as I continued to stare into my phone, I spotted something moving along the top steps as if ascending.

I quietly tossed the covers off me and glided into my slippers as I grabbed my robe. I cautiously strode to the spiral stairs to peer upward into the stairwell. It was not as dark as I had expected, but a muted light from the moon struggled to illuminate it. I glanced downward to discover it was darker beneath me. Turning my attention again to the stairs leading upward, I remembered the curvature in the design prevented me from seeing to the top. How, then, my mind argued, could the moonlight find its way down?

I stepped onto the staircase. My right hand clenched the phone, while my eyes continually moved from the image on my screen to the steps above me. My naked eyes could see nothing out of the ordinary. The steps appeared just as they had a few hours earlier. But my phone displayed a shadow moving upward.

As I reached the uppermost stairs, I realized the image picked up by the security camera was not a human, but rather a human form. It was opaque, but I detected the outline of a man's broad shoulders, his torso, arms, and legs. His legs were misshapen, as though he were wearing breeches that ballooned slightly from him. There was something else that extended beyond his body, like a waistcoat. I could see the outline of his head, but it was shadowy, with facial details absorbed into the darkness.

I froze on the step. I could see the image clearly on my phone's security app. But when I used my naked eyes without the benefit of the phone, I could see nothing at all in the spot where it should have appeared. Shakily, I climbed to the next step and then the next.

The figure moved just beyond me as if to entice me to follow him. As my head topped the floor, it turned to me, as if he was looking straight at me, though I could see nothing but darkness where his face should have been. Then, the shadow began to pulse, and it turned into an orb that glided around the room.

I blinked, unable to comprehend what I was seeing. Nothing was before me except the room I'd left a few hours earlier. Yet on my camera app, I watched the orb move from window to window, pausing slightly at each one.

I stepped onto the floor, convinced there was something in the night sky that created such unusual effects. But as I stopped to gaze out one of the windows, the moon and the stars remained distant and stationary. They couldn't have created such an illusion.

I turned around to face the room just as my laptop swung open and came to life, the screen casting a blue glow throughout. Then, the lantern burst into a brilliant light that rotated outward through the windows, illuminating the gallery beyond.

The orb was gone.

I felt the blood draining from my face as I surged forward. I must have tossed my phone onto the table that held the lantern as both hands searched frantically for a switch to turn off the light. There had to be a short somewhere. My thoughts became disjointed, as though they had somehow separated from my body.

Finding no switch, I rushed to the light switch on the wall, but jiggling it had no effect. I found myself back at the lantern, determined to shut it off for no reason other than to take control of this crazy situation. I shook the tall, slender table that was only slightly larger than the lantern itself. My phone thudded to the hardwood floor. My fingers groped along the bottom of the lantern; it was permanently affixed to the table stand. I tried to pull it up and out, but it was anchored to something beneath it. My hands sought each side of the table, prodding and grappling for something to shut off the light that seemed to have a mind of its own.

Then, one side swung open.

I dropped to my knees in front of it as the light went out. The beam's intensity was so bright that the loss plunged me into an inky blackness, with murky dots dancing in front of me. As my eyes adjusted, the room took on a muted purple hue, and I realized my laptop was closed again. Had I only imagined that it had opened?

My heart pounded so forcefully that my chest ached. Despite my urge to run down the stairs, I groped inside the stand until I located the electric cord coming from the lantern. I tried to follow it to a plug only to find the lantern was already unplugged.

I grabbed my phone and shone its flashlight into the hollow stand. An outlet had been installed, but it was unused. Only one electric cord dangled within, and I held that in my hand. As I continued shining my light from the top of the interior to its bottom, I noticed the wood inside was older than the exterior, as if a new sheath had been installed atop the old one. The interior consisted of several boards held together by thin strips of wood.

I don't know why I began disassembling it. Perhaps I thought I would find something that had somehow managed to short the lantern into alighting. But I pulled at the strips of wood until they popped away from the boards, and then the interior began to fall away like a house of cards.

A spider scurried across the back of my hand, startled by the intrusion into its well-hidden home, and I frantically shook it off me. I pushed the lantern out of the crevice at the top of the stand. Just as I started to stand up to pull it the rest of the way out, something caught my eye. It was dark and rectangular at the base of the stand. I pulled the remaining boards away to find a small, leather-bound book covered in a thick layer of dust.

I grasped it and unsteadily came to my feet. My heart was still palpitating, and I placed a hand over my chest in a vain effort to calm myself. The lantern had shorted, I told myself. And I knew how to take care of that. I'd pull the whole dang thing out of the stand and place it on the ledge. Tomorrow, I will remove it from the room entirely.

I placed the book and my phone on a ledge while I snaked the electric cord out of the stand, wrapped it around the base of the lantern, and moved it to the top step of the spiral staircase. Then I left the mess I'd made behind me, grabbed the phone and book, and made my way back down the stairs.

I should have been wide awake from the frenetic activity, but I felt almost drugged as I reached my bedroom. I placed the items on the nightstand, lay back atop the bed, and promptly fell asleep.

6

It was an unusually balmy day for April, even by coastal North Carolina standards. I sat outside the lighthouse at a wrought iron table sized for two on a petite flagstone patio. Crepe myrtles, hydrangeas, and seasonal flowers surrounded me in varying stages of spring awakening. I recalled Billie's comment about the absence of fauna on the mound when Harry found it, but he'd obviously been successful at changing that. There was a pleasant, earthy aroma in the air. I took a sip of hot tea and leaned back in my chair. Mingled with the scent of fauna was an undeniable tang of wood burning. My eyes scanned the treetops surrounding me, but I saw no telltale wisps of smoke. The wind was almost imperceptible, so it was difficult, but not impossible, to imagine the aroma wafting for miles to reach me.

I gingerly divided a biscuit and spread blackberry jam on one half. Although I may no longer be in Ireland, certain customs, such as tea and a scone-like biscuit, felt part of my soul now.

I ran the fingers of my left hand across the leather-bound book, careful to keep my right hand from accidentally marring it with my breakfast. Feeling like an archeological historian, I'd gently cleaned off the dust earlier in the day with a fresh cosmetics brush. The leather appeared handcrafted, with edges that were not perfectly straight, and a pattern created with a leather puncher of sorts. I pulled the book onto my lap and opened it to the first page.

It was not a published book but a journal. The words were written carefully, each letter painfully correct, the lines straight. Despite the lengthy entries, it appeared to have been written with a quill and ink, giving it the appearance of calligraphy.

On the first page was the name Jonathan Corbyn, followed by the year 1776. I turned the page to the first entry dated January 3, 1776.

"Those who advocate war are those who have never fought in a battle. They puff their chests and speak forcefully against the King and Crown as though they could snap their fingers and replace one with another. But they do not know the horrors that await a man in battle. They have never witnessed swords severing hands and limbs, bayonets piercing a man's gut while the enemy stares into his face with sheer hatred—or worse, in childlike terror. They have never observed the indiscriminate damage of musket fire. For each man who is wounded or killed, a family somewhere will also feel the pain; their lives will be forever altered, the void never filled, and the struggles to survive often just beginning. They have not trampled through mud and swamps, borne the pain and humiliation of dysentery while marching, a hunger that cannot be fully met, or the shock of a man calling himself a battlefield doctor who may not own the qualifications to be operating.

"These men calling themselves patriots believe if they lose—and surely, they will—they will simply return to the lives they once had. They do not comprehend by the declaration of war that those lives are lost forever. Even if they return home,

*everything will be transformed. The most profound
changes will be inside themselves. Those shifts will
rise during the dead of night to haunt them. They
will relive the ravages of war again and again as
their minds frantically seek to experience a different
outcome. But the result will be the same, again and
again. Then, the terrors will seek them out during
broad daylight. A sudden noise, a specific odor, or
the sight of something otherwise mundane will
pound into them until their minds have returned to
the battlefield, and they will relive it anew.*

*"I have received word of the burning of
Norfolk, and though it is over two hundred miles
from where I sit, I know war is coming for us here
in Nova Dunglen. It is inevitable. The British
have burned Norfolk; the businesses and homes of
those so puffed for war, nothing but smoldering
ruins. The so-called patriots have, in retaliation,
burned a loyalist stronghold. England will win, as
she always has. God save the King."*

I held the book in my hands, my fingers lightly
skimming his words as if I could touch his soul with my
fingertips. The emotion in his words echoed within me, his
frustration lingering in the air. I think it was safe to say that
I might have found the identity of the portrait in the
lantern room, though, of course, I couldn't be certain. I
could almost see his furrowed, dark brows, flashing black
eyes, and tight lips as he wrote, occasionally dipping his
quill into the inkwell with quick jabs of anger.

He had known war. He had seen or experienced all
that he wrote. That much was obvious.

I returned to the mention of Nova Dunglen. I knew
the word "nova" was Latin for "new." Recalling that the
Canadian province of Nova Scotia was Latin for New

Scotland, I wondered whether Dunglen had existed in Europe, since "dun" was Scottish Gaelic for a fort. The name, then, was New Fort Glen. I grabbed my mobile and ran a quick search. There was indeed a Dunglen situated in the Scottish Highlands.

Next, I searched for Nova Dunglen in North Carolina. I found scant, aged information, suggesting it had existed at one point. I wondered if it had become extinct over time or simply renamed. Certainly, Dikshita was a highly unusual place name for America, as it had Hindu origins; could that have once been Nova Dunglen? As I recalled the aura of the nearly abandoned intersection, my author's mind raced at the thought of it as a ghost town.

With the book resting in my lap, my eyes skimmed the horizon, but my mind was elsewhere. Could this Jonathan Corbyn have been the lightkeeper during the revolution? Otherwise, it was a stretch to understand why this journal had been hidden here.

Hiding it made sense in his day, I realized. Jonathan was wrong, of course. The British did not win, which probably placed a bounty on his head if he had been a loyalist, and from his opening words, he certainly was one. I knew little about the Scots in North Carolina, only that many had fled north to Canada during the Revolution. Others had settled here after the war was won. But, I countered myself, not all Scots were loyal to England. Many, after all, had fought against the monarchy only thirty years earlier.

My eyes dropped back to the journal. The words, "God save the King", stared back at me. It was a phrase that had emerged to support King George II against the Jacobite rebellion, which originated in the Scottish Highlands. A paradox existed already, as Scottish Highlanders were highly unlikely to use the phrase. Yet, Jonathan had seen war, or he would not have begun his journal in such a way. He had experienced the heat and horrors of battle, which had left their imprints upon him; of that, I was sure.

A stiff, cold breeze encircled me despite the warmth of the sun. As it swirled around me, I looked at the tops of the trees silhouetted against the blue sky, but they remained stationary as if there was no breeze at all. I found myself shivering and rubbed my forearms in a futile attempt to warm the goosebumps that had appeared there.

It was hard to imagine the events of last night as I sat in the bright sun, yet the persistent chill felt like an insistent voice. I found myself accessing the security cameras on my phone. The surreal events of the night before would not be as I recalled them, and the cameras would not lie. There would be a plausible explanation.

The lantern room camera had recorded events as I'd lain sleeping. My laptop case had opened on its own, casting a blue light around the room, before closing a moment later. I leaned in to watch it again. There was a figure in front of the laptop. It was opaque, just as the shadow that had led me to the lantern room last night had been. I compared the top of the figure to the windows as it moved around the room; it must have been close to six feet tall. It hesitated in front of each window as though it was gazing outward. Only when it reached my laptop did it turn its attention to the room and what must have been a strange device that rested on the ledge.

It appeared to fade. The following recording, taken a few minutes later, picked it up again, pacing the room before it began to descend the staircase toward my bedroom. It must have been this recording that had awakened me.

The camera also detected the figure returning to the top floor, and the moment I emerged. This time, however, I had the benefit of watching myself near the silhouette. Rather than continue pacing, it was as if it was attempting to lead me upward, hesitating every couple of paces until I began to catch up.

My laptop opened again and closed, just as it had before. And then the lantern burst into a blinding light. I watched myself race across the room, searching for a way to turn off the light, flicking the wall switch to no avail, and finally, half-destroying the lantern stand.

This time, however, I watched an orb hover around me where the shadow had been. It was bright white and appeared to pulsate. It moved to the floor level as if peering over my shoulder while I pulled out the wood, and it moved upward toward the ceiling as it circled me. When the lantern light went out, it remained, and yet, I hadn't seen its maneuvers the night before. I must have been too preoccupied with the stand and the destruction I wrought upon it.

It must have been a reflection of an airplane, I told myself. There was no other possibility, as I was in the middle of nowhere—or, as the Irish say, in the back of beyond. Anything on the ground, such as a vehicle, could not have shone its light on the third floor. But I knew even as I raced through probabilities that none of them were plausible. An airplane, drone, or helicopter could not have moved as this orb had. It could not have hovered in such a way to reach the floor, come back up, and rotate around me. Or could it?

In any event, it was clear from the videos that I had made a monumental mess and destroyed someone else's property. I held onto the book in my lap. I would have to turn it over to Billie, but I didn't want to do it immediately. I'd read through it first for no reason other than curiosity about the region's politics—after all, I was there researching my ancestors who had fought in the same war. This certainly fell into the realm of research.

I set it on the table, determined to finish my cooling tea and biscuit before climbing the stairs and assessing the damage.

7

Sometime later, I climbed the stairs to the lantern room. Before I reached the top, I gazed out of one of the windows at its sweeping panorama of the surrounding terrain, and my heart skipped a beat. I could not have asked for a more perfect setting to write my next book.

But as my eyes peered over the top of the floor, my heart sank, and my breathing grew shallow and accelerated. Instead of viewing the shambles I had created the night before, I stared at a perfectly tidy room.

My footsteps grew slower as I took the last few steps. My fingers grasped the smooth wood railing, leaving prints of perspiration that had suddenly leached out. My mind wrestled with what my eyes conveyed. It wasn't true, my mind argued. I would walk around to the other side and see the mess spread across the floor. But as I methodically rounded the lantern stand like a predator stalking prey, I found the lantern cabinet reassembled as if it had just been installed.

I refused to believe a phantom lived in this lighthouse who was capable of tidying up my messes.

The only plausible explanation was that Argo Dikshita had fixed the lantern while I sat outside enjoying breakfast. But wouldn't I have heard his vehicle? The area was remote and, therefore, quiet, save for the evening crickets and toads. Wouldn't he have called out to me or walked around the lighthouse when he saw my vehicle parked here?

I strode to the window overlooking the patio. The windows leaned slightly outwards, providing an excellent view of the grounds below. Had he looked, he might have seen me there.

I made my way to my laptop and sat heavily in a chair. My case was closed, the computer silent.

Stunned, it took me a moment to realize my cameras would have picked up his presence. I quickly retrieved my mobile from my pocket and accessed the security app. There was no history after my presence in the lantern room last night. The shadowy figure, the orbs, or another human being had not returned to the room after I left it in disarray. I watched the video again as I ripped apart the wood inside the cabinet, strewing it across the floor. It was impossible for it to go back together without detection.

No; there was another video. I opened it only to see myself rounding the top of the stairs just a moment earlier, my mouth agape, my eyes wide, and my face pale. A glance at the green light on the security camera told me I was being filmed even now.

I spun around, opened my laptop, accessed a browser, and searched for Dikshita General Store. I quickly added it to my phone's contact list—address, phone number, and names. I wanted this place on speed dial.

Then I rang the number. It was answered on the second ring.

"Dikshita General Store," a melodious voice called out. "Argo speaking."

"Hello, Argo," I started. Hearing the breathlessness in my voice, I consciously attempted to slow my speech. The last thing I needed was for him to think I was an overly excitable, hysterical woman.

"Ah, hello, Miss Hunter. What may I do for you?"

"How did you know it was me?" I demanded.

"Caller ID. Don't you have it?"

I felt my skin flush. "I was wondering if you might have come by the lighthouse to fix the lantern we spoke about yesterday."

It sounded as if he took a sudden intake of breath. "No. No, I'm not sure if it can be made to work…"

"You haven't been to the lighthouse?"

"Not since I met you yesterday, no."

"You didn't fix the lantern."

"No." I could hear the puzzlement in his voice. "Is it working now?"

"I'm going to bring the lantern to you."

"No, no, I don't think that is a good idea—"

"Okay, then, I'll see you shortly."

"No—"

I cut him off as I hung up the phone. My hands were shaking as I returned the phone to my pocket. I returned to the lantern stand and stared at the offending light for a long moment. It was a beautiful piece of work, consisting of multiple intricately patterned panels that appeared to be crystal. The panels were joined by metal, possibly brass. The octagonal lantern grew narrower with a small dome constructed of the same materials. I could clearly see the lens inside the lamp.

Shay and I had toured Ireland together and often stayed overnight in lighthouses turned into holiday residences—or, as Americans would consider them, bed and breakfasts. One lighthouse, in particular, had extensive information posted in the gallery to educate visitors on the lanterns and their operation. I felt the knowledge seep back into my consciousness.

This was a Fresnel lens with dioptric prisms that rotated between four beams set in all four compass directions. As it rotated, it would have set off a pattern of beams or flashes to warn sailors navigating up the channel.

I leaned in more closely. When the lighthouse was constructed in the latter half of the 18th century, the lamp would have been powered by oil, most likely whale oil. Yet something about this lamp led me to believe it was not a new replacement. It had an energy about it. I couldn't quite put my finger on it, but it was the difference between studying an antique and a modern replica. It just didn't add up.

"To whoever is here," I said aloud, feeling a bit crazy for speaking to unseen spirits, "I plan to unplug this lamp and take it in to be repaired."

The slightest chuckle surrounded me. It had only lasted the briefest of moments. My eyes scoured the windows to find one blown slightly ajar. I exhaled in an attempt to steady myself. There had been no chuckle; it was only the wind.

I found the opening to the stand more readily this morning than I had the previous night. The lantern was affixed at the top with a piece similar to the base above. I found a large thumb screw. I attempted to turn it, but it was fixed tightly. I pushed against it, attempting to put my whole forearm and shoulder into turning it, but it remained stationary.

"Jonathan," I said, exasperated. "I need to remove this."

"Jon." The single syllable was spoken so fast, I almost missed it.

I froze. The most sensible thing to do was to leave this room immediately and take my laptop with me. If there had been a door to the room, I should have closed it shut and never ventured up here again, light or no light. Better yet, I should have flown down the stairs, packed my bags in record time, and gotten the heck out of there.

My hand was still on the thumb screw, and it suddenly rotated. It was such a minute action that I thought I had imagined it. Yet, I was able to continue unscrewing it. With the screw removed, I could easily take out the piece that had secured it to the lamp above. I stood shakily. Setting down the pieces from underneath, I lifted the lamp off the stand. It was surprisingly heavy, and I wondered at my ability to carry it down the stairs. I snaked out the electric cord, took a brief moment to screw the pieces together again once it was out of the stand, and without so much as another look around, I planted it against my torso and took the spiral staircase all the way to the ground level, careful to remain on the outer edges of each stair.

~~~~~

The lantern felt even heavier as I lifted it from my vehicle and hauled it into the Dikshita General Store. It seemed silly, but it was almost as if it hadn't wanted to be removed from the lighthouse, and it was fighting my efforts every step of the way in the only way it could.

As the screen door slammed behind me, I caught the top of Beckett's head just before it slid behind an aisle endcap. "Hello, Beckett," I called out in my most jovial voice. "Mind helping me with this?"

There was no response from Beckett, but as I trudged across the store, Argo appeared behind the counter. Witnessing my heavy load, he quickly came to my rescue. When I transferred the lamp to him, it appeared as if his knees might buckle. He moved to the counter and deposited it with an audible huff.

"Is this—?" He stopped short, his face growing pale.

"The lantern from the lighthouse," I offered. "I was wondering if you could plug it in here to see if it works?"

"Oh. No. I'm afraid I can't do that." He wiped his brow. Grasping the cord, he followed it to the plug. "It takes a different outlet, I'm afraid. Had you allowed me to explain, I could have saved you the trip."

"Well, the thing is, Argo, this lamp comes on when it isn't plugged in. I can't seem to shut it off. Does it have a power pack inside—an independent power source?"

He shook his head and continued to peer at it as though we'd just placed an odorous carcass on his counter. "Is it incompatible with the solar panels?" I offered. "Maybe it needs to be wired into them?" As he shook his head, I continued, "Are the solar panels perhaps shorting it out? You said you wired the lighthouse, right?"

He planted both hands on the counter. "I wired the lighthouse. I did. It had been wired previously—in the 1950s, I believe—but I rewired the whole house when I installed the solar panels."

"Was the lamp there when you rewired it? Or was this installed just recently?"

"Miss Hunter," he said, wiping his forehead again, "I suggest you return the lamp to its rightful spot. You are renting, no? This wasn't yours to remove."

"I intend to put it back where it belongs," I said, a bit miffed, "after it's fixed. It comes on by itself in the middle of the night. It's quite alarming."

"Yes. Yes, I suppose it is. But you should have called Billie about it. She would have asked you to keep it where it was." He shook his head at me. "You shouldn't have removed it."

"Well, now that we have established that I shouldn't have removed it, why does it come on when it isn't even plugged in?" I tried to rotate the lamp, but it felt glued to the counter. "There must be an alternate power source. I just want to flip the switch or remove the battery—or whatever it takes to keep it from coming on."

"There is no alternate power, I assure you."

"Then, how—?" Out of the corner of my eye, I spotted Beckett's head sliding out to stare at us before it glided back behind some merchandise.

"Miss Hunter," Argo was saying, "Is there anything else you came for? I'm afraid I'm very busy today."

I glanced around at the lack of customers. "Yes. I see that you are." I sighed heavily. "Actually, yes, there is something else. Can you tell me if this place was once known as Nova Dunglen?"

I saw the recognition flash in his eyes, but he remained as still as a stone.

"You said your family had been here for a long time," I added, forcing a smile.

"Two hundred years." His voice sounded almost robotic.

"Dikshita," I said, trying to keep my voice light. "It is a Hindu name, isn't it?"

"Sanskrit."

"Oh. I'm a historian, and I'm very much interested in genealogy. If you don't mind me saying so, you don't appear to be of Indian descent."

"And how are we supposed to appear?"

I could see a flush moving across his cheeks, and I sought to break through his defensiveness. "It's just that you seem so very—*local*—to me." I forced myself to smile politely.

He sighed. "You will find it all online, I'm sure." His eyes searched the room, though I remained the only customer. "An ancestor married a man from Nepal, not India. His ancestors had taken on the Dikshita name, which means they are scientists. My ancestors took it as well."

"Oh," I said, leaning forward in what I hoped was a friendly way. "So, your ancestor was a woman, and she married a man with the surname Dikshita?"

"That is correct. Now, if you will excuse me—"

As he turned away from me, I continued, "Was your other ancestor—the female—Scottish, perhaps?"

"No." His answer was abrupt and too harsh. "Beckett," he called out. The young man slid his head out. "Take this lamp to Miss Hunter's car for her. She's leaving." With that, he disappeared into the back room behind the counter.

"I can manage—" I started to say, but Beckett had already lifted the lamp as if it didn't weigh more than a few ounces.

I followed him to my vehicle. I opened the trunk and watched him deposit the lamp into the center. His eyes took on a glassy appearance as he studied the lamp. I moved to lift the cord into the trunk, but he beat me to it, wrapping the long cord around the base of the lamp as gently as he might wrap a baby in a blanket.

I placed my hand on the top of the trunk, ready to lower it, but he stood there a moment longer. "Thank you," I began.

"Ask Jon to stop shining it."

With that, he was gone. I turned quickly but only caught a glimpse of his back as he disappeared into the store.

Maybe, I thought as I closed the trunk and returned to the driver's seat, I had been speaking to the wrong Dikshita.

8

I might have said that I lugged the lamp back into the lighthouse, but lug wasn't the right word, as it felt half the weight it had when I took it out. I could have sworn that as I drove down the long dirt drive, someone was watching me, and I kept glancing at the top of the lighthouse, expecting to see someone there. Even when the house appeared empty, I felt uneasy.

I set the lamp on the dining table inside the front door. I simply didn't feel like carrying it back up two flights of stairs. Instead, I grabbed the journal and headed up the stairs, intent on doing some research and then reading another journal entry.

I had to admit the lantern table looked sad and forlorn without its beautiful crystal lamp. I glanced around the circular room. Then I took a deep breath.

"Jonathan," I said, knowing full well if he answered me, I would fly down the stairs or jump off the gallery, "Jon. I want you to know that I brought the lamp back home. It belongs here," I added in appeasement. My eyes dropped to the security camera. I would delete this recording for sure. "I'll bring it upstairs later today or tomorrow, and I promise to set it back in place. But, I have a favor to ask." I took another shaky breath before continuing. "Please don't make the lantern come on, at least not at a time when I'm likely to see it. It makes me... uneasy." I hesitated, but there was no reply.

Of course, there wasn't. I stepped briskly to the laptop and sat down heavily in front of it. I had a sudden desire to go back downstairs and retrieve the lantern, but I opened my laptop instead. There must be some information on Nova Dunglen online.

An hour later, I was no closer to discovering the location of the mysterious village. I was replaying the conversation with Argo in my mind when the phone rang. "Shay," I said as I picked up.

"Is this a good time?" His Irish accent was unmistakable. How I'd missed that familiar Irish lilt. Every voice in Ireland contained a melodious quality. It occurred to me precisely what an Irishman would have said had I brought the lantern in to him. He would have informed me that no self-respecting lighthouse would be without a ghost and to leave it—the lantern and the ghost—alone.

"Perfect timing," I said. "How are things going with the conference?"

"Just grand. I should be finished and on my way to you in a couple of days. Is that still working for you?"

"Absolutely. In fact, I have a bit of a mystery here that perhaps you can help me with."

"A mystery, 'ey?"

I told him of the journal I found and the reference to Nova Dunglen, but purposefully omitted the details of a possible haunting. After all, that part might be a component of my active imagination. Perhaps I was curious to see if he would sense one here without me planting the idea in his head.

When I finished, there was a brief silence before he began. I could detect his expertise in history in his tone. "The American Revolution is not my forte, as you know… However, I do recall there was an exodus of Scots after the Battle of Culloden in 1746. A good many of them were wanted by the British for treason, and they hoped to disappear in the Americas or elsewhere."

"But," I countered, "wouldn't they have fought against Britain? This man was a loyalist."

"Ah, that's where it gets complicated. The Scots have always believed in a king. They fought against England, not because they didn't want one. They simply believed that King James II—James VII in Scotland—and his descendants were the rightful heirs to the throne."

"Enlighten me, please. I don't know anything about that war."

I could hear his voice pick up in tempo, and I knew he relished the opportunity to share his historical knowledge. It was difficult, if not impossible, not to feel his unbridled enthusiasm. "King James II was deposed in 1688 after William of Orange, who happened to be his nephew and son-in-law—long story—arrived with an army to oust him. The supporters of King James thought the ouster was illegal, and they sought to restore James to the throne. They became known as Jacobites, and the Jacobite Uprising began a year later, in 1689.

"There was also a religious undertone to it. James was Catholic, you see, although he had no apparent issues with Protestants. However, William of Orange was what you might call extreme, a Protestant who believed the Catholics should be converted, annihilated, or moved from Britain and her colonies."

"So, the Jacobite rebellion ended with the Battle of Culloden?"

"It was a pivotal point for sure. There were battles after—none so heavily fought—but Culloden killed about a third of the Jacobite forces. That's when an exodus began in earnest, as every man who fought for James had a bounty on his head."

"But—" My brain calculated the difference between the Battle of Culloden and Jon's entry. I felt a strange sensation move through me as I realized I was thinking about him by his first name as though I'd known him.

"Thirty years isn't a long time in European minds. Why would they fight for England here when they fought against her there?"

"Ah. It's a tangled web, you see. Jacobites in Scotland lost their lands, and clans were stripped of territorial rights. But, once the Scots landed on American shores, they were often allowed to acquire land if they swore allegiance to the king."

"So, they fled Scotland to escape the yoke of Britain—or the hangman's noose. But once they reached America, they could start over, but they had to swear allegiance?"

"Aye."

"So, when the revolution began here, they had a choice. They could fight for the king—"

"—or lose everything they'd built in America. They really were between a rock and a hard place, you might say. Or, as we say in Ireland, between two rocks."

"Noted," I said, chuckling. "Did any fight against England here?"

"Undoubtedly. Scots were on both sides."

I told him about Argo and the name of the crossroads, and I mused whether it might have been Nova Dunglen.

"The thing of it is," Shay answered thoughtfully, "if the inhabitants of Nova Dunglen had been British loyalists, they most certainly had to flee the area when the Americans prevailed. They would have been seen as traitors. Many were hanged without trial, so there was an immediate incentive to get out." He hesitated before continuing, "A number of them fled to Canada, which remains loyal to the English crown to this day."

"I see. And the name of the village, had it been Scottish, would have been erased as well?"

"Absolutely."

"But," I countered, "what of the volume of Scottish place names throughout this country today?"

"Those would have come later. Scots began to immigrate long after your American Revolution. The difference is that the new generation would not have sworn allegiance to an English monarch upon arrival, because America was a separate and independent nation. They were free to purchase land or worship as they pleased, and they were out from under England's yoke."

"Well, for someone who said he didn't know much about the American Revolution, you have certainly enlightened me."

Shay chuckled. "I'll do more than that when I arrive. My flight lands in Raleigh. Will you be available to pick me up there?"

"I wouldn't have it any other way."

"Grand. I'll email you my itinerary, then."

We chatted for a few more minutes, but my mind began to wander. It had been a warm day, unseasonably warm even for coastal North Carolina, but I started to feel a chill in the air. It was becoming quite common, and I found myself glancing at the windows to ensure they were closed. When we finally clicked off, I sat for a long moment, hugging myself against the chill. It almost felt as if a draft moved past me, though there could be no source for it.

Finally, I stood, closed my laptop, and headed downstairs.

9

The light was waning when I finished dinner and the requisite cleaning. The teapot whistled just as I placed a nice chunk of peach cobbler on a plate. I added the boiling water to a tea infuser, plopped it into a cozy porcelain pitcher, and brought it to a snug chair by the window. I'd say it was in the corner of the room, but there were no corners. Yet, as I made myself comfortable, it felt like it was. With my platter of dessert and tea on the table beside me, I turned on the lamp and picked up Jon's journal.

And there it was again, I thought. It wasn't Jonathan but Jon, and somehow, I felt closer to him.

Before I opened the journal, my eyes fell upon the lantern still on the dining table. Was it my imagination, or did it really seem as though it was happy to have been returned to the lighthouse? Tomorrow, I noted, I will carry that thing to the third floor and pray that it is lighter going up than it was coming down.

But for now, I thought, I wanted to know more about Jonathan Corbyn.

The second entry was dated January 7, 1776.

"War surrounds me.
"I swore to my soul and my God above that when I departed Scotland, I would live out the remainder of my life in peace. I thought I had

succeeded as I managed to remain far from others.
I swore allegiance to King George when I purchased
this lot, and others thought I was a fool for buying
it. A channel cuts down the length of my property,
but I managed to turn it into a lucrative business,
for it slices off a length of travel from the Atlantic
Ocean to the Cape Fear River, speeding small
ships along their way. I have been content alone in
the lighthouse, satisfied to remain far from others,
surrounded by only my animals. My mare Justine
is the sweetest creature, gentle and patient. And I
never would have suspected that my closest
companion would be a large white wolf-dog, the
most loyal of friends. I found Win when he was just
a pup. How he'd survived, I'll never know. 'Tis a
miracle, for certain. I fed him milk until he was
weaned, and proper food thereafter, and a closer
friend I could not have hoped for.

"I only seek peace now. Gone are the days I
advocated for war along with the rest of them, a
folly led by Charles and ending in death to so many.
Ah, but that was thirty years ago now, a lifetime
between myself and a field of battle. I was naught
but a foolish lad in those days."

I thought for a moment I'd heard something, but
when I looked up from the journal, only the intimate room
met my gaze, the glow from the lamps a cozy amber. I felt
almost as if I was stepping into his shoes. I wondered if
Jon had built the original structure with his own hands.
Had he earned his livelihood charging ships to traverse the
channel alongside the lighthouse, only to find a few years
later that the channel had been diverted, leaving him with
nothing more than useless swampland? Or, I mused, he

might have fled long before the channel was closed, a hunted traitor to the American cause.

I could almost picture him at the table, eating by candlelight, his dog Win at his feet gnawing on a bone. There must have been a stable or barn on the mound for his horse. It would have been wood, I surmised, and long ago succumbed to the elements.

His tone was quite a bit different from his first journal entry. This one sounded melancholy, as if he was becoming resigned to the war surrounding him. There was also an evident, weary longing to live out the remainder of his life in peace with his animals.

I poured a cup of tea from the pitcher and added a bit of cream. Taking a sip, I relished how smoothly it warmed my throat, then turned back to the journal.

"Now war has come for me. It has skirted around my slice of heaven to rear its ugly head at Haddrell's Point, South Carolina. I have received notice from one of the ship's captains passing through Corbyn Channel that two ships of His Majesty's, the Tamar and the Cherokee, sought to detain a fishing boat suspected of gun smuggling. However, the First and Fourth South Carolina Regiments engaged the British. The fishing ship managed to escape, and no one is the wiser about its cargo. The patriot regiments were forced back to the island. It was a draw, it appears. The following day, it was said that the British ships had departed the harbor.

"The normal channels are bottled up with patriots and loyalists, with one or the other defending while the other attacks. Soon, they both will search for alternate routes. I am sandwiched between the fighting in Virginia and that in South

Carolina, and tensions are high. North Carolina is next.

"I have already received a dispatch alerting me to King George's desire to make good on our oaths. It was only last year that Generals Donald MacDonald and Donald McLeod reiterated the oaths we had agreed upon years ago—and for the newer arrivals, recruit them along with us. We had each been granted 200 acres of land with the promise of no taxes for a twenty-year period in return for fighting for King George. None of us expected it to come to fruition. Would I have signed it otherwise?

"Yet, here I sit in my idyllic home thousands of miles and years away from Culloden, and it appears I am doomed to fire upon those that oppose the King when I once vehemently opposed the succession."

I paused once more. The first entry had appeared staunchly in favor of England, but this entry was more in line with Shay's assessment of Scots in North Carolina. They had been placed in difficult, if not impossible, positions. They had fled the tethers of England, the King, and the Crown. They had traveled halfway around the world to begin anew. And now, it appeared that they were to be rounded up to fight against their new countrymen.

I sipped a bit more tea and returned to the journal to find the question was on Jon's mind as well.

"I am too old for war, and yet age is not considered. I swore an oath, and now I must attend meetings and ready myself for battle. The alternative is to leave what I have built here. Where

would I go? Across the mountains and to the west,
it is far more challenging to find a man who doesn't
want to be found. Canada beckons if I remain
faithful to the Crown, for her people do not rise
against England... for now.

"Tomorrow, I take my boat and head to the
village of Cross Creek, where Scots loyalists will
plot their movements against the patriots."

I bookmarked the page and returned the journal reverently to the table beside me. I gingerly dipped into the peach cobbler. It wasn't bad for Dikshita's frozen food section. As I ate, I found myself musing about Jon's age. Assuming he fought the English at Culloden as a young man, he would now be in his fifties. That was already ancient by 1700s standards, when the average lifespan was only thirty-eight years. Life back then could be brutal. I wondered if he had been injured at Culloden. If he had been imprisoned, it would have truly been a miracle that he survived, as the merciless treatment, half-starvation, and dungeon-like conditions were well documented. Now he lived in this idyllic lighthouse with only Nova Dunglen nearby, and he might be on a collision course with war again.

I was tempted to turn to the last entry in his journal to see how his story ended, but I stopped myself. I was tired and a bit sleepy. Tomorrow would come soon enough.

I rose, brought the dishes into the kitchen intending to clean them in the morning, and started for the stairs. Just as I placed my foot upon the first step, something caught my eye just outside. I leaned toward the glass, trying to make out the image. My heart quickened when I realized it was a dog romping inside the fence line as though chasing a firefly. Hadn't Billie told me there were alligators on the other side of that fence?

I sprang to the door. My nearest neighbor was miles away. I couldn't leave that dog running loose in these parts. It might be hungry, thirsty, or in need of medical care. I could certainly provide all of that, and a cozy and safe place for it to sleep this night.

I rounded the lighthouse to catch another glimpse of him. It was a large white German shepherd; of that, I was sure. Could it be a descendant of Harry's dog? I rushed forward, calling to it. It hesitated in its romping and turned toward me. Then, as I stared directly at it, it simply disappeared.

10

The rain awakened me before dawn, the steady pitter-patter of raindrops against the windowpanes oddly reassuring, as if Mother Nature was in her proper place. I lounged in bed a bit longer than usual, the gray skies misleading me about the time as the darkness remained settled in my round bedroom.

When I finally arose, I donned a cozy fleece robe and hesitated by the window. Of course, I didn't see a white German shepherd traversing the lawn below. It had been just a figment of my imagination, a trick played on the eyes by encroaching fog and a tired mind. I really had to get a grip on myself and be in denial with the best of them. I had always been the logical one, all the way until I rented that troubled cottage in Ireland. Since then, it often felt as though a supernatural portal had opened and sucked me in. I needed to close it if I was going to maintain any semblance of self-control.

I made my way downstairs, my blurry eyes fixated on the coffee maker in the surprisingly modern kitchen. I popped in a pod and started it up while I heated a couple of fruit pastries in the toaster oven. It was the perfect morning for comfort food.

It wasn't until I had arranged my morning breakfast at the table and sat down, ready to read the morning e-news, that I froze my cup in midair. I blinked twice, thinking my eyes were lying to me. I returned the cup to the saucer with a clatter that was too loud for the otherwise quiet room.

The lantern was gone.

My eyes darted to the doorway in the vestibule on the other side of the room, where I found the deadbolt in place and the chain across the door. My eyes abruptly came into focus from their blurriness as I gazed at the spiral staircase. From this angle, I could barely see beyond the first bend, and I shivered when I thought of myself alone, sleeping soundly in the bed between this table and the lantern room.

I stood, my heart pounding and my knees too shaky to support my legs. I lunged for the staircase and grabbed onto the railing as though it were a lifeline. I haltingly climbed the highly polished steps. I wanted to quiet my heart as it pounded in my temples, convinced the sound echoed in the stairwell and amplified its way to the uppermost floor to herald my approach.

I almost expected to find someone there—not a ghost, but a living, breathing human being. I anticipated a maintenance man or perhaps Argo himself, setting the lantern back into place. That had to be the answer, I told myself. Someone has a key to this lighthouse. They let themselves in, quietly made their way up the stairs, and were installing the lamp at this very moment.

Then how, my mind countered, did they manage to get past the security cameras and the chain on the door? There was only one entrance unless someone climbed in through a window, and the window locks were next on my to-do list. And Argo, after all, had sold me the cameras and may know exactly how to disable them.

My eyes peeked over the floor as I neared the top, and I stopped and hugged the railing. The lantern was there, back in place as it had been the day I arrived, as though it had never moved.

I surveyed the rest of the room. My laptop was precisely where I'd left it the day before, the chair slightly askew. The nearby portrait swayed so slightly that I wondered if I'd imagined its movement. The man stared back at me, his black eyes almost one of merriment.

The storm cast shadows of raindrops through the windows and onto the ledge, where they continued like tentacles across the floor. I was tempted to turn around and rush back downstairs, but I felt frozen to the step. After a moment that felt too long, I climbed the rest of the way. For the first time, I noticed that the railing did not extend to the top, forcing me to release my grip as I stepped onto the polished floor.

I quickly moved away from the stairs as if I might tumble down them if I didn't, and I made my way to the lantern stand. As I stared at it in disbelief, a gravelly male voice with a thick accent said, "You're welcome."

I whirled around, expecting to see Argo standing there, though once I registered that the room was empty, I knew the accent and timber had been completely wrong. Had it been a distinct Scottish accent I heard, or was I hallucinating?

I pulled out my desk chair and unsteadily lowered myself into it. Then I reached into my robe pocket and extracted my mobile. Opening the security camera app, I noticed there were no newly recorded videos other than me, the wide-eyed wonder, popping my head over the railing. I clicked through to view the historical notes, which should have alerted me if the cameras had been placed on snooze and then re-engaged. Nothing was in either place.

I stared back at the lantern. There was no way it could have been carried from the dining table to the stand two stories up without a human being doing so. The voice had been my imagination. I dialed the number of the Dikshita General Store. Argo answered it on the second ring.

"Argo, this is Hayley—"

"Hayley Hunter. Yes, we have caller ID."

"Of course you do."

"How can I help you this beautiful morning?" His voice sounded light and friendly.

"Did you, by any chance, have someone install the lantern last night or this morning?"

There was a moment of silence in which I could almost sense his confusion. Finally, he said, "No, but I can be there later today."

"Don't bother. It's back in place," I said flatly. Then, "Can you access my security cameras? The ones you sold me?"

"No, but if you bring your phone in, I can help you set them up."

"They're already set up on my phone."

There was another silence. "I don't understand what you are asking me," he said finally.

"I was wondering if the cameras might have been used," I said, my internal dialogue reminding me not to accuse anyone without evidence.

"No. They are brand new. When you installed the app, you should have set an original username and password. No one else would have access."

"I see."

"Is there something wrong?" He asked the question hesitantly as if he genuinely did not wish to hear my answer.

"Nothing is wrong," I said. A beam of light slipped across the floor in front of me. I followed it to the window, where I observed the sun bravely attempting to peek out from behind rain clouds. "Nothing is wrong at all."

"Then, is there anything else I can assist you with?"

"No. Thank you. Goodbye." I clicked the phone off. Then I turned on my phone's video, which would automatically engage the audio as well. "Jon?" I asked hesitantly. "Jonathan?" I waited as I rotated the phone so that it caught every part of the lantern room, and then I rotated it back to its original position. "Thank you." I waited a moment longer and then stopped the recording. I grabbed my laptop and headed back downstairs, mindful of the uneven stair tread and making sure to stay at the broadest part lest I foolishly trip myself in front of a ghost. I began to breathe a sigh of relief when I reached the familiarity of my bedroom, and I let out an audible sound when I stepped onto the ground floor.

I set the laptop on the table across from my cooling breakfast. I sat down and pulled up the video recording. I listened to my voice, which sounded far more confident than I'd felt. There were no images captured on the video, and no responding voice was heard on the audio; instead, the constant refrain of the rain against the windows and the raindrop reflections across the room were all that remained.

11

I settled into the chair with a fresh cup of coffee, hoping the caffeine would prove more grounding than the tea I'd become accustomed to drinking. I'd spent the last hour attempting to research Jonathan Corbyn, only to find it was a surprisingly common name. The results included a decent number in Canada as well as the United States, spanning from the 1700s to the present day. The sheer volume was frustrating as my hopes for quick results were dashed.

I turned back to his journal. Opening it felt somehow sacred, and I realized I was becoming protective of the journal.

"January 10, 1776

"I have returned from Cross Creek. My beloved Win discovered me a short distance from the lighthouse and rollicked along the shore, keeping pace with my boat. How happy I was to see him! Justine stopped munching on hay to trot across the mound to greet me as I pulled ashore. I have carved out a piece of heaven in miniature, and yet, if I had a drop of coward's blood or common sense, I would be packing at this moment instead of placing quill to parchment. It is an enticing

thought, for one of the men present at the meeting sought me out afterward and asked if I would join them on a journey northward to Canada. I answered neither yay nor nay, as spies are in abundance in these parts, and I knew not his true intention.

"I considered his offer on the journey home. While others traversed the countryside on horseback or carriage, I departed alone in my boat. I navigated the Cape Fear River until I arrived at an opening that appeared little more than a gap between palmetto and cypress; yet, I knew it to be the Corbyn Channel. I knew every inch of it, and as the hours passed and the moon arose, I knew it would lead me home to my lighthouse, my sanctuary, my beloved animals.

"However, there was more to consider. Another sought me out, my own sister's husband. I would trust—I have trusted—Alasdair Glenn with my life. We grew together from wee lads playing in the wilds of the Highlands. We fought side by side as foolish young men convinced of our immortality during the Jacobite battles.

"We crossed the Atlantic as brothers, along with old friends and new. By the end of the voyage, we all had sworn allegiance to one another in this new and strange land, filled with tribes and peoples with whom we shared no common culture.

"At Cross Creek, Alasdair informed me that his convictions lay with these independent-minded, stubborn rebels, despite his stature in the King's service. Cuddy was there, making up our trio of misfits, nodding his approval without uttering a word.

"We met Cuddy on the voyage. A modern Marco Polo, he was, and someone I'd have aspired

to be like had I been younger and the aches and pains of aging bones been absent. He was Asian but spoke English with a flawless, upper-class British accent (though we would have preferred Scottish!) Whenever we asked how he came to be in Europe, learned English, and now embarked for the uncertainty of a New World, he launched into a thoroughly entertaining yet riotously inconsistent tale of his travels.

"Yet, at Cross Creek, Alasdair and Cuddy placed me in the most difficult position. As a loyalist, I am bound to report them both immediately. They would be apprehended, tried, no doubt convicted even if scant evidence was to be had, and swiftly executed. Too many have already suffered that dire fate based only on a single accusation.

"During the official portion of the meeting, of which a few hundred attended, I was also informed in front of all present that only loyalists are permitted to use Corbyn's Channel. And what should I do if a patriot were to find his way to my lighthouse? I asked. Turn them around and report them, I was told. For, if I permitted them to cruise past my lighthouse in any direction at all, I would be branded a traitor just like the patriots, a coconspirator guilty of aiding the enemy. I was instructed to maintain a detailed list of all boats entering the channel, including their manifests and the names of their occupants.

"I felt like the ball in a game of cricket, the competing sides up for bat to whack me to one side or the other. Yet the two teams acted as one in the presence of others, only revealing their true natures in the shadows.

"I feel like a tool whose existence belongs to King George. Perhaps that is the fundamental idea for which the patriots fight, for they see the democratically elected official as belonging to and serving the people, whereas the people belong to and serve the monarch."

The entry ended there. I wanted with more pressing urgency to discover his decision and fate, but my phone rang rudely, interrupting my thoughts and the lighthouse's tranquility. I realized it was my editor as I checked the caller ID, and I let out an audible groan.

"Hi, Lindsay," I answered, trying to keep my voice light.

"How's the book coming along?"

It always disconcerted me when folks dove right into the meat of a conversation. I noticed it more since returning from Ireland, where it was impolite to get straight to the point without asking about the other party—and the other party's mother, whether you knew her or not. I became accustomed to hearing, "How's your mam?" at the start of every conversation. "Research heavy," I answered.

"Does that mean you haven't begun writing yet?" She sounded distracted, and I could hear the rustle of papers. "Will you have the first five chapters to me by the deadline?"

I glanced at my phone's calendar. "Absolutely," I said, trying to convince myself it wasn't an outright lie.

"I'm due to check it off," she said.

"By the way, how's your mam?" I asked.

"How's my what?"

"Your mam. Your mother. We always ask that in Ireland."

"You never asked me."

"Maybe I should have."

"You're not in Ireland."

"Maybe my heart is."

There was a slight hesitation during which I could hear her wheels turning. Then Lindsay answered, "She's fine. She's still in remission."

"Oh. She had cancer?"

"They think they got it all. She also underwent therapy, which was tough on her, but she's done with that round now and starting to feel better."

"I'm sorry about the diagnosis, but relieved she's in remission."

"Yeah. Well. So, I'll indicate in our system that you're on target."

"Yes," I answered, my mind circling back to the call's original intent. "I'll have it to you."

"Okay. And—thanks for asking about my mom." Before I could answer, she added, "So long."

As I held the phone in my hand, I wondered why more Americans didn't show an interest in their fellow human beings the way the Irish did. Of course, Ireland was a small island roughly the size of South Carolina, while the United States could quite literally fit 116 Irelands within its mainland. I wondered if the larger a place grew, the more impersonal it became.

I set down the phone. I realized I had a hefty assignment to catch up on. Not only did I need to gather a lot more information on my ancestors during the Revolutionary War period, but I had to write the first five chapters. And it was due at the end of next week, right in the middle of Shay's visit.

I turned back to my laptop, opening it once again on the dining room table. About two minutes in, I abruptly closed it and packed it under my arm. This was ridiculous. I loved the lantern room, the 360-degree windows, the scenery just outside, and the overall ambiance. I wound my way upstairs without so much as a glance at the lantern, set up my laptop, and pulled up my chair. I did, however, steal a glance at the portrait and almost expected it to wink at me, which, thankfully, it did not.

A few clicks later, I was settling into the North Carolina Digital Collections on the State Archives of North Carolina's website.

12

The sun was setting when I finally looked up from my research. The skies still roiled with clouds, transforming the sunsets I'd become accustomed to seeing into shades of purple ranging from amethyst to indigo. The thinnest slice of red appeared on the distant horizon, and the adage came to mind: "Red sky at night, sailors' delight." I hoped this would be the case, and the long day of rain would quickly come to an end.

The wind had continued to intensify as the day progressed. It occurred to me that the windows in the lantern room were so tight that I couldn't even hear the wind howling. Yet, the trees and rushes beyond the mound bowed in unison to an unseen god.

As I gazed out at the landscape, something odd caught my eye, and I stood to take a closer look. Leaning toward the window, I made out the figure of a man standing just outside the fence line. As I stared at him, I realized he was peering back at me. My initial inclination was to duck out of view, but my feet felt bolted to the floor, and my blood went cold.

He was short in stature. He wore no shirt but appeared to be wearing a strange pair of leggings, nearly the color of his skin, which blended seamlessly with boot moccasins. But what stood out to me was his hair. It was the color of a raven, and it reached past his waist. As the wind kicked up, his hair blew outward and away from his face in thick, rich folds.

A flash of lightning lit up the sky, and for the briefest of moments, my attention turned to the heavens. When I looked back, the man stood a good twenty feet inside the fence line.

My mind tumbled over itself. There was no way anyone could traverse that fence and cover the ground he had in a fraction of a second. He remained nearly in the same position he had a moment earlier, his face still upturned toward the window where I stood. His hair still billowed with the breeze. My gut told me that a ghost would be oblivious to the wind. Wouldn't it?

My feet flew down the stairs before I realized I'd left the window. Somehow, I must have skipped every other stair, and I don't even remember passing the bedroom landing. I reached the door on the ground floor, threw back the chain and the deadbolt, and bounded onto the lawn. He had been on the other side of the lighthouse, and I stretched my legs like an Olympic runner as I rushed to confront him.

Then, just as quickly, I landed on my backside after running straight into what felt like a brick wall.

I heard my breath whoosh out of me, and for a moment, I lay stunned on the soft, muddy ground. Something screamed inside me to get up, but it felt as though I'd cracked a rib.

Then, a hand appeared seemingly out of nowhere.

I felt the blood drain from my face. My mouth gaped open, but I was unable to scream. As a voice inside me demanded that I not look, my rebellious eyes traversed the pale, open palm, the faded denim long sleeve, the metal buttons, and the slightly askew collar. His eyes were large and kind and almost golden in the waning light. I was still taking in his closely cropped blue-black hair when he reached down, grabbed my hands, and hauled me to my feet.

"Beckett," I managed to croak. "What are you doing here?"

His brows quickly knit.

When he didn't answer, I continued, "Did you see anyone? On the other side?" I pointed in the general direction.

Then his hands dropped from mine, and he began to run toward the open gate. I called after him, assuring him that he hadn't done anything wrong, though I doubted it, but I desperately wanted—needed—him to help me check the grounds. He continued as if he hadn't heard me, pausing only long enough to retrieve a dirt bike leaning against the chain link fence. I watched as he rode out of sight, his figure disappearing into an emerging mist.

I felt as though I was losing my mind. The door to the lighthouse remained open, just as it had when I bounded through it a moment ago. I considered returning to the comfort of the lighthouse, the cozy chair, and a comforting cup of tea, but something compelled me to turn away from the door to peer across the expanse of lawn.

I suppose one really couldn't call it a lawn because it was covered in a hodgepodge of bare sod and ground cover, which looked more like weeds than grass. I found myself gingerly stepping across it to avoid the mud that had formed from the rains, my eyes darting from my feet to the area in front of me. I circled the lighthouse, not once but twice, the second time reversing my steps as if it could give me a different perspective.

It was easy to see that the mound upon which the lighthouse stood was empty. There were no trees or thick brush to hide behind; all of that was beyond the fence, and only a few ornamental plants, not large enough to obscure a body, remained inside it. I came to stand beside the chain link, measuring its height against my own. It was at least six feet in height, and it leaned inward on one side and outward on the other as if decades of strong winds had forced it to tilt. Not even a superhuman could have traversed that fence as quickly as the figure had, and it had been on the opposite side from the open gate. Additionally, there had been no footprints in the soft, wet soil.

When I returned to the gate, I pulled it shut. A padlock hung on the links, and I closed my palm around it for a reflective moment. I couldn't use it, as the key was missing, and the last thing I needed was to get myself locked inside. Yet, as I stared at it, I realized it could be the answer. Tomorrow, I would make my way not to the Dikshita General Store but to another in a proper town, and I would buy a padlock. Then, I would keep it locked to prevent someone like Beckett from simply strolling inside, as if it were a public park.

As I made my way back to the door, mental scenes began to play out in front of me: scenes of the lantern on the dining table and then upstairs, of the lantern coming on oddly, and of security cameras that didn't record obvious breaches.

I closed the door behind me until I heard the solid click into place. Then, I bolted and chained the door before turning to the windows. If it took me the rest of the night, I would ensure that every one of these windows was properly locked and secured.

13

I was blurry-eyed as I slid behind the steering wheel, having spent the better part of the night working on my next book. I remained on the ground floor, which was blissfully silent. There were no sudden flashes of light penetrating down the spiral staircase, and I kept my attention on my laptop's screen and away from the open windows. It was odd living in a place that had no curtains or blinds. It wouldn't have struck me as odd while I researched this property online, as it was clearly advertised as remote, the closest neighbor several miles away as the crow flies. But when I first began writing the chapters my publisher required, I found myself willfully pushing the idea out of my mind that someone was just outside, watching me work. As the last of the light faded, however, and I became more engrossed in my story, everything else faded into the background before seeming to disappear completely.

I should have been at my laptop even now, and I felt a pang of guilt as I started my vehicle. The more logical part of me thought of returning to the lighthouse, phoning Billie, and asking that she change the locks. The impulsive, independent character on my shoulder urged me to do it myself to ensure no one else had the key.

So, here I was, under a bright and happy sun, ready to drive an hour away to buy a new door knob and the tools to install it.

I turned the vehicle around on the lawn in front of the lighthouse, pausing momentarily to scan the landscape beyond the fence line. I felt that familiar guilt of wasting time and effort to fix a problem that didn't truly exist. There had been no half-naked Native American standing outside my home; it had only been Beckett, and God only knew why he had been lurking about. Well, that would stop after today as well, once I installed a padlock on the gate that only I could open.

I found myself driving even more slowly than the pockmarked dirt drive required. Despite my better judgment, I felt compelled to peer into the tree lines and underbrush on either side of the road. What I anticipated seeing there, I don't know. I certainly did not expect a tribe of Native Americans with white German shepherds to weave their way through the trees as if following me as I retreated.

Yet, with every wave of a tree and burst of a breeze, my foot instinctively hovered over the gas pedal as if ready to gun it. It seemed to take much longer to reach the county road, which was graveled, and even longer to arrive at a proper asphalt road that took me past Dikshita.

I slowed at the Dikshita General Store, my eyes scanning the parking lot for signs of customers or perhaps for Beckett. However, the lot contained only Argo's aging truck forlornly sitting at the edge as though leaving room for the rush of customers that would never come. I turned at the intersection, marveling at the tiny spot in the road that seemed more like one man's private acreage than a proper village, and I found my mind wandering to what it might have been two hundred and fifty years prior.

It wasn't until I reached a state road that the phone's navigation system kicked in, directing me closer to civilization.

I wasn't far from Wilmington, and signs along the way reminded me that I was often driving somewhat parallel to the Cape Fear River as it wound its way from Fayetteville to Wilmington and eventually to the Atlantic. I envisioned Jon navigating these parts from the lighthouse through the channel to the river. The waterways had been the highways during the revolution, especially in these sparsely inhabited parts. It was still underpopulated, I reminded myself, as I passed occasional simple houses surrounded by various crops, without a single vehicle passing me in the opposite direction.

Eventually, I came to a much larger and highly traveled road. It felt odd to accelerate to the speed limit and still have vehicles flying past me. Perhaps I was settling into my remote setting better than I'd realized.

The traffic in Wilmington cemented this, and I couldn't wait to return to my tiny plot of land. I found a decent hardware store, where the aroma of potting soil, freshly cut lumber, and wood polish mingled in a cozy way, drawing me in to linger in the aisles. I found myself pausing over varied candles as I attempted to find just the right one for my little abode. I discovered an old-time furniture oil with a heady scent of lemon and pine. And I even stopped at a welcoming corner offering free coffee, a combination of caffeine and fragrance to awaken my senses.

Nearly an hour later, I rolled a cart to the register filled with things I hadn't intended to purchase, along with a new and shiny door knob, a fancy padlock with digital buttons in place of a key, and four new security cameras operating on lithium-ion batteries that I could place in strategic positions.

The drive home felt as if it flew past, but it was early afternoon before I turned once more at the Dikshita General Store. It appeared oddly forlorn after driving around Wilmington, and I wondered how Argo could possibly remain in business. The truck hadn't seemed to have moved since that morning, and the screen door at the corner entrance looked like something out of an old movie set from the '40s.

I had a fleeting feeling that in my quest to replicate the isolation I'd enjoyed in an Irish village, I'd gone too far in the wrong direction. Perhaps, I thought, I should have looked for a small but proper town. The feeling subsided as I got closer to the lighthouse, and I felt a warmth rising in my chest as I spied it past the trees, the clearing welcoming, and the structure gleaming in the sunlight.

My first order of business once I parked the car and even before I carried in my purchases, was to rifle through the bags until I located the padlock. I walked back to the gate, pulled it closed, and slipped the padlock into place, spinning it around. Then, just for good measure, I unlocked it to make sure I could, and then keyed the combination into my phone for safekeeping. Satisfied that I had effectively blocked anyone from suddenly appearing on the property, I returned to my car and carried the bags into the house.

Changing the lock went surprisingly quickly with the tools I had purchased. I took the old door knob and deadbolt and placed them into one of the shopping bags and carefully stored it inside the kitchen pantry on the bottom shelf. Then I mounted one security camera outside the front door so it had a good view of the gate, another monitoring the door from outside, the third on the ground floor, and the fourth in the lantern room. I disconnected the cameras I'd purchased from Argo, placing them in bags alongside the original door locks.

It was dinner time before I finished, but I felt proud of myself. Now I could turn my attention to finishing those first five chapters and completing the work I had been contracted to perform, without the worry that anyone or anything would disturb my progress.

14

There is no greater motivation to complete an assignment than the thought of the man I love traveling halfway across the world to see me, and I would be forced to cordon myself off from him while I write—and fume. I was determined that would not happen, and I felt a surging sense of accomplishment as I hit the *Send* button to send the first five chapters into cyberspace. Before I could close my laptop, they would be waiting in my editor's inbox.

The lighthouse had remained surprisingly silent. Without the lantern beaming on its own accord and apparitions manifesting on the ground below, it had become tranquil, serene, even. The grass grew green as the weather continued to warm, and the plethora of plants beyond the mound began to flourish; I dared say I was falling in love with it.

I carried my laptop down the spiral staircase and deposited it on the dining table on the ground floor. It was going on noon, but I wasn't that hungry. I made myself a cup of tea and an English muffin with jam and butter and headed out to the patio. On my tray was also Jon's journal, which I had neglected as I wrote the requisite chapters for my publisher.

Now, I was eager to find out what Jon's decision had been.

However, I discovered he was still pondering the fate of the nation and his role within it.

"January 11, 1776

*"It is insanity; is it not? For, so many of whom
I fought alongside at Culloden and elsewhere are
willing to risk everything—even their heads—to
fight the most formidable force in the world. Every
name on Britain's patriot list is equivalent to a
death sentence, and the family could fare no better.*

*"Alasdair visited me this day at great cost to
himself. He trusts that I will not turn him in, and
he is right. I could not do that to him or my sister.
But there are eyes everywhere. I feel them when I
am in the lantern room, especially at night when
the light must show my every movement. I feel
watchful eyes as I step outside my home to tend my
small garden, though I know Win would surely
have alerted me had there been anyone about. The
most normal and mundane tasks have become
elaborate, as I seek to show that I exist fully in the
light.*

*"But, that is untrue. For the darkness comes
for me, and I know I must decide quickly."*

I hesitated, glancing up to survey as much of the
ground as I could from my chair. I could see no evidence
that a garden had ever been planted. Of course, I reminded
myself, that was almost two hundred and fifty years ago,
and Billie had never mentioned that Harry had engaged in
the activity. Could I grow something here? I pondered. It
was spring, the ideal time to plant tomatoes, peppers,
perhaps even romaine.

I made a mental note to discover the types of
vegetables that would grow in this soil. I imagined that
Argo would know. I hadn't been to his store since I
discovered Beckett at my door. It was just as well, I told

myself. I took a sip of tea that was cooling too quickly and returned to the journal.

"I must be honest with myself and God. It is fear that keeps me loyal to King George. Fear of the unknown—this concept of a republic. It is not a novel idea nor even an original one. Rome became a republic over a thousand years ago when the Roman monarchy was overthrown. Ah, but what happened to the Roman Republic, but for it to collapse after the War of Actium? Who is to say that this new country the patriots envision will last as long? If it does not persist for the rest of my life, I will be a hunted man with nowhere left to hide.

"Even England herself was a republic for the briefest of times following the execution of King Charles I. That lasted—eleven years, I believe? Eleven years. That is what this new country faces. Threats from every direction. Spain has settled in the south. The French have settled in parts, as have the Germans. The patriots proclaim that France is on their side, but where are the French ships? I see no one fighting the English but the settlers, and they are woefully outmatched. The English have had hundreds of years to hone their army, while the settlers are comprised of shopkeepers, farmers, and the occasional blacksmith. What do they know of fighting—and governing?

"It is fear that keeps me from joining their ranks. It is the fear that the colonists will lose and lose badly, as we did at Culloden. And then there will be Hell to pay."

I hesitated once more as his words sank in. It would be only 85 years before the country would erupt in a war that would make this revolution pale in comparison. It had been a miracle that the country was not ripped permanently in two during the American Civil War, and even today, we continue to deal with its consequences. We rose to superpower status at the end of World War II, mainly due to the atomic bomb; however, like Rome and Athens, superpowers ebb and flow, rising and dying. It was difficult for me to imagine present-day Italians, Egyptians, and Greeks once ruling generous parts of the known world.

Perhaps he was right to be afraid.

But then, I reminded myself, he must be in his fifties or sixties by now; hadn't I read his age somewhere? If he lived out his natural life, he would be gone 50 years or more before Fort Sumter fired the first shot to start the Civil War. And that's all he had to do, I realized. He just needed to make peace for his remaining days on earth.

Isn't that what we all must do? I pondered as I spread thick raspberry jam on my muffin. I hesitated as I held the muffin a few inches from my lips. Had Jon never married and had children? I wondered. I had assumed he lived here completely alone; hadn't he said that himself? But then, if Argo and Beckett were descendants, who did they descend from? Could they have been from Alasdair's lineage?

It was an uncommon name. Perhaps I could research him and discover Argo's lineage. After all, everything was online these days.

There were more entries made that day, the only telltale sign that he had returned again and again, a slightly different lilting cursive, as if his mind had begun to think faster and more frantically. For the first time, I realized how tenuous life must have been in those times. There were no guarantees that either party would win. The losers could be summarily executed, as habeas corpus would not become law until the Judiciary Act of 1789, precisely to prevent hasty executions, deportations, or punishment.

Until then, neighbors could turn on neighbors, unleashing a hellish experience for them all. And, even if the colonists did manage to expel English rule, what was to say that another country would not arrive to fill the void?

15

As it turned out, Jon's future was about to take a dramatic turn. He would be visited twice on the same day, once by a small sloop captained by a smaller man, and then by a tiny, deteriorating rowboat that would accidentally find its way down the channel to his lighthouse.

"January 12, 1776

"A small sloop made its way down the channel today just before dusk. I had ascended to the lantern room and was preparing the lantern for the night when I spotted it moving eastward from the Cape Fear region toward Wilmington. I would normally have remained as I was and allowed it to pass through undeterred, but a voice inside me urged me to take the newly acquired logbook and stand on the shore.

"It was a good thing that I did, for two men navigated the sloop while a third stood at the bow, his hand inside his jacket like Napoleon himself, cutting a ridiculous caricature atop the small boat as though he considered it a battleship. As they approached the lighthouse, he held up his hand in a sign for them to stop and pull ashore.

"I called out a greeting to them, my eyes naturally moving upward to the British flag flapping in the wind. The man in charge did not respond in a similarly friendly manner, either by word or expression, as he stepped onto the shore.

"I asked for his name, dutifully poised with my ink to record the first visitors since given my orders at Cross Creek, but he grabbed the book from my hand and demanded to know why it was empty. I attempted to explain that this was not a well-traveled channel, and I had just received my orders, but he refused to listen.

"For the next half hour, he inspected the grounds and eyed me suspiciously, questioning my allegiance to King George. I responded with the pledge I was committed to upholding.

"His name, once it was finally provided for my logbook, was Captain Hugh Horton. I recorded the others' names as well, but it was Horton's that seemed to stick in my soul. I knew instinctively the man was trouble. He was short in stature, perhaps not much over five feet in height, and I towered over him. From the way his dark, beady eyes surveyed me, I suspect he resented my height and bearing. He maintained a brooding scowl, which was curious, considering I should have been considered an ally.

"As he returned to the shore where the sloop was waiting, I breathed an inward sigh of relief, but he suddenly turned to me as if to catch me in an act of treason. Then he quite suddenly marched to the stable and retrieved an armful of hay set aside for my horse and deposited it at the base of the lighthouse. Before I could stop him or recover from my shock, he pulled a fire striker from his pocket and deftly set the hay on fire.

"As I scrambled to put out the fire lest it set the whole lighthouse ablaze, he laughed—cruelly, I thought—and told me that was nothing compared to the fate that awaited those who cooperated with the colonists.

"I singed my hands and nearly caught my legs afire as I stomped out the blaze and pulled the hay away from the wooden lighthouse. I pulled it all the way to the channel and watched as the food for my horse simultaneously went up in flames and sank to the bottom. His laughter continued as the sloop continued out of sight.

"I have been left shaking with rage."

I discovered my own hands shaking as I read the entry. Though I owned no animals at present due to my travels, I was an unabashed animal lover. I'd ridden horses all my life and considered past dogs and Shay's current dog, Sadie, among my most cherished relationships. It took a cruel person to harm another's property, but to burn an animal's fodder and stable was especially egregious. Captain Horton might have left Jon and his animals homeless, with nowhere to go and possibly scant materials with which to rebuild.

There could be no logic for it. My historical work suggested that anyone who committed such gratuitous cruelty against others was likely a small and petty person attempting to appear powerful. Such power never lasted.

I contemplated this new development for some time before turning back to Jon's journal. It appeared there was much more in store for him.

"January 13, 1776

"It has been a long night and day fraught with danger. Shortly after Horton left the lighthouse, a rowboat appeared. It was a miracle that it had remained afloat, as it appeared unseaworthy and likely to sink at any moment. The man who navigated it through the dusk appeared as surprised to see me as I was to see him. It hadn't occurred to me until then that I had neglected to light the lantern due to Horton's interruption.

"His name was Ben, and he was a runaway slave. Needless to say, I did not record him in the logbook. I warned him against continuing down the channel, as I was quite convinced Horton would be a cruel fate for him to come upon.

"I invited him inside while I hid his boat under firewood. I did not have much to offer him, but I shared what I had, and he ate as though it were his first meal in a very long time. He also drank a considerable amount of water and ale, and I noticed his hands shook as he raised the cup to his lips as if his nerves had gotten the better of him.

"It turned out that he did not know the lighthouse was there, which was not surprising. He had intended to get lost in the swamps where the dogs could not follow his scent, hoping to find his way to the sea by God's grace. Once there, it was unclear to me how he planned to leave the mainland or how he could find his way to the islands, which were also ruthlessly governed by slave traders.

"The cruel fact of the matter was that he could not possibly escape if he continued eastward. I explained this to him as he ate. Initially, he eyed me suspiciously, as if expecting me to tackle him to the ground, bind him, and return him to his master, and he appeared ready to bolt at any moment. But his eyes began to show an inner light when I

suggested instead that I take him to a tribe known for helping runaway slaves.

"Ben washed in the channel before falling asleep in my bed while I kept watch. I had thought of placing him in the cellar in the event Horton returned, as I had a bad feeling about the snake of a man, but thought better of it. The cellar spooked me even in the light of day. I could not imagine the total blackness of it during the night. Even a lit candle could not cut through the gloom. There was wind in the cellar, of which I could never determine from whence it came, and it took on the characteristics of whispers so that I felt there were others there speaking to me. But I have digressed.

"We waited until the dark of night had settled in. I never lit the lantern. I did not wish for the light. I knew these waters even in blackness. What may appear to another as a random patch of marsh grass was a marker to me, indicating whether to turn left or right. As we continued westward, we eventually came upon Drowning Creek, which led me to the tribe I sought.

"Warriors met me along the shore, but I had gifts to present to them. I was taken to one of their leaders, who immediately agreed to welcome the slave. I noticed that as the members gathered, there were several black men and women among them, while others had the appearance of both black and tribal descent. I knew Ben would not be treated as a slave but would become, if he remained, a member of their tribe.

"I stayed for a while, partaking of a meal and swapping news, and I even acquired some hay from them to replenish my horse once I returned home. Long before dawn, I was impatient to return, as I did not know whether Horton or his men might

return to burn my home down or take my horse and chickens.

"However, my worries were for naught. A violent storm blew in from the sea, a threat to anyone unlucky enough to find themselves upon the water. The marshes morphed in the darkness and rain, and it was only my intimate knowledge of them that allowed me to navigate the narrow, shifting channels. I felt like I needed two more arms as I alternated between navigating and baling water, but eventually, I found myself back at my home. I carried the wet hay to the stable, intent on pulling it out into the sun once it reappeared. Justine had been, it appeared, blissfully asleep while I was absent. Win must have spent the night chasing rabbits and returned home shortly after me. My two hens, Henrietta and Basille, were quietly nesting.

"I returned to my bed, gratefully collapsing into it. I knew in my soul that I would see Horton again, and I slept fitfully despite my exhaustion."

16

I awakened to find Jon's journal lying across my torso, open to the last entry I'd read. I had spent the remainder of the night dreaming that I had traveled back in time, and it was I who experienced the cruelty of Hugh Horton and the kindness of the tribe who accepted a stranger—and a runaway slave, at that—into their midst.

I wondered as I lay there halfway between full wakefulness and sleep, whether Jon's bed had been in the same spot as I now lounged and whether it had been in this very room where the slave had spent the night before Jon had transported him westward. Then I remembered that the original lighthouse had been constructed of wood, and this one was made of masonry. As I became more fully awakened, I found myself studying the walls and windows, wondering whether the old lighthouse beams were beneath the newer construction. Surely, I thought, Harry would have repurposed the wood or kept the original bones. Or would he?

Then, there was the matter of the cellar. Each floor was comprised of beautiful hardwood, and I was certain it had been installed during the renovation. Moreover, each story was relatively small, consisting of only one circular room. An entrance to the cellar would have—or should have—been easy to spot.

My phone alarm beckoned me from my thoughts, and I swung my legs over the side of the bed. I needed to change the sheets and straighten up before I left for the airport in Raleigh, where I would greet Shay as he arrived from Ireland.

~~~~~

I first met Shay, whose full name is Seamus MacGregor, in person during my visit to Ireland last year. He was, and still is, a renowned historian, particularly in the field of Western Europe, sought after for his detailed knowledge and encyclopedic memory. He had assisted me in my quest to uncover facts regarding my ancestors during O'Doherty's Rebellion of 1608, and, well, we'd become intimately acquainted.

I spotted him easily as he descended the escalator to the baggage claim area. He stood nearly head and shoulders above most of the people around him, and his broad shoulders appeared even more impressive in his heavy wool coat. It had obviously been quite a bit colder when he left Ireland than it would be in North Carolina.

He wore a herringbone tweed cap, and as he reached the bottom of the escalator and spotted me waiting, he swept his cap off his chestnut hair so he could encircle me within his arms and kiss me so deeply that I could feel other passengers glancing our way. When he pulled away, I cupped the side of his face in my hand, his soft beard caressing my open palm.

"Oh, and what a sight for sore eyes you are!" he exclaimed.

I laughed. "I can say the same for you!"

The time and distance that had separated us slipped away, and by the time we retrieved his luggage and reached my car, it felt as though we had never been apart. He quickly shed his heavy coat and cap, tossing them atop his luggage before rolling up his sleeves. Shay was understandably hungry after the flight from Europe to

New York and the connecting flight to Raleigh, so we dropped into an Italian restaurant just southeast of the airport.

The lunch crowd had come and gone, and it was blissfully serene as we slipped into a booth. The dining area was dim, despite the windows at the front of the room. The dark paneling and burgundy seating muted the light. Soft Italian operatic instrumentals wafted through the restaurant.

Shay reached for my hands immediately. "I've missed touching you," he said. He had the slightest bit of a brogue mixed into his Irish accent.

The waitress's appearance abruptly reminded us that we were not alone, as much as we wanted to be. We ordered our drinks and perused the menu for a few moments.

"And how is your research coming along, 'ey?" Shay asked after we ordered.

I told him about my Raleigh research into my ancestors and provided a quick overview of the first five chapters of my book. He listened attentively, but his eyes lit up when I mentioned the journal of the man who had built the lighthouse.

The waitress returned with our iced teas and a sliced loaf of casareccio. We watched as she poured olive oil into a dish containing a mixture of Italian herbs and spices. As she left us on our own, we dug into the delicious and warm homemade bread. I could feel my eyes rolling back in my head as I tasted the bread and dipping oil.

"I've been experiencing some activity," I said hesitantly when our main meal of agnolotti arrived.

"Activity?" Shay repeated, puzzled.

As we leisurely consumed our meals, I told him of the white German shepherd, the Native American, and my discovery of Beckett Dikshita outside my door. I held back from mentioning the disembodied voice I thought I'd heard. For some reason I couldn't explain, I felt that discussing Jon was a betrayal of him. He might have died over two centuries ago, but he felt very much alive to me.

When I was finished, Shay's eyes were narrowed in thought. "I'm relieved you changed the locks and set up the cameras," he said thoughtfully. "I think we should make it a habit for the locals to see us together, don't you think? Give them the impression that there are two of us there. As isolated as you say it is, I don't fancy the idea of the village folk believing you're there all alone."

"I agree, though the locals so far have consisted only of Argo and Beckett Dikshita." I didn't want to ask exactly how long he would remain before he was due back in Ireland for his job at the university. It seemed that doing so would hasten his departure. "And what do you think of the—unexplained—" I hesitated.

"Ghosts?" he offered. "Apparitions? You didn't believe a Native American and disappearing dog would get past me, did you? Well, you've come to an expert on that as well."

"Oh?" I chided. "You're an expert?"

He chewed his food thoughtfully before becoming serious. "The Irish have a different mindset when it comes to spirits, they do," he said, his voice softening. He cleared his throat. "You Americans have such a physical approach to life; you tend to think that when a person's body ceases to function, their soul is taken away as well."

I thought of my father, who had passed away shortly before I went to Ireland. What he said was true. We buried my father as if his presence was completely gone from our lives; as though every aspect of his being had passed from us. On phone calls with my mother, she often mentioned that she could feel his presence. She'd step into a room and smell his cologne or the aromatic blend of cherry and Bourbon tobacco from the ornate pipe that perpetually rested between his side teeth.

My brother and I chalked it up to the fact that our parents had owned that home for decades; of course, his scent would remain there shortly after his death and dissipate soon after. It didn't mean, as our mother inferred, that he was still there. In fact, it only served to redouble our efforts to get her to vacate that rambling, drafty old house outside of Boston. It was way too big for her anyway, with its dark, basement laundry room that had scared us as children, to the overstuffed attic with ghostly sepia portraits.

My mom and dad had owned two other homes, one in New York and another in Los Angeles, and she eventually moved back to her penthouse in Midtown Manhattan.

It occurred to me that maybe the creepy colonial Boston house was why I was so susceptible to otherworldly occurrences. Perhaps it had been bred into me from the home that had belonged to my ancestors.

"So you see, the Irish," Shay was saying as though oblivious to my sudden mental departure, "with the centuries of history, our myths and legends, we believe the body might pass from this earth, but the soul remains. You experienced that yourself in that rural cottage you rented."

"That feels like a lifetime ago," I said as the memories rose within me of a woman's disembodied voice crying for her lost sons.

"I don't know as much about American history as I do Western Europe," he continued. "But don't be fooled by the new world moniker, for the North American continent is just as old as any other. It's my understanding that the United States was divided into roughly five hundred Native American tribes, each with their distinct territories, before they ever laid eyes on a white man. They may have lived in the area of the lighthouse for centuries. Perhaps it is not that unusual that you've seen the ghost of one; perhaps it would be more unusual if you had not seen more."

I considered his words as we continued eating. "What could they want?" I asked. I felt a chill rush through me as if someone had opened a door. I wondered if it was possible for a ghost to follow a living being. I had a vision of me dutifully driving up the interstate while a spirit sat in the back seat. I hoped one could not attach itself to me. The thought of him listening to our discussion was disconcerting.

Shay shrugged. "It's impossible to tell. Each spirit was once a human being. Each one could have a different reason for hanging about. Perhaps they are simply passing through with the fancy of seeing their old home," he added quickly as if my expression was giving away my angst, "and it's nothing more than that."

"And the dog?"

"If it were a spirit, it would be the same for him, I suppose. The dog might have been quite happy living there and might have returned to see if the bone he buried might still be about." His voice grew deeper. "No one has tried to hurt you in any way, have they?"

"No," I said quickly. Then, more forcefully, "No. Not at all."

He observed me for a long moment. "No poltergeist, then. In that case, I don't believe they mean you harm. They may not even know you are there. Some believe it takes a portal on both sides for each to move through to see the other."

I opened my mouth but closed it abruptly.

"Is there something you're not telling me, love?"

"Well." I felt like I was betraying Jon as I took a deep breath. "Jonathan Corbyn, the man who wrote the journal."

"The one who built the lighthouse originally?" Shay added.

I nodded. "Beckett—the odd young man at the general store—told me to ask Jon—Jonathan—not to turn on the lantern anymore."

Shay put his fork down. "And did you do that?"

"I did. I felt pretty silly. But…"

"Let me guess. After you asked him, and I assume you did it respectfully, the lantern didn't come on again?"

I nodded.

We chewed in silence for a moment before Shay spoke again. "I'd like to pop into a hardware store on our way to the lighthouse."

"Oh?"

"I want to buy an EMF detector." Seeing my confusion, he continued, "We only assume the electricity was run to code in the lighthouse, 'ey? An electromagnetic meter can determine whether magnetic and electric fields are leaking from any of the equipment there—a refrigerator, television, appliances—"

"—lantern—"

"Aye. And we can test the power boxes as well. It is entirely possible there is a heightened electromagnetic field there that can completely explain the feeling of ghosts."

"What do you mean?"

"Well," he shifted in his seat, "suppose you had a basement and every time you went down there, you had an uneasy feeling. Maybe the air feels different. Maybe you feel like you're being watched. Or you just have a sense of unease, 'ey? An EMF detector might identify electricity leaking from the basement's power box, which is what is giving you 'the creeps.'" He motioned with his fingers to form a quote. "It is quite common in older homes."

Ah, one more reason for my mother to sell that old house. The basement is leaking an electrified field. Maybe my brother and I glowed in the dark after venturing down there. "Speaking of a basement…" I hesitated.

"You have one and it feels creepy?" he laughed.

"I haven't found one, but Jon—Jonathan—the man who wrote the journal—he mentioned a cellar. But I haven't found one."

"Ah. If the lighthouse was built in the late 1700s, the cellar would have been very small. It likely would have been filled in during an extensive renovation. Especially if it was in the moors, the ground might have shifted to fill it in naturally."

I smiled at his use of the word moors. It sounded so much better than swamps.

The server returned to take away our plates and offer dessert. We eagerly selected Panna Cotta and coffee with Bailey's. As she stepped away, Shay asked, "So, am I to understand you're on a first-name basis with Jonathan Corbyn?"

I felt myself blushing. "I suppose I am," I admitted. "There's something about reading his journal—it all seems so personal—that I have begun to feel like I know the man." I related the story of the runaway slave to Shay, how Jon had offered his own bed to him, and then transported him to a local Native American tribe for safety. "He must have done this at great risk to himself," I finished. "Had anyone discovered them—patriots or loyalists—I shudder to think what might have happened."

"Assisting a runaway slave?" Shay added. "There would have been grave consequences."

Our dessert and coffee arrived. Though I was already full from the bread and pasta, I was very happy that we'd chosen to have dessert. It was the perfect end to the meal. The Panna Cotta was served in fluted glass bowls with delicate stems. We took a moment to admire the layer of jam on the bottom, custard in the middle, and raspberries crowning it with the perfect dash of powdered sugar. As we dove into it, our conversation turned to gentle moans of admiration. I realized just how much I'd missed Shay's moans, and I was suddenly eager to arrive home where we could experience total privacy.

At least, I hoped our time would be private.

17

I awakened at the first promise of dawn. I lay on my side as the window just beyond the bed took on the slightest shade of indigo. As I watched the color creep up the windowpane, I became aware I was being watched.

I glanced over my shoulder. The covers were pulled back, and through the gloom, I made out the indentations in the mattress and pillow where Shay had lain. An odd scent in the air reminded me of wet pine and tobacco. I started to pull myself to a seated position when a movement caught my attention.

A figure stood across the room. I squinted to see better, but they were encased in shadows. The figure appeared shorter and slighter than Shay's imposing physique. I couldn't see his face, yet I knew he was observing me.

Then it turned and started up the spiral stairs.

"Shay?"

"Aye?"

I cried out and jumped completely out of bed as the voice came from behind me. Shay appeared at the bathroom door on the other side of the room.

"Are you alright, dear?"

My heart pounded frenetically, and it took me a moment before I could speak. I pointed frantically toward the staircase. "Someone was standing there," I managed to get out.

Shay walked to the stairs with great strides, confidence oozing from him. A man could never understand the vulnerabilities of a woman, I thought as I slid my feet into my slippers and reached for my robe.

He peered down the stairs and then up. "Right here?" he asked quizzically.

"Right there," I insisted. I joined him at the landing. "He went up there."

Shay reached behind me to the nightstand and yanked the lamp cord from the socket. It was a heavy lamp that appeared to be solid brass, and I watched as he quickly pulled off the shade and wrapped the cord around the base.

"Is that your weapon?" I breathed.

"You have a better idea, do you?"

Before I could respond, he was taking the stairs two at a time. I followed behind, my tentative steps causing me to drop back. I hesitated at the last swirl as I caught a glimpse of him standing on the top step, the lamp in both hands, almost as though he wielded a sword. He glanced down at me and then nodded to me, holding out his hand to encourage me to join him.

"There's nothing here," he said as we both stepped onto the hardwood floor.

The lantern room was awash in purple and blue shadows that almost danced across the floor.

"You saw, perhaps, an optical illusion," he said, setting the lamp onto the floor by the top step. "'Tis only the sunrise."

"No," I insisted. "No. I know what I saw. There was a man standing there staring at me. He was watching me in bed. It wasn't the sunrise."

Shay made his way around the room as he checked each window and the door leading onto the gallery deck. "Everything is locked," he announced, though I could clearly see it was. I could also peer out the windows in every direction from my spot near the center of the room; had anyone been on the outside deck, it would have been impossible to miss him. After dutifully checking every lock, he came from behind and wrapped his arms around me. "There's nothing at all up here, darling. And if it would make you feel better, I'll check the other floors as well."

"It will make me feel better," I admitted.

"Isn't the sunrise gorgeous?" he murmured against my hair.

Despite the circumstances, I had to admit it was. The land was flat, providing an expansive view. As we gazed toward the horizon, the colors of the sunrise were morphing as they rose. What I had witnessed only moments earlier had turned into shades of red and orange. It was impossible to tear myself away from his arms, and I wrapped mine atop his as he pressed against my back. We watched as the skies seemed to part, allowing the brilliance of the morning sun to greet us. It was hard to believe that only moments ago we had been stalking an intruder. Maybe, I thought, it had been only a trick of the eye.

After a few moments, he whispered in my ear, "Wouldn't this be even more beautiful from the bed?"

I turned in his arms to catch the twinkle in his eyes. "I can think of something else that might be beautiful there."

He chuckled. Taking a step back, he grasped my hand and we made our way toward the staircase. He reached forward to retrieve the lamp, and we descended to the bedroom level, where he set it back on the nightstand. Before I could assist him by plugging it back in, he whirled me around to hold me. His lips were nearing mine when a sudden flash of light caught both our attention.

I felt the blood drain from my face as the EMF meter on the nightstand fully lit up. We both stared at it. It remained inside the preformed, plastic blister packaging. An image on the front of the meter ranged from green to red with a light above each color to form five in a row. It remained solidly lit.

Shay stepped away from me. As he picked up the package, the lights went out. "What the devil?" he breathed. He carried the package to the chair where he'd laid his pants the night before and dug out a Swiss Army knife from one of the pockets. It took him a few moments to break through the packaging. I was reminded of the frustrating thoughts I encountered every time I had to slice through a blister pack, convinced the manufacturer never intended the consumer to open it.

When he finally broke through, a 9-volt battery next to the meter popped out. After I bent to pick it up from the floor, I rose to find Shay's face ashen. "What is it?" I asked.

He turned the meter toward me. He had opened the battery compartment to reveal that it was empty.

I felt the room begin to spin, and for the briefest of moments, I detected the scent of pine and tobacco as though someone had just brushed past me. "Do you smell that?" I meant for my voice to remain a whisper, but it croaked as it left my lips.

"What is that?" he asked.

Though I remained perfectly still, my eyes scanned the room. As it was circular, I could see nearly every inch. The only thing breaking up the perfect circle was the bathroom, and I could see through the door to the sink and bath. "Jonathan Corbyn," I said, my voice trembling more than I would have preferred. Then I felt a jolt through me. "Jon," I said more forcefully. "Are you playing games?"

There was no answer, and had there been one, I'm pretty sure I'd have been halfway to Dikshita in the blink of an eye, padlocked gate or no. I'd have jumped right over it like a pole vault, and I wouldn't have even needed the pole.

Shay stared at me for a long moment before he seemed to snap out of his thoughts. He retrieved the battery from me and placed it into the housing. Then he held it beside the nightstand where it had been. The lights remained off.

He made his way slowly around the room, pausing at intervals along the wall, bending at times to the external outlet levels, checking at waist-high, and extending his arm to verify the levels above his head. One light registered as the meter neared the outlets, my charging station, and a clock radio. He stepped into the bathroom, slowly waving the meter past the outlets, the sink, the bath, and the fixtures. When he returned to the bedroom, he stepped back to the nightstand where it had first lit up. The lights remained off.

After a long moment, he spoke. "This lit up as I would have expected," he said quietly. He turned toward me. "Every piece of electrical equipment emits magnetic fields. You want them on this low end here," he pointed to the lowest level, "and that's exactly where it registered at the outlets and small appliances." He pointed toward the clock radio. "I'm going downstairs to check it there."

I followed him down the spiral staircase. He took the stairs slowly as he raised and lowered the meter. The results in the living area were similar to those in the bedroom. When we reached the kitchen, the meter registered three lights near the refrigerator and other appliances. Four lights flickered when he stepped to the fuse box and opened it.

He stopped in the middle of the living area and stared at me. "What precisely did you see?"

"He was staring at me," I insisted. "I couldn't see his face, but I knew he was watching me."

"He was watching you sleep?"

I nodded.

"I don't believe I approve of that at all."

I laughed nervously. Then I became somber. "You don't think—last night—"

"No," he said forcefully. "No. No. No."

"It's a 'no' then." Our eyes met. I raised my voice. "Jonathan," I called out. "Jon. Maybe I've no right to ask this, since this is the house you built—kind of—but—"

"—but we don't need you spying on us while we're sleeping—or otherwise," Shay completed.

"Do you believe he's here?"

Laughter split through the air, causing us both to jump. Before I could ask if Shay had heard it too, he pointed toward the stairs. "It came from up there."

"Your meter," I cried out.

All five lights were lit. Shay took the stairs to the top floor, and though I was two steps behind, my eyes never wavered from the meter, and it never stopped its full glow. When we emerged onto the top floor, the sunrise had been replaced with daylight. Then the meter abruptly grew dark.

18

I settled into the dining table next to the window as Shay slid a plate in front of me. There must be a special place in heaven for a man who cooks. He'd done wonders with what he'd found in my pantry, and now I inhaled the fresh aroma of hot peppermint tea, Crème Brûlée French toast, proper European bacon, and Orange Creamsicle juice made with a touch of vanilla and cream.

He slipped into the seat across from me, his eyes roaming across the landscape outside our window before settling on my face. "Have you walked the perimeter of your property?" he asked.

I told him about my cursory inspection the day Beckett had wandered onto my property. He listened intently as he ate. When I finished, he chewed his food for a moment and then took a long sip of tea. "Would you mind if I took a look around after breakfast?"

"Not at all. Would you like for me to join you?"

"I'd enjoy nothing better. Well, unless—"

I chuckled. "We might have to get a hotel room." I shuddered. "I don't want to think of a ghost watching us."

"Do you think ghosts have X-ray vision?" he asked with a grin. "I could cover you up nicely. Do you gather they can see through blankets?"

"Do I really want to find out?"

We ate in silence for a moment, save for my instinctive groan of pleasure as I tasted the French toast stuffed with creamy, rich custard and caramel sauce.

"Now, that sound is familiar," Shay said with a crooked smile.

It was surprisingly normal sitting at the table after the way in which we'd awakened only a short time ago. The sun had risen, heralding a warm day as it burned through the Carolina morning haze. There was a plethora of birds soaring over the swamp brush, from the outstretched wings of turkey vultures to the gentle glide of seagulls, their calls intermingling in the morning air.

"I'd like to try something, if you don't mind," Shay said.

"If it's anything like this breakfast, I'm game."

He took a sip of juice. "It would be quite different."

"How so?" I looked up to find him with a pensive look on his face.

"I want to try a séance."

"A what?"

"A séance. It's where—"

"I know what it is. But, why?"

He set down his fork. "I'm concerned about you here, Hayley. I can't hide it, nor do I think I'd want to."

"Because of the ghost."

"The ghost, for sure. And Beckett. And whoever else is wandering about."

"Would we be opening a Pandora's box?"

He shrugged. "Not if we do it right."

"I don't want to anger Jonathan—or whoever is with him."

"Well, and that's the thing of it, isn't it? We're assuming it's the man who built this structure and wrote the journal, 'ey? But what if it isn't?"

"Who else would it be?"

He laughed softly. "How long has the Earth been here? How many souls might have traveled through these parts centuries ago?"

"Spoken like a true Irishman."

"But it's true, isn't it? In more recent history, there have been Americans, British, Native Americans, and African slaves... Who knows how many were here during times we know little to nothing about?"

"How would we do this?"

"I'm still thinking about it. But here's what I'd like to do. After breakfast, say we go for a bit of a stroll around the mound here, perhaps even down the lane beyond the gate. When we return, we gather a few things and go upstairs to the lantern room. I want to open the windows and doors and let the fresh air in. And see if we can connect with the spirit that lives here."

"In broad daylight?"

"Why not?"

"I don't know. I thought séances were done at night."

"In the dark. With candlelight." He raised one eyebrow.

I nodded.

"But this spirit has a strong presence here, wouldn't you say? And we'll have more modern means of speaking with him." Before I could question the details, he finished his breakfast and stood. Seeing that I was also finished, he asked, "I'll wash, you'll dry?"

~~~~~

The land was just as it had been when I'd walked it alone, though the combination of grass and ground cover was becoming slightly greener and longer with the Carolina spring. Shay hesitated at various points along the way to lean against the chain link fence and peer into the reeds and underbrush. He spotted an alligator whose eyes peeked slightly above the water as it watched us, its form nearly immobile. A cardinal landed on a tree branch and burst into song, while a woodpecker drilled into a neighboring tree. He also thought he spotted a blue heron walking in the shallows, perhaps searching for minnows.

We unlocked the gate and strolled down the lane. I felt more vulnerable there without the protection of the fence between me and whatever wildlife might fancy me for dinner. Perhaps because we were looking, we seemed engulfed in bird sightings. A possum scurried into the swamps, and a garden snake coiled around an upper tree branch. I shuddered as we came upon a bright yellow spider basking in the sun, its legs outstretched in its intricate web.

"That looks large enough to kill me," I whispered.

"It's an orb spider," Shay said thoughtfully. "I didn't think they came out until the fall."

"If I looked like that, I'd come out whenever I wanted."

Shay laughed. "It should be harmless to a human. Give it a wide berth, but if you're bitten, it should be no worse than a bee sting."

"Oh, I'll give it a wide berth, alright."

"So, where do you suppose the channel once was?" He stopped at a clearing between some trees and peered through.

"I haven't the slightest," I admitted. "Maybe Billie—Harry's niece—could shed some light on it. She mentioned that the original lighthouse had only been in use for twenty years, right around the time of the Revolutionary War. Then the water was diverted, and I suppose the channel dried up."

"Do you have a boat here?"

"At the lighthouse? No. I haven't seen one."

"Aye, and we've walked the property," he said thoughtfully. "Perhaps, later today or tomorrow, we can visit the village near here to see if they have rentals?"

"Dikshita? I'm sure Argo would know where we can get one."

"Just a canoe or a kayak," Shay said as he started to walk again. "Something we can use to get back into the brushes."

"Are you sure that's safe?"

"Not at all," he chuckled. "But we'll have our oars to whack anything that tries to get in our boat. A canoe would be more stable," he mused as if to himself. Shay stopped and turned around to peer at the top of the trees. "Some of those trees appear to be forty feet tall."

"I suppose."

"How fast do they grow, though?"

"What do you mean?"

"I mean, what did they look like two hundred years ago? Were they even here? Or could all of this—" he waved his arm "—have been water? How far away could you have been and still seen the lighthouse lamp?"

"I never thought about that."

"Is it the same height as the original?"

"As far as I know. I had the impression Harry built the new one right over the old one."

"Right over it, you say? He didn't tear it down and rebuild?"

"I don't know. I don't know why I said that." I took a couple of steps before whirling back around to face Shay. "I believe she told me he tore it down because it was collapsing in on itself. It was made of wood and was over 150 years old when it was discovered. Surely, they didn't rebuild on top of the old bones. I don't know why I said that." I shook my head.

"People make mistakes all the time," Shay chuckled. "Don't be so hard on yourself."

"I don't make mistakes like that," I insisted. "Not when it comes to history."

"Well, if you're willing," Shay said as he joined me, "I'd like to have a chat with Billie. Perhaps she has some old drawings somewhere. Harry must have needed licensing and inspections, wouldn't you think?"

"Back then? I mean, it was only a few decades, but out here in the middle of nowhere, I don't know."

"We'll find out where the county seat is and have an ask."

We continued on for a few more minutes. I suppose we must have walked a couple of miles at least, and by the time we turned back, my legs were already aching. I'd become accustomed to walking while in Ireland, and I was surprised I'd gotten out of shape so quickly.

The kitchen was welcoming as we made our way through the door, and the cool pitcher of tea in the frig was exactly what we both needed. We poured some glasses, took a few long swigs of it, allowing it to cool our throats, before Shay turned to me.

"Are you ready for a séance then?"

19

The sunny skies had given way to an approaching summer storm, with dark, roiling clouds on the horizon. As we opened the windows in the lantern room, the wind felt brisk and heavy with imminent rain, and the trees beyond the lighthouse swayed and dipped.

We pulled two chairs into the middle of the room facing the lantern. Shay pulled two items from his pocket, and though I could easily ascertain their uses, he felt compelled to describe them. Yet, as he started, I realized he spoke not to me but to Jonathan—or any other spirits inclined to participate.

"We are here in peace," he began. "We mean you no harm, and we ask the same of you." He placed his phone upright on the ledge behind us so it was facing the room. "This device will record our voices and images. If you have something to say, we might not hear you, but this device might record you. We are interested in anything you have to say to us."

I felt apprehension wash over me and fought the temptation to leave. It wasn't that I had experienced relative calm at the lighthouse; it was quite the opposite. But I was reluctant to topple the apple cart and unleash whatever forces might be there. They had not yet harmed me, and I suppose I was beginning to fear negative energies crossing a boundary.

Before I could react, Shay continued by placing the EMF meter on the lantern stand. "This meter will record your presence," he said. "We know that you know how to use it."

The meter suddenly lit up with five full bars.

Shay swallowed as the meter went dark. "Alright, then. We ask that the Holy Spirit surround us," he said, giving me a sideways glance. "Make sure we remain in the light and keep us safe from harm." His voice became a bit louder as he reached for both my hands. "I am going to ask a series of questions that require a yes or no response. If the answer is yes, please light up the meter as you just did. If the answer is no, please allow it to remain dark. Are you understanding me?"

The meter lit with five bars.

Shay squeezed my hands as the winds whistled outside the windows and sent a cool chill through the room. "Are we speaking with Jonathan Corbyn?"

The meter lit again.

Shay waited until it went dark before he continued, "May we call you Jon?"

The meter lit. I felt my mouth go dry as though I'd walked Death Valley at high noon. I struggled to calm my heart, which had begun to beat so forcefully that it took my breath away.

"Are you alone, Jon?"

The meter remained dark. Our hands were moist, and I wondered whether it was Shay or I who had suddenly begun perspiring. Glancing at the calmness in Shay's face, I knew it was me.

"Are there other spirits with you?" Shay asked.

The meter lit.

"Are all the spirits friendly?"

The meter remained dark.

"Okay," Shay said slowly. "Do any intend us harm?"

Only three bars lit up. Shay glanced at me, but he had a strange look in his eyes, as though he wasn't seeing me at all. "A neutral response, then. We ask that the Holy Spirit keep us in the light and protect us from harm."

It didn't escape my attention that he'd asked this twice, and I began a refrain in my head asking for protection. Years earlier, I had written a historical book that unexpectedly veered into divine light and protection from evil and darkness. The images came to me now as I envisioned the Holy Spirit's divine light surrounding us. Nothing can heighten a person's belief in God faster than a ghost.

The trees beyond the lighthouse swayed more forcefully as the storm approached. Had this been nighttime and we had candles lit, this would have been the part where they blew out and I flew down the stairs screaming like a banshee.

Shay's voice interrupted my thoughts. "Jon, do you have a problem with us being here?"

The meter remained dark.

"May I ask a favor of you?"

Three bars lit.

"Okay. The answer is 'maybe.'" Shay took a breath and continued, "Could you give us some privacy on the second floor? The bedroom and bath?"

Three bars lit.

"Is that also a maybe?"

Three bars lit again. "So, you're funning with us now, are ya?" Shay asked. Oddly, there was no response. After a moment, he asked, "Is there a reason you remain here?"

All five bars lit.

"Do you need our help?"

The wind whooshed in like a locomotive, filling our ears. Before we could react, the window nearest the stairs closed with a bang that caused me to jump. Then the latch was thrown into the locked position. The sequence continued around the room, one window at a time.

Both Shay and I leaped from our chairs as the banging continued downstairs. It was insistent and so loud that it overpowered the storm. He rushed to the spiral staircase, and as he started his descent, I grabbed the meter and phone and quickly followed. My hands were shaking, and my knees felt weak. I could feel something behind me in the stairwell, but I didn't dare look. I tried to focus on Shay's back, and each time he rounded the spiral and I lost sight of him, I hurried to keep up.

But as we descended below the bedroom and the banging became more insistent and intensified, I realized someone was at the door. By the time I stepped onto the first floor, Shay was already at the door. "Are you expecting anyone?" he asked, his voice taut and his brow furrowed.

I shook my head.

"Let me answer it," he barked as though I'd have it any other way.

I positioned myself behind him as he opened the door. My heart was beating frantically. I expected the wind to zoom into the lighthouse and form a figure before our eyes. I wanted to run to the car and leave this place. Then the realization hit me that whatever it was, it was between the car and us. There was no way out.

As I peered past his shoulder, a figure came into view on the front stoop. She was a little shorter than I. Her trim figure was clad in a dirt-streaked tweed Versace suit jacket, paired with a matching skirt that fit her like a glove. Her voluminous, layered bob was getting reduced to soaked platinum tendrils by the storm's sudden onslaught. She dangled two Christian Louboutin heels in one hand, the iconic red soles staring me in the face, the stiletto heels covered in mud and grass. Her brusque voice cut through our shock. "Your gate is locked. You forced me to climb the blasted fence."

As she pushed past us into the room, I gasped, "Mom?"

~~~~~

Shay and I sat in the living room like two teenagers awkwardly caught in an intimate act. Despite the storm, he had dutifully unlocked the gate, driven my mother's car to the door, and unloaded three matching Louis Vuitton suitcases from the trunk. While my mother showered in the bathroom, he placed the suitcases where she could clearly view them. Then, he returned downstairs and attempted to dry his hair from his soaking.

I made a kettle of tea and arranged some sweets on a tray. I set it on the table, but as the minutes crept past, the water began to cool. Eventually, we heard the unmistakable sound of a blow dryer. It was another half hour before my mother descended. She had changed into a lightweight Chanel dress in pink and gray. Several pearl strands of varying lengths spilled over the neckline. She was the only woman I'd ever known who could make the color pink into a power color. She had also changed out her stilettos and was now wearing sandals whose four-inch heels comprised the letters YSL and were woefully mismatched to the rural swamps.

Her hair had been washed, dried, and arranged into her trademark bob. Her makeup was impeccable, the violet eyeshadow and false lashes expertly emphasizing her sharp blue eyes.

Shay stood as she entered the room. Mom marched straight up to him and held out her hand. "I'm Mae Hunter," she announced as though this were a professional networking function.

As he shook her hand, he managed to murmur, "I'm Seamus MacGregor—Shay, for short."

"I much prefer Seamus," she said. "But I do love the accent." She dropped his hand and turned toward me, raising her eyebrows and widening her eyes in a sharp appraisal. "Dear Hayley," she said, her eyes perusing me, "whatever happened to your clothes?"

As words failed me, I shook my head. It took me a moment to find my voice, and when I did, I pivoted the conversation. "What are you doing here?"

She strode to the table, seated herself in a faux demure fashion that was so like her, and poured herself a cup of tea. She took a moment to study the porcelain design before placing a dessert plate in front of her and gingerly extracting a scone.

Shay and I joined her. My stomach flipped inside me, and though I was no longer hungry or thirsty, I poured Shay and myself cups of tea. We both dutifully retrieved some sweets from the tray, but they sat untouched in front of us.

"I can see you two were in the middle of something," she observed as though she had caught us behind the bleachers at the local high school.

"Mom, why didn't you tell me you were coming?" I asked.

"I phoned on my way down. You didn't answer your phone," she said. Glancing at Shay, she smiled wickedly and added, "Now I see why."

I pictured my phone on the nightstand beside my bed, where it had lain all day.

My mother wiped the edges of her mouth with a napkin. "Well, now that we've had dessert, what's for dinner? I haven't eaten all day."

20

I finished drying another plate and slipped it into the cabinet.

"That does it," Shay said, wiping down the countertops.

"You were so gracious to cook dinner for us," I said. I glanced out the window. My mother stood at the patio's edge with an old-fashioned in one hand and a cigarette in the other. I followed her line of sight to the muddied fence area where she'd managed to climb over. I still couldn't picture it.

"It was my pleasure," Shay said, gathering me in his arms. "But I must say, it will cost you dearly."

I smiled. "I will gladly pay."

My mother turned toward the lighthouse. Spotting us in the window, she made her way to the door. "I could do with another drink," she announced.

"I'll make it," Shay said. "Why don't you ladies have a seat, and I'll bring it to you? Hayley, would you like anything, dear?"

I hope he caught the gratitude in my eyes. "Bourbon. Straight."

Mom and I moved into the living area, which really was not so much a room as a small space designated by an area rug. I plopped into the chair at the window, my eyes falling briefly on Jon's journal, while Mom stood in front of the sofa with her cigarette still in hand. "Well, I suppose

I will be forced to sleep in here tonight," she announced, taking a puff. "Then, tomorrow I'll be off."

"No, I'll—"

"There isn't enough room for the two of you," she interjected. "This sofa is barely large enough for me. Where is your ashtray?"

"We do not have one," I said emphatically, glancing at Shay as if warning him not to be too hospitable. "We don't smoke, and I'd prefer if you didn't inside, either, Mom."

"Ha!" She strode to the door, only a few feet away, and cast her cigarette outside.

"Good thing the ground is wet," I observed. My mind wandered to Jon putting out the fire the British captain had started, and I involuntarily shuddered. I noticed Shay kept his eyes on something outside the window as he made our drinks. I hoped he was watching for smoke as I fought the urge to go outside and ensure it was stomped out.

Mom sat gingerly on the sofa, briefly running her hand over the fabric as if judging it.

"So, Mom, you said you're only spending the night? You didn't drive all the way from Boston just for one night, did you?"

Shay joined us, handing us our drinks while he sat in the opposite chair with his.

"Well, I am so glad you asked." She took a deep breath and smiled conspiratorially. "I am moving to a retirement community."

"I don't believe you," I said.

"Believe it. It is here in North Carolina and only, I don't know, a two-hour drive from here, perhaps?"

"On the coast?"

"Inland. Between Interstate 95 and the Pinehurst area."

I frowned. "Mom, you're a city girl. It's too quiet here for you."

She rolled her eyes. "Well, *here*, yes. But I'm not moving here. I'm moving there."

I noticed Shay remained conspicuously quiet. "Mom owns a company in New York with offices in Boston and LA," I said. While Mom nursed her drink with a sly smile, I continued, "Mom was a model. She did all the runways—Paris, Milan, New York, London—and she was also the model for a number of high-end colognes and clothing, high couture, of course."

Shay nodded and murmured appreciatively.

"After twenty years in the business, she decided to open her own modeling agency," I continued. "She represents a fair number of very high-profile models." I turned toward her. "What about your company, Mom? You can't run it from a retirement village."

"Ha! I could run it from anywhere if I so choose." Before I could respond, she continued, "But, as it happens, I have sold it. For an ungodly sum, I might add."

"Why?" I breathed.

Mom set down her drink and picked up her cigarette pack in its sleek silver case. Catching my eye, she tapped it once or twice and set it back down. "I know this may be difficult for you to believe, dear Hayley, but I am tired. I am tired of rising every morning at five to go to the gym and then arrive at work by seven. I am tired of the stream of calls and emails and texts and all the challenges that go into keeping my company viable. I am tired of poring over the day's analytics every evening when I should be relaxing. I'm tired."

"Have you thought of a vacation?"

She pursed her lips.

"I'm just saying, Mom, you're not the kind of person who can go from sixty miles an hour to zip."

"I won't be."

I raised a brow.

She leaned forward secretively. "I want to tell you all about this community." Her voice sped up as she talked, her tone brimming with enthusiasm. "Midway between the interstate and Pinehurst, a farmer sold all his land—hundreds of acres—for this retirement community. It's a planned community with a historic Main Street filled with arts and crafts stores and unique shops of all kinds. Beyond it is a man-made lake with homes all around it, mostly townhomes like those in England's Cotswolds region.

"But," Mom continued, "it has a decidedly Scottish flair. In fact, Scottish immigrants once owned the land before the Revolutionary War, and it maintains a strong Scottish heritage."

"Oh, really?" Now I leaned forward, my curiosity piqued.

"And that's not the best of it." She sipped her drink and waited until the warm fluid moistened her throat. "Every person there is living the life of their dreams. That's right," she said, reading our expressions. "After working a lifetime to achieve what society dictates, each resident retired and started over in this community. One man always wanted to run a pub, so he has one now, right on the water. Several others wanted to be in a band, so, guess what, they play every weekend at the pub. Others wanted restaurants, so there are plenty of them. Crafts and artsy shops, too. A retired city detective is now their Chief of Police. A big city mayor is now their mayor. There's even a fire department for those who always wanted to live their childhood dreams. I'm told they have a Dalmatian."

I chuckled. "So, what's your dream, Mom? I thought you were already living yours."

"Ah. But that's the beauty of life, isn't it? We can always start a new dream."

We waited with bated breath for her to continue, but she expertly allowed the anticipation to rise before announcing, "I am starting another modeling agency."

"But—what—?"

"This one," she continued, "will be for the senior market. Seniors in this country account for more than sixty-five percent of consumer spending. Did you know that? That's nearly ninety-five billion dollars *a year.*" She let that sink in before continuing, "So, I plan to recruit senior women—and men, no discrimination—for models. Real-life models, not these six-foot, hundred-pound skeletons on the runways today. Heads on a stick! No, my models will be short, tall, big bellies, small bellies, big boobs, sagging boobs, wilting asses—"

"Mom!" I laughed.

"That, my dear, is my next chapter."

"So, are you driving there tomorrow to purchase a place?" Shay asked. He'd been silent through the discussion, but I could tell he was interested in this vision.

"I've already purchased it. Sight unseen." She held up her hand in case there were protests. "I am confident it will be exactly what I want."

"And, you're going there tomorrow to—move in?" I pictured her car in front of the house and three suitcases upstairs.

"A moving truck will arrive in a few days. Until then, I'll stay at the bed and breakfast—which, incidentally—"

"—is also owned by a retiree living their dream," I completed.

Mom smiled.

"Mae," Shay said, setting his drink on the table. "Would you mind terribly if we went with you tomorrow?"

21

We left shortly after breakfast, after wrestling Mom's suitcases back into her car. Then Mom and I headed off while Shay followed to give me a ride back afterward. Mom was quite clear she was remaining at the village, and this, I had to see.

Three hours later, a bit longer than Mom had estimated, we had crossed under Interstate 95 on Route 20, breezing through the tiny towns of St. Pauls and Lumber Bridge, before driving through a swath of farmland. We were alone on the country road, save for Shay, who remained dutifully behind us despite my mother's heavy foot. She drove like an obsessed New Yorker on a mission, and while I would have much preferred to slow down and observe my surroundings, I only caught blurs of color as we whizzed past, like driving through a Monet. I held onto the overhead grab handle as we swerved around the winding road, more than once veering over the double yellow line.

"It's a two-bedroom, two-bath duplex," Mom said, breaking the silence.

"I can't picture you in a duplex," I said, holding onto the grab handle with both hands to keep from sliding off the seat.

"Look for a group of trees," she said.

"Are you kidding?" I studied the blur of farmland dotted with trees, which I supposed marked the boundaries. There seemed to be no other good reason for them to remain standing. A wave of nostalgia washed over me, and for a fleeting moment, I wished I were back in Ireland. Finding trees in the middle of fields usually meant they were fairy trees, sacred places for the fairies who lived there. Allowing them to remain untouched brought prosperity to the farmer, while disturbing them could bring doom and misfortune, or so the myth went. I found myself wondering if the original Scottish settlers had similar myths and legends. Certainly, these trees could easily be more than two hundred years old.

"Until twenty years ago," Mom was saying, "these were all tobacco fields."

"Were?" I realized as I stared at the blur outside my window that I wouldn't know a tobacco leaf from a cornstalk.

"The place we're going is called Midland Cove. It's a *non*-retirement village where people come to live their dreams."

Mom didn't often repeat herself, so I stopped looking out the side window and observed her as she drove. She was clearly excited. Her resting face was intimidating to most people and hard to read, but now, she was actually smiling.

"So, tell me more," I said.

"These are people just like me. They may have worked at jobs they may not have loved or perhaps even hated because that was what was expected of them."

"But you always said you loved your job."

"I said 'they'." She glanced out her side window before focusing back on the road.

The first car I'd seen since Lumber Bridge passed us in the opposite direction. I glanced into my side mirror to ensure that Shay was keeping up. He was, and I imagined he wouldn't be too happy if we were both stopped for speeding.

"It puts cans in the cupboard and keeps the hat on the house," Mom continued. "Now it is *our* time."

"And what did you say these other people do now?"

"Whatever they had always dreamed of doing just for the love of it—opening a bookstore, becoming a dogwalker, growing pumpkins, designing jewelry…" She slowed as she entered a darkened stretch of road. Giant oak trees on either side stretched toward the heavens before bending toward one another to touch their branches in the center of the road.

"These must be the trees," Mom murmured almost to herself.

With the moonroof slid back, I could glance upward and see the branches intertwined as if they were people grasping outstretched fingers. A sudden surge of apprehension washed over me. The wipers came on, though there was no rain.

"What the—?" Mom said, glancing down. She made a motion to turn off the wipers, but they were already off.

As we plunged more deeply into the grove of trees, the air felt as if it was swirling around us. I nervously watched the speedometer gain speed and wished the wipers would stop their frantic pulsing across the dry windshield. When I glanced back at the road, only a few yards away, a man dangled from a tree.

"Stop!" I screamed. The car fishtailed as her foot slammed on the brakes. We came to a complete stop just feet from where he hung. Behind us, I could hear the screech of tires as Shay barely avoided rear-ending us.

The wipers swept to the left and then back to the right before coming to rest. Time seemed to have slowed. He was facing away from us, his wrists tied together behind him, the rope trailing toward his feet, which were clad in heavy black boots with dirty black pants tucked into them. A dusty red coat swayed in the breeze as if the front was unbuttoned. And as my eyes traveled upward, I saw his hair. It was deep auburn and long, reaching past his shoulders. It had been drawn into a ponytail, but the strands had come loose, so the material that once bound them appeared ready to slide off.

"What the hell?" Mom shouted.

I stared at her. "Don't you see him?" I shouted back in panic.

"Who?"

I looked back through the windshield. He was gone.

A tap on Mom's window caused us both to nearly jump out of our seats. As she rolled down the window, Shay asked, "Are you two okay now?"

"I am," Mom retorted. "She isn't." She turned to me. "Get out of my car. You nearly killed us."

"I did not!"

"Get out!"

I dutifully opened the door and slipped out. Shay met me in the front seat of his car. Mom had already taken off like a NASCAR driver before we had the chance to settle in.

"What the devil?" Shay asked as he pushed the gas pedal to the floor, attempting to catch up to her. "Were you arguing?"

We cleared the trees, and I turned around to stare behind us. "A man was hanging from a tree," I said shakily.

"You couldn't have told me that before we drove off? Where's my mobile? How the devil could I have missed that?"

"Your—no, we don't need to call the police."

He half-turned to stare at me.

"Road, please," I said, pointing at the upcoming curve. As he focused on the road ahead, I added, "I don't understand it. It looked like a British soldier. He was in uniform—a Revolutionary War uniform."

"That's it. No more séances for you."

"I swear. I know what I saw."

"And what were you thinking just before you saw him?"

"I don't know; fairy trees."

"Ha!"

"She's turning," I pointed out the obvious. We slowed at a small village that had seemingly sprung up in the middle of nowhere. The entrance was marked with a brick wall on either side of the road, each with an inset that proclaimed:

Welcome to Midland Cove
A *non*-Retirement Community

"Well, I can certainly see the appeal," I said as we continued to decelerate. To ensure that we would, Center Street was marked with periodic speed bumps that even my mother had to observe to avoid throwing her luxury car's front end out of alignment. In front of us loomed a three-story, elegant building within a traffic circle, and as we approached, I noticed two large parking lots on either side of Center Street, which were nearly vacant. At the top of the building was an exterior sign announcing Town Hall. We followed Mom's car past the police station, which was housed within it. Mom pulled into a parking spot beside the mayor's office, and we followed suit.

As we slowly exited the cars, I stretched my legs and took the opportunity to peer down Main Street, which ran perpendicular to Center Street, branching off from the traffic circle to the east and west. I sucked in my breath. It appeared as though we had been transported into another dimension. The tree-lined street was lined with tan brick buildings with slate roofs that looked like they were straight out of the Cotswolds, just as Mom had said, instantly transporting me to Europe. A glance at Shay's face told me that he also felt it. His face softened from the harshness he'd sported only a moment ago.

I turned back to admire the three-headed street lamps, which reminded me of Victorian London. I longed to see them lit up after dark as I imagined a cozy golden glow beneath them. Quaint signs hung at intervals, marking the shops located just off the shady sidewalks.

"Welcome to Midland Cove!" The man's voice startled Shay and me back to the present. Mom had already reached the mayor's door and was holding out her hand to shake his. He was dressed as if he'd just come off the golf course, his shirt fitting snugly across a slightly paunchy middle. "Mark Reynolds," he said as he shook hands all around. "Well, I have the keys right here," he said, dangling them for us to see before handing them over to my mother. "The house is just two blocks over. It's a nice stroll, if you've a mind to."

While my mother declined, as I knew she would, Shay and I eagerly accepted the mayor's offer to join him on a stroll through this suddenly intriguing little village.

22

The homes in Mom's new neighborhood were certainly unique. Unlike Main Street, each structure was a duplex straddling a city block. As we strolled, Mayor Mark, as he preferred to be called, explained to us that the driveways accessing the garages were along the side of the house while the front doors faced opposite streets. It meant there was no backyard at all, but ample side yards and a generous front. It gave the illusion from the front that each house was detached, and the shared back wall down the center was primarily adjacent to garages and laundry rooms.

As we approached, I realized how much larger they appeared than I had imagined. It was no wonder Mom had been drawn to them. They looked to be two stories tall, but as we strode through the open front door, we found ourselves in a living room with a soaring two-story ceiling, which accounted for the outside appearance.

"I'm back here!" Mom called out.

We made our way through the living room to a dining room before reaching the kitchen and laundry along the back.

"Isn't it quaint?" Mom gushed, gesturing at cabinets made to appear vintage. She opened one to reveal a modern refrigerator expertly blending into the cabinetry. "It reminds me of Paris."

As we each murmured our approval, she walked briskly through the rest of the house as though she were giving a tour. "Off the living room," she said, opening a door, "is a master bedroom and bath, and that door in the dining room leads to another en-suite, so one bedroom faces toward the driveway while the other faces a courtyard." She stopped at the floor-to-ceiling bedroom window and pointed admiringly to the well-kept courtyard. "You see," she continued, "This privacy fence separates one side of the duplex from the other, so we each have private living accommodations. Of course, it is much smaller than my old place, but it's perfect, don't you think?"

"Mom," I said as we strolled back through, "have you already purchased this?"

"I told you I have. Is there something wrong with your hearing, dear?" She said the last word not as an endearment but with barely contained impatience.

"Had you seen it before today?"

"Only online."

"You bought the house sight unseen?" I couldn't help but gape.

She stopped and turned toward me in a stance that could intimidate people far more powerful than I. "You are repeating yourself. Once more: of course I did, dear. That is one of the advantages of the internet, is it not?" She smiled at Mayor Mark with that expert flash she'd perfected on the runway so many years ago. "Everyone has been quite accommodating. I had 3D tours, a complete inspection, a few minor adjustments, and—" she gestured to the space around us "—it is move-in ready. I even had it repainted and the floors repolished."

"And your furniture?"

"It will arrive tomorrow or the day after."

"What about your old place? Did you sell it?"

"Of course not; don't be silly. Real estate is an investment. I am renting it out."

"Where will you stay until your furniture arrives?" I asked. I couldn't picture her in a sleeping bag on the floor, even one with rhinestones.

Mayor Mark spoke up. "We passed the B&B on our stroll here."

"Of course," I said, remembering. I wiped my forehead of perspiration. It wasn't like me to forget things. Perhaps it was the interrupted séance from the evening before, coupled with what appeared to be a mighty step back in time to the precise era I was writing about. I felt disassociated from my body.

"You probably didn't recognize it as such; it blends in so seamlessly," Mayor Mark was saying as he beamed. "This is a planned community in every respect." He held up another set of keys. "And I also have the keys to your new modeling studio, Ms. Hunter, should you care to walk through."

"You also bought a studio?" I asked. I gave a sideways glance at Shay, whose face was conspicuously blank.

"Of course not," Mom answered. "I leased it." She smiled broadly. "First, I am famished. Mayor Mark, where shall we eat? I hope you are joining us."

~~~~~

In the end, we spent the entire afternoon at Midland Cove. I had to admit, I fell in love with it, and Mom, usually the skeptic, uncharacteristically seemed over the moon. We dined in a cozy café on Main Street overlooking an expansive park filled with walkers with and without dogs, as well as the occasional jogger. The café owner had been a career advertising executive who always wanted to own a little café, and my meal of tortellini caprese salad and hot, homemade yeast rolls was divine. Afterward, we each had leisurely cups of maple pecan lattes and slivers of chocolate-dipped key lime pie. Fortunately, as the owner was eager to inform us, all the portion sizes had been downsized for an older generation, so we could—theoretically—indulge.

Afterward, we popped into Mom's new modeling studio. There wasn't much to see, as it currently consisted of two rooms, a front room overlooking Main Street and a back room that I assumed was for stock or office space. Mom was rather mysterious regarding her plans for it, only assuring us she had a local contractor lined up to transform it. No doubt, he was retired and living his dream of remodeling; I felt like I was beginning to catch on. She assured us that it would give us a reason to return, and Mayor Mark seemed eager for her new and unique business to join the others along the historic downtown area.

I was feeling exhausted at the end of it all as we stopped on the sidewalk in front of the bed and breakfast.

"How long are you staying in America?" Mom asked Shay as Mayor Mark waved his goodbyes.

Shay glanced at me. "I haven't yet decided."

"Well," she said, her eyes gleaming, "I hope to see more of you." She turned to me. "You must come back after I'm all settled in."

"I'm actually impressed, Mom," I said. "I think you've made a wise choice. This place has a great feel to it."

"Once you get past the apparition in the road," she said. Her chuckle had a bit of a bite to it, but it served to remind me that we had things yet to do.

"You saw—?"

"Don't be ridiculous."

I hesitated. She had half-turned toward the inn. "I'll call you tomorrow," I said finally, leaning in to kiss her on the cheek. She reciprocated, which surprised me, and then Shay and I watched her stroll into the bed and breakfast. I stood for a moment, observing the old-fashioned screen door, the porch swings and rockers, and the variety of flowers. It made me want to grow a green thumb and learn how to decorate. But let's get real.

"Are you ready to go, dear?" Shay's voice was melodic.

"I am," I said, surprising myself with my reluctance to leave. "But we have a stop to make."

~~~~~

When Shay pulled the car onto the shoulder and turned off the ignition, the sun was already lowering in a blaze of red and orange. We sat for a moment in silence.

"Are you sure you saw something?" Shay asked quietly. "It wasn't your imagination from all the goings-on at the lighthouse?"

I hesitated. "Of course, I'm sure." My words did not even persuade me, but I avoided looking at Shay as I opened the door and stepped out. I could see for miles in each direction; although the road had bends, the surrounding area was perfectly flat. Other than this particular group of trees, there appeared to be little else than agricultural fields filled with various plants I couldn't identify. Unless, of course, I looked more deeply into the fields to observe America's version of fairy trees. Why were these ancient-looking trees with their deep and mangled underbrush left intact?

"So, tell me what you saw," Shay said as he joined me along the side of the road.

I looked upward. The trees were exactly as I remembered them. Their trunks were broad, and the bark aged, as though they had stood in place for a century or more. Their branches were mottled and sometimes curled backward, yet some had managed to stretch across the road to meet those from the other side, like fingers stretching outward in an attempt to hold hands.

"You see how those branches appear?" I asked, shielding my hand from the setting sun to peer upward.

"I do."

"Somewhere along this stretch, I swear to you that a man was hanging. He was hanging, Shay, like someone who had been lynched."

I watched his face closely. His eyes were somewhat veiled, and I wasn't sure if it was the setting sun or if he was intentionally hiding his view. But when he spoke, all doubt was gone. "I believe you."

"You do?"

"I do."

I glanced back at the overhanging branches.

"What was he wearing?" he asked.

"I think he was a British soldier during the Revolutionary War."

"That would be entirely too convenient." He smiled.

"I know. Maybe it was just my imagination. All the happenings at the lighthouse, like you said, and then, the fairy trees…" My eyes wandered to the trees scattered throughout the fields.

"Fairy trees, are they?" He followed my gaze. "I hate to break this to you, darlin', but those trees were most likely kept in place to prevent soil erosion."

"Oh." I could feel the heat rising.

"It was a long drive," Shay said softly. "And the sun might have been in your eyes."

"No. The sun was behind us." I sighed. "But, I get your point."

"In any event, he isn't hanging now, is he?"

I took one last look at the trees before returning to the car. Shay stood for a moment longer, peering curiously into the overhead branches. Then he shook his head and joined me, sliding behind the wheel.

"Shall we? We'll be back after dark as it is."

I nodded silently. He turned the key. A moment later, we were easing onto the road and heading east as the sun silently set behind us.

23

I had fallen asleep. When the tires bounded over the uneven driveway to the lighthouse, I awakened to the dashboard casting its blue light over Shay's face. He appeared deep in thought, his lips somewhat pursed.

I stretched. "Sorry I wasn't much company on the drive," I said.

He glanced at me with tired eyes. "That's quite alright, darlin'." He suddenly pointed. As I followed his gaze, an alligator, caught in the headlights' glare, slithered off the drive and disappeared into the swampy underbrush beside the road. "Glad we didn't come across him on our walk."

"Me, too! Shay…" As I said his name, the car rolled to a stop. Both of us stared at the gate in front of us. It was drawn completely open. The padlock dangled unlatched from the gate lever. "Did you…?" I couldn't finish the question.

After a brief silence, he answered. "I distinctly remember closing the gate and locking it when we left."

I thought back to that morning, which seemed so long ago now. Mom had taken off like a racecar driver, but I'd glanced back to ensure that Shay was following us. He hadn't right away; he had pulled the vehicle through the gate and slipped out to close it back. I was certain I'd seen him lock it. Or had I?

"Who else—?" he started.

"No one. Only you and me."

"The people at the general store?"

"Absolutely not them. Beckett was one reason I wanted it locked. And," I added, "I bought the padlock in Wilmington, so they should not even know I have it."

"Was it a generic passcode?"

I gave him a side-look as I pursed my lips. "Absolutely. I left it 1-2-3-4."

"Point taken." Shay's eyes skimmed the surrounding area. A full moon cast a buttery glow on the lighthouse. Between the moonlight and our headlights, the lighthouse appeared as though it was glowing. The lantern room was darkened, and its contents in shadows. After a moment, Shay eased the car through the opening. Rather than head straight for the door, he veered to the other side, brightening the headlights to see into the swamps beyond the fence. We slowly drove completely around the structure until we were both satisfied that there couldn't be anyone lurking there.

When he parked the vehicle, the headlamps shone on the gate a few yards away. As I exited the car, the chill night air descended upon me, and I involuntarily shivered. I glanced across the car's hood to see Shay on the other side, staring at the gate. As I followed his gaze, we both watched as the gate began to creak. It swung back until it latched with a loud clang, as though it had been blown shut by a strong wind.

We continued standing there for what seemed a protracted time. Then Shay took a step forward. I quickly followed. "What are you doing?" I asked.

"Locking the gate," he answered.

"Maybe—"

"Maybe I didn't lock it correctly," he finished curtly. "Maybe the wind blew it open."

"But, Shay," I said, stopping just feet from the gate. "Look at the trees. The wind isn't blowing."

He continued moving forward, but I saw his head tilt upward to peer at the canopy. It was true; everything was completely, utterly still and silent. Not even the crickets and frogs dared make a sound.

I hurried after him, determined not to be left alone, even if I would be only feet away.

As we descended upon the gate, both of us stopped abruptly. The padlock was through the gate latch, and it was locked.

"I don't care for that padlock," Shay said in a hoarse voice.

~~~~~

"I'm dead serious," Shay said as we readied for bed.

"Please don't use that phrase."

"I'd feel much better if, when I return to Ireland, you move out of here. Maybe even before."

I pulled back the covers on my side of the bed. Rather than lie down, however, I fluffed the pillows and sat up in the bed, drawing the covers around me. As he joined me, my eyes wandered around the room. The moon illuminated the circular room seemingly from all directions. It had become familiar to me. Now, it felt warm and cozy. My eyes fell on the spot where I'd seen the figure watching me. As Shay wrapped his arm around me, I turned to him.

"Shay, I don't think Jonathan means us any harm."

"Whether you're on a first-name basis or no, I don't see how you can arrive at that conclusion."

I hesitated. I felt as though Jon was there in the room with us, silently listening. "He hasn't hurt me," I said thoughtfully. "And, I think… I think he wanted me to find the journal. I think he's trying to tell us something."

Shay made a noise somewhat like a muffled guffaw.

I turned to him. "Maybe, he opened the gate for us, knowing we were home."

"Do you realize how illogical that sounds, Hayley?"

"I do," I admitted.

"Do you really now?"

When I looked into his eyes, I saw deep concern etching his brow. "There's a part of me that feels uneasy," I conceded. "But," I added quickly, "there's another part that feels like he's okay with us being here. I mean, Harry lived here for decades."

"How did Harry die?"

"You don't think—?"

"I don't know what I think. But I'll tell you this, I'd be finding out as quickly as possible. Perhaps as we're driving away."

"No," I said a bit shakily. "I don't think Harry... I mean, his niece would have told me. Don't you think?"

"Would she now? She inherits a strange structure in the middle of the beyond, and she does not know what to do with it. She's given a chance to lease it, buying her a full year to determine its long-term fate. Wouldn't you have taken advantage of an eager renter?"

I felt a wave of sadness envelop me. But as I lay there in his arms, my head coming to rest against his chest, I realized the sadness wasn't inside me. It was just beyond. I straightened. "I want to watch the video from our séance."

Shay sighed. "First thing in the morning, I suppose."

"No. Now." I leaned forward and grasped the phone from the nightstand.

"You have got to be joking me."

"No. I just have this feeling." I turned on the nightstand lamp to bathe the room in amber light before settling back into his arms. The lantern room appeared brighter on video than it had felt when we had begun our séance yesterday, and I wondered how much had been my imagination. But when the meter started lighting up in response to Shay's questioning, it was unmistakable that we had indeed been communicating with an unseen force— and a highly intelligent one.

"You see," Shay said, tapping the video to pause it, "Jonathan said he was not the only one here."

"He didn't respond when you asked if he was alone," I said quietly.

"Which was a negative, meaning, he is not alone. And then three bars when we asked if the others were friendly. Don't you see, Hayley? Even if Jon means you no harm, there are others here. We have no idea how many there are, and I can't protect you from them. You have to leave when I do. Maybe you can stay with your mother until you find another place."

"I don't know," I said, but my voice did not sound convincing, even to me. I pressed the button to continue watching. As we neared the end, I watched as Shay asked, "Do you need our help?"

"The parlor tricks are over. You have a guest."

The windows closed one by one, slamming and locking. Shay and I stared at the video. Seconds later, the screen rotated and then went blank as we rushed from the room amid distant banging.

"What was that?" Shay and I asked almost in unison.

"Back it up," I urged.

Shay went back a full minute. As we listened to him ask if Jon needed our help, a deep voice with a thick Scottish accent responded, "The parlor tricks are over. You have a guest."

He backed it up again as we listened for a third time. Then he paused it and leaned back against the headboard.

"I don't remember hearing that before now," I said shakily. I attempted a chuckle to lighten the mood, but it fell flat.

"I most definitely did not," Shay said emphatically.

I resisted the urge to leap from the bed, run downstairs, and flee in my flimsy nightgown. It occurred to me how often I'd wanted to flee from this house. Fight or flight, wasn't that it? I wasn't prepared to fight whatever this was. The air grew colder around us in a familiar embrace, and I wrapped my arms around my chest in a vain attempt to stay warm. I began to wonder if Jonathan was manipulating us.

Shay retrieved the phone from my grasp and returned it to the nightstand. He opened his mouth as if to say something. Instead, he shook his head.

"But," I said as we lay down and drew the covers around us, "he is able to move things."

"Meaning?"

"Meaning," I continued, "he can open and shut the gate—and the windows. He can even latch them shut—or apparently, unlock them."

"One more reason for us to get out of here tomorrow."

"So then," I asked hesitantly, "why does he need our help?"

24

I awakened before dawn. Shay's measured breathing told me he was deep in slumber despite the lamps illuminating the room as if it were already daylight. Though neither of us vocalized it the night before, I doubt either of us wanted the darkness to encroach around us, and so we'd kept the lamps on while we eventually fell asleep.

I slipped from beneath the covers and grabbed my thick fleece robe. I made my way to the landing. I paused to peer up the spiral staircase toward the lantern room. I came close to climbing the stairs and talking with Jon, if 'talking' was the right word for it. I realized what stopped me from doing so was the possibility that he was not alone, and therefore, neither was I. I hesitated, not knowing who the others were, looking back at the cozy bed that beckoned me. But I was wide awake and knew that even if I were lying in Shay's arms, I could not sleep.

In the end, I descended to the living room.

I could still feel my mother's presence there. Perhaps it was her perfume, a signature scent of florals, vanilla, and—dare I say? Bourbon. The covers she'd used were folded neatly at one end of the couch, and I sat down and drew the blanket around me. It was darker here than in the bedroom, but it was peaceful. From somewhere in the distance, I thought I heard the hoot of an owl and another answer.

"Jon," I said in a barely audible whisper, "is there something you're trying to tell me?" I immediately regretted the question; if his voice had responded, I think I might have had a heart attack. I realized that, at first, I had been in denial about a ghostly presence, despite the evidence. I knew since Shay was here that I had not wanted to face the possibility alone. Yet, a large part of my psyche still wanted to leave the dimensions separate.

Thankfully, I was met with silence. My eyes roamed the room. There were no shadowy figures, much to my satisfaction.

Then my eyes fell on the journal. It was sitting on the table between the couch and the chair, exactly as I'd last left it. I leaned forward and took it in my hand. I flipped on the lamp, opened it to the next page, and began to read.

"January 14, 1776

"Word reached me today that two days past, a colonist boat named Hibernia had been conducting reconnaissance off the coast of Sullivan's Island in South Carolina, when she discovered a British fleet at Charlestown Harbor.

"The three British ships were identified as the HMS Raven, HMS Rittenhouse, and HMS Syren. Not seeing the Hibernia as she lay in wait, a small boat was dispatched from the HMS Syren. The colonists waited while the boat entered the harbor, speculating that the fleet might have come in support of the HMS Tamar, which the colonists had apparently already removed.

"As the boat returned to the fleet, the Hibernia opened fire. In turn, the HMS Syren pursued the Hibernia to Sullivan's Island, where

*another colonist ship lay in wait. It is said the 2ⁿᵈ
South Carolina Regiment chased away the Syren.
"I know this because colonist boats passed
through the channel today. I did not note them in
my logbook. I would have allowed them to pass as
though I were away and did not detect them, but
they stopped, and I witnessed Alasdair and Cuddy
disembarking. Oh, if only they had continued! I do
not wish to be drawn into this war!"*

I hesitated. Only you *were* drawn into the war, Jon. I
positioned the bookmark, closed the journal, and held it
against my chest. It smelled of old paper, pine, and
tobacco. It was also frigid, as if it had been stored in a
freezer and only now removed. The cold permeated my
chest, and I shivered, drawing the blanket closer about me.

I shut my eyes and leaned against the back of the
couch. Inhaling the aroma, I could almost see Jon in the
lighthouse. It would have been less solid; perhaps the stairs
were not as substantial, with thinner steps. I could see him
in the lantern room, dressed in an ivory broadcloth shirt
with ballooning sleeves, over woolen breeches that reached
just past his knees. His hair was pulled back in a ponytail,
revealing strong sideburns and a squared jaw. He held a
spyglass in one hand as he watched the boat ease its way
westward. The trees were shorter and the channel wider.
The chain link fence that surrounded the current structure
fell away until there was nothing between the lighthouse
and the surrounding swamps.

Jon stepped away from the window and pressed his
back against the wood between two windows, but they
could not shield his broad shoulders from view. He turned
his head and watched as the boat slowed and pulled
alongside the bank. I could see several men in the vessel as
if I were watching them from the lantern room above,
when one stepped ashore.

He looked at me standing there, and I knew he had seen me. I could not remain in the shadows like a coward.

A wave of emotions washed over me as though I were suddenly inside Jon's heart and mind. I felt his irritation that Alasdair would endanger him. Yet, I knew he would not dare do so if it hadn't been urgent. War was not coming. It was already here.

25

Shay finished washing the last dish and handed it to me. "But don't you see, Hayley?" he said, his normally genial expression replaced by knitted brows and darkened eyes. "I can't protect you here."

I dried the dish and placed it on the open shelf with an assortment of mismatched dinnerware. "I'm not asking you to protect me," I said for the umpteenth time.

"Hayley, I hope you know that if I could cancel my commitment in New York tomorrow, I would."

"I know. But you can't. You're the keynote speaker."

"It's been on my calendar for months," he sighed.

"But you enjoy these conferences," I said, attempting to make my voice lighter. I made an effort at a smile.

"Yes, I do. Normally. But that is only if my girlfriend is not trapped in a house with a ghost with nefarious motives."

I laughed. "First of all, I am not trapped. I can open this door and walk right out at any time. And second, we don't know whether Jon's motives are 'nefarious.' What does that even mean, anyway?"

"It isn't just him, though one ghost is certainly one too many. It's the others that we know nothing about."

I made my way into the living area and sat on the couch, drawing the same blanket that had kept me toasty during the night back around me. It had been where Shay had found me sound asleep when he awakened this morning. The blanket felt comforting, almost like warm arms wrapping around me. Could I possibly be starting to have feelings for Jon? Certainly not romantic ones, I thought as Shay joined me. They were almost like familial affection.

"Hayley," Shay said, grasping my hands, "I can't keep you safe here."

"You've already said that," I said, though I smiled reassuringly. "And you won't have to. Tomorrow morning, I'll drive you to the airport in Raleigh. You'll be in New York in time for lunch. You'll only be there overnight. The next evening, I'll pick you up. I'll be fine here overnight."

"Is there nothing I can say to convince you to stay with your mother?"

"Nothing. Which reminds me, I promised I'd phone her today."

"Then, a hotel. Perhaps one by the airport."

"The truth is, I don't want to leave." The statement surprised us both. As it hung in the air, I continued, "It's kismet. I came here to write about my ancestors during the Revolutionary War. What are the odds that I'd find a journal written during that time? After I've dropped you off at the airport, I plan to come back here and work. I have tons of research yet to do, and my publisher will be clamoring for the next installment."

Shay sighed heavily as if unconvinced. "If something happens to you, I am going to be very angry that you didn't listen to me."

"Nothing will happen." I retrieved my phone from my pocket and dialed my mother, not because I especially wanted to speak with her but because I wanted this conversation to come to an end. Shay's brow darkened further as he turned away. Mom answered on the third ring, but she was speaking to someone else. "Mom?"

"Hayley, is everything okay?"

"Everything here is fine. I'm calling to check on you." I caught a few words as she held the phone away from her mouth. "Mom?"

"This isn't the best time," she said. "My furniture is here, and the movers need me."

"That didn't take long."

"It never does with me, dear."

"So, everything is okay at your new place?"

"Better than okay. I love it here. You'll have to come back and visit."

I glanced at Shay. It was obvious that he overheard the conversation. "I will, Mom."

"Gotta go, Hay. Chat later?"

"Sure." I clicked off the phone.

"Are you sure—?" Shay started.

"Don't even start."

Shay fell silent. Then, "Well, I might not be able to protect you from spirits, but I can certainly protect you from the young man lurking around your house the other night." He abruptly stood.

"Not without me," I said, throwing off my blanket.

"You stay here," he ordered as he moved into the kitchen and retrieved my car keys.

"The hell I am," I answered as I followed him out the door.

⁓⁓⁓⁓⁓⁓⁓

We approached the intersection in Dikshita just as a pickup rolled through it. "That's Argo," I announced. "I don't think he saw us."

"Is that the man—?"

"No," I answered. "It was his son Beckett."

Shay parked my car beside a beat-up copper-colored truck that had appeared to have seen a lot of time off-roading, judging from the dried mud and rusted panels. We made our way into the general store. I caught the screen door just before it nearly slammed behind us. A man at the counter glanced up from an assortment of items laid across the counter, a pencil in his hand.

"Argo will be back in a bit," he said by way of a greeting. He returned to a pad of paper in front of him. He was rather short, especially when compared with Shay, and his stomach seemed ready to burst through his overalls. "You new around here?" he continued without looking up.

I watched as he wrote down each item he was taking, along with the price. "We're at Harry's place," I said, careful to make it seem as if Shay had moved there, too.

"Oh?" He glanced up as if truly seeing us for the first time.

"Is Beckett about?" Shay asked.

The man pushed the pad of paper to the opposite side of the counter and gathered his things in one arm. He held out his hand to Shay. "Travis Tyler."

"Shay MacGregor," Shay reciprocated as he shook his hand.

"Scottish?"

"Irish, of Scottish descent."

"Ah." Travis narrowed his eyes as if concentrating. "I visited both a few years ago. Nice places. Friendly people."

"We try to be welcoming," Shay answered. "Beckett—?"

"He's around here somewhere," Travis said. "God only knows where." He nodded toward the paper and pencil. "If you buy anything, just write it down and Argo will put it on your account when he gets back."

"Our account?" I asked. I held out my hand. "Hayley Hunter."

"The writer?"

My eyes widened. Word traveled fast in these slow parts. "Well, yes, as a matter of fact."

"I've heard about you. Doing research up at the lighthouse, are you?"

"Mostly in Raleigh," I said, though I didn't know why I preferred to keep my latest research secret.

Travis didn't seem to notice as he shifted his supplies into both hands. "Yeah. Argo will send a bill out at the end of each month. It's an honor system."

"Well, it's nice to have met you," Shay said. "Do you need help getting those to your truck?"

"No, I've got it, thanks." Travis seemed to have taken the hint as he started through the door. We were already searching the store for Beckett before I glimpsed Travis's truck pulling out of the parking lot.

"Beckett?" I called as I lifted the swing top at the end of the counter. I made my way past the mailboxes to peer in the back. A dark midcentury desk was pushed against the equally dark paneled wall, its contents overflowing with piles of paper. I glanced around the room, taking in the metal file cabinets, a wall clock stopped at a quarter to two, and a metal rolling chair with ripped vinyl seating. Boxes were stacked precariously along one wall. It smelled of oil, bagged soil, and freshly formed rubber.

I returned to the shop floor, shaking my head as Shay glanced in my direction. He strayed to one end of the store as I began to walk down the opposite end. I caught glimpses of him as I peered down aisles filled with buckets of paint, garden tools, and plumbing supplies. Really, I needed to come back just to tour these aisles. The merchandise alone was like stepping into a general store of the last century.

I caught a glimpse of Beckett stepping backward. I almost called out to him before realizing his eyes were firmly fixed on the aisle he was exiting. With his back still to me, he nearly plastered himself against the end cap as he stuck his head out horizontally just far enough to see down the aisle he had just left.

"Beckett?" Shay's voice rang out.

I stopped in my tracks, afraid to move lest the young man realize I was behind him. He was dressed similarly to the other occasions, with a red plaid shirt and faded jeans speckled with paint and oil. His shoes were scuffed, the leather worn, and I suspected the soles contained remnants of dried mud. His closely cropped black hair appeared almost midnight blue under the fluorescent lights.

"Beckett," Shay was saying. His voice grew softer. I could tell he was moving down the aisle toward the young man. "Please don't leave. I came to speak with you. My name's Shay. Shay MacGregor."

Beckett paused with his head sideways. His eyes had to have been just barely visible beyond the merchandise. I held my breath and stepped closer.

"Beckett," Shay continued, "Can you tell me why you went to the lighthouse? Were you looking for something there?"

Beckett stepped backward, oblivious to me behind him.

"Don't go, Beckett," Shay said. "I only came to talk to you. What did you hope to find at the lighthouse?"

Beckett stepped back again. This time, he stepped on my foot, and I instinctively cried out. Startled, he whirled around just as Shay appeared from the aisle. Beckett's doe-like brown eyes were immense. He slung his hands across his chest as if protecting himself, but as he spun back around, Shay caught him by the shoulders.

"Are you alright?" Shay asked me, stopping Beckett in his tracks.

"I'm fine," I said. I could see the panic on Beckett's face. "It's okay, Beckett," I added. "This is Shay. He—lives with me."

His eyes darted from me to Shay and back again.

"We just wanted to know why you came to the lighthouse the other night," I said. My voice was soft, and for a moment, I wasn't sure if he'd heard me.

"Harry's lighthouse," he said. His voice was thin and reedy, like a boy's not yet through puberty.

"Yes," I said. I hoped Argo did not return to find his son trapped between us. Shay relinquished his hold on his shoulders but continued to block his exit. "Harry's lighthouse. Why were you there?"

He rubbed his chest with one hand. "Harry said I could come."

"Did you used to visit Harry there?" I asked. My eyes met Shay's.

"Still do," Beckett answered.

"You—still do? When was the last time you saw Harry?" My throat constricted.

"Two days," Beckett answered. He shifted from one foot to the other. His head bobbed as if he were looking for a way around us.

"You saw Harry two days ago?" I asked. "Was Harry at the lighthouse?"

Beckett nodded. "He's always at the lighthouse. He said I could come."

I sensed the puzzlement on Shay's face even before I glanced at him again. I looked back at Beckett and forced a smile. "Of course he did," I said gently. "But Harry said I could stay there while he's gone—"

"He isn't gone," Beckett interjected, vehemently shaking his head.

"He isn't... gone." My words hung in the air.

He continued shaking his head. "He said I could come." His voice grew breathy and insistent. "I brought Lola a bone. I always do."

"Lola?" Shay asked. His voice had softened as if he were afraid to break the spell.

"Lola," Beckett said. "Harry's dog."

"Harry's white German shepherd," I said. My own voice had taken on a robotic monotone.

Beckett nodded. "I always do. Harry said I could."

"And you saw Lola while you were there two days ago?" My words felt glued to my lips as if they had more meaning for me than for the young man.

He nodded again. "Harry said I could. I brought her a bone."

~~~~~

Shay and I sat in my car, our eyes riveted on the Dikshita General Store.

"He's... a bit challenged," Shay said haltingly, groping for the right words.

There was a moment of silence before I responded. "I think he's harmless."

He turned the ignition and backed out of the parking lot, guiding the car in the direction of the lighthouse. "I have to agree with you."

"You do?" I don't know why I felt pleased. "So, you agree that I have nothing to worry about?"

Shay kept his eyes on the road. "I didn't say that."

"But, you said—"

"I don't think that boy will hurt you. At least not intentionally," he added. "I feel it in my gut."

"Then—?"

"What do you know about Harry?"

26

Harrison Ellsworth Cooper's passing was, as it turns out, huge news. I was in Ireland when he passed away, where he wasn't well known, at least in the newspaper I read. But now I found a large spread on him in *The New York Times* online, as well as several video clips about his life.

"I wonder if my mother knew him?" I mused after Shay and I viewed a video about his real estate ventures. "I mean, she spent a good deal of time in New York, and it appears they once traveled in the same circles."

"Maybe," Shay said, scrolling through his phone. "Or maybe not." He sat up a little straighter on the living room sofa. "This says that he largely disappeared from view around twenty years ago."

"That might have been a few years after he began living here full-time." I glanced around the cozy room. "This would be a nice place, I suppose, without the ghosts. But I can't imagine a city guy retreating to this lighthouse, especially one who'd made his fortune in New York real estate. Certainly, he traveled back to the city on occasion?"

"Did his niece say he'd been ill?"

I shook my head. "I don't remember. I don't think so. I would have recalled if he'd been here wasting away."

"Then, his death was sudden?"

My eyes met Shay's. "Do you think—?"

We both became riveted on our devices as we searched for a cause of death or a nefarious end to Harry. Finally, I sighed. "I'm calling Billie."

"You're not thinking that's a wee bit direct?"

I hesitated with the phone in my hand. "I'll think of something." I dialed Billie's number, and she picked up on the third ring.

"Hi, Hayley," she said by way of greeting. "Is everything okay? Anything wrong?"

I hit the speakerphone icon so that Shay could listen in. "Everything is great," I said, hoping my voice wasn't artificially cheery. "I was just wondering about something, and I thought you'd be the best person to ask."

"Ask away."

"I was at the Dikshita General Store today."

"Aren't they great? If you need something and they don't have it, they'll order it for you. I hope Argo told you that."

"He did, yes. I think. Anyway, Argo wasn't there today, but Beckett was."

I heard something like a chuckle on the other end of the phone. "You'd best go when Argo is there."

"Why is that?" I locked eyes with Shay.

There was a moment of hesitation. Then Billie answered, "Argo knows the inventory."

Now, it was my turn to hesitate. My mind stumbled for the proper segue. "Actually, I spoke to Beckett—my boyfriend, Shay, and I did."

"He didn't run away?" Billie asked in an incredulous voice.

"Does he usually?"

Billie sighed. "Beckett is a little bit introverted." She hesitated briefly before adding, "He's a good kid, though. His mom died giving birth to him, so it's always been just him and his dad."

"Oh. Sorry to hear that. Well," I took a deep breath, "he apparently had a good relationship with Harry." Shay and I strained to hear Billie's breathing, and I wished we'd arranged to see her in person so I could read her body language.

"Yeah. He visited Harry now and then."

"He said," I took another deep breath. "Beckett said he saw Harry and Lola just a couple of days ago."

Billie snickered. "That would be difficult to do."

"Because Harry's—" I struggled for the kindest way to put it.

"Precisely."

"And his dog?"

"Lola's been gone for ages."

"She passed away?"

"I suppose. She just disappeared."

"Disappeared?" I thought of the white German shepherd I'd seen just outside the lighthouse. Instinctively, I peered out the window as though I would see her chasing butterflies on the lawn.

"Harry was beside himself with panic and grief. He said he looked everywhere for her. He took a rowboat over every inch of those swamps, I think, but he never found any sign of her."

"He didn't keep her in the yard?"

"No need to. She stayed right there, all the time. Unless Harry went somewhere, and then she was with him."

"Is it possible that Beckett found her?"

There was a long silence. "I don't think so. That was some time ago, and she seemed ancient."

I had a fleeting thought of the alligators, but debated whether to mention them. Then, my curiosity got the better of me. "Billie, didn't you tell me the fence was to keep the alligators out?"

There was a long silence before Billie answered. "When she was a puppy, yes." She did not elaborate, and I decided that train of thought wouldn't get us anywhere.

Instead, I pivoted. "What do you think Beckett was referring to when he said he'd seen Harry and Lola recently?"

"I don't know." It sounded like a car door opened. A moment later, I heard the car start and the phone switched over to Billie's car speakers. "Maybe he meant he visited their graves?"

"Did you say 'their' graves?"

"When Harry couldn't find Lola, he had a tombstone erected for her. He was buried beside her."

"Oh. That would make sense."

"He probably rode his bicycle to the gravesites. Maybe he talked to them. You know, how some people do."

Shay mouthed the word 'where?'

"Is the gravesite close by?" I asked.

Billie sounded a bit distracted. "It's on Harry's property."

"By the lighthouse?"

"About a quarter of a mile from there. It's not hard to find, but you can't drive there. Walk down your drive about a hundred yards and veer off to the right. You'll find the footpath. It will lead you straight to the cemetery."

"You don't mind if we visit, then?" I asked. I immediately regretted it. It would have been far easier to do it and beg forgiveness later if I'd overstepped.

"Of course not," she said. "Look, I have to go. I'm meeting a buyer in a few minutes, and traffic is a bit heavy."

"Of course. Oh, one more question, Billie?"

"Shoot."

"How did Harry die?"

"How did he die?" she repeated.

"I mean, did he have cancer, or—"

"No. Physically, he was in perfect health. He'd become obsessed with finding the stairs to the cellar. He was dead when we found him."

"He was on the stairs to the cellar?"

"He never found them. Look, I really need to go—"

"Of course. Hey, thanks, Billie."

After we both hung up, Shay and I stared at one another for a long moment.

"She said he was in perfect physical health," I said, though Shay had been a witness to the entire conversation.

"What does his obsession with the cellar have to do with his death?" Shay asked.

I shook my head. It didn't make sense. "So," I said after a moment, "What do we do first? Find the cellar or Harry?"

~~~~~

As we left the lighthouse, the sun shone bright and the air was heavy with humidity. We found the footpath just as Billie had described it, and we both marveled at how we could have overlooked it on our earlier stroll. Once we stepped off the lane, however, the trees seemed to close around us, cutting off our light and casting us in semi-darkness. The soil was spongy, and I imagined how easily a heavy rain could wash out the footpath, leaving us tramping through the swamps in circles. I considered turning back, but something compelled me to keep moving. Perhaps it was Shay's shadowy figure just ahead of me, while the branches appeared to hinder our exit behind us.

Shay picked up a long stick that had fallen. He broke off some of the twigs and handed me the stick. "Walking stick," he said. He glanced around us. "And it might be useful if a snake gets too close."

"I can't imagine burying someone out here," I mused. "I'd be too afraid of alligators—or something else—getting to the body."

Shay looked at his watch. "Twenty minutes, and then we turn back if we haven't found it by then."

I nodded.

I don't know how he managed to identify the path before us. The cypress trees were gnarled so severely that they created a puzzle around us. The roots poked straight up from the ground in a phenomenon known as cypress knees. They were so plentiful and uneven that I had to watch every step. And if watching for alligators wasn't enough, the mosquitoes decided to come out in full force. We swatted and slapped at them as if attempting to march through the Amazon rainforest. What a time to have forgotten we might need insect repellent. I hoped I didn't catch some deadly disease.

Something brushed the back of my neck, and I nearly squealed as I swatted it away.

Shay stopped and peered back at me. "You okay?"

"Tell me that was not a spider."

"Turn around."

As I dutifully turned around, he said, "I don't see anything on you. If it were a spider, it went down your shirt."

"Don't tell me that!"

I caught a glimpse of his grin as he continued to push through. I followed more slowly, running my hand up my back beneath my blouse. "You won't be smiling for long if a tarantula kills me!"

"You have wild tarantulas here in the Carolinas, do you?"

He came across a fallen trunk and paused to survey our predicament. As I joined him, he instructed me to turn around. He lifted my blouse, running his hand along the fabric and my skin. "No tarantulas," he declared.

I was about to suggest we turn back, but as I tried to peer around the thicket, my eyes caught something white. "Look!" I said, pointing.

Shay followed my gaze. "I bet it's a mausoleum," he said. "Why would anybody in their right mind put one in a swamp like this?"

"I think the key phrase in that question is 'in their right mind'," I pondered.

After a moment, Shay turned his attention back to the fallen trunk and pointed at the ground. "Look. A footprint."

"Beckett?" I asked.

"Possibly. It's a bit smaller than my own. It might be exactly as Billie suggested. He came out here to visit Harry's gravesite." Shay stepped next to the footprint and turned around to offer me a hand. We half-climbed, half-scurried over and around the trunk until we found ourselves on the other side. Beckett's footprints continued for a few more yards before disappearing into an area covered in moss.

The trees cleared out, and we discovered the ground had risen here just as it had at the lighthouse. "It's almost like someone built another mound," I said.

"It does, does it not?" Shay agreed. "These mounds are a source of curiosity to me, they are." He stepped forward and then came up short.

"What—?" I looked down at our feet.

"It's a grave marker." He held out his hand. "Might I borrow the walking stick, darling?" I handed it to him and watched as he squatted and cleared moss and debris from the stone with the sharper tip of the stick. We were unable to make out the faded name, but the dates were 1801 to 1829.

I snapped a picture of it with my phone. "I might be able to enhance the image on my laptop."

Shay remained squatting in front of the marker. "Someone lived here after Jonathan—Left? Died?" Shay ruminated. "This would be a fascinating job for an archaeologist. Imagine how many stones there might be here."

"The year this person was born might have been when Jon was in his eighties or older," I said. "If he lived that long. His journal hasn't mentioned living here with anyone else."

Shay stood. "Perhaps he abandoned or sold the lighthouse."

"Maybe… But Billie said it had only been used for about twenty years. The channel was diverted, so it ended up in the middle of an unnavigable swamp. By the time Harry discovered it, it had been abandoned for decades, perhaps a century or more."

After a moment, Shay nodded. His brows were knit, and he appeared deep in thought as he began moving forward again.

We moved more slowly now, shuffling our feet as we went, in a rudimentary attempt to discover more stones. We found eight in all, including one with an erect tombstone. Although we could feel the etching on it, we were unable to read the inscription. I felt a heavy weight settle on my chest as I wondered if it was Jon's grave. I took additional photographs of each one. I wish I were more of an expert at photographic enhancements, but perhaps I could manage to enhance them enough on my laptop to glean something from them.

The mausoleum might have been white granite once upon a time, but it was now so covered in moss and lichen that I wondered how we could have seen it through the thicket. It appeared as though a jungle was attempting to reclaim it; even the door handle was covered in lichen. Shay scraped a bit of it off with his pocket knife, but it was locked. In fact, the bronze door was so solid that it seemed to be sealed. It, too, had turned as green as the surrounding foliage. An odor wafted upward of wet soil and sulfur.

We made our way around the small structure until we came upon a small window. A compact trunk had been rolled against the building as if someone had stepped atop it to peer inside. Shay glanced at me before stepping onto it to test its strength. It had not begun to decompose. He placed his full weight onto it and grasped the bottom of the window.

A grate was anchored across the opening, but the glass inside it was now in shards. Shay reached into his pocket and retrieved his phone, using the flashlight to look inside. "There are two crypts," he announced. He angled for a better look. "I can't read anything… One is a standard size; the other is very small."

"Let me try?" I asked. He stepped down and assisted me onto the trunk. It was wobblier than it appeared, and he reached out to my waist to steady me. I used my phone in a vain attempt to light up the interior, but it remained dark and foreboding. I could barely make out the two crypts he'd described. As I angled my flashlight app, I felt a sudden sensation along the back of my neck. I had the strangest feeling that we shouldn't be there. "Let me down," I said curtly.

"What is it?"

"I think we're being watched." I hopped to the ground and turned off my flashlight app. A crow broke through the treetops nearby with a loud caw. Afterward, there was nothing but an eerie silence. We both stared into the same area, where thickly spaced cypress trunks and underbrush dominated. An odd white blur raced among some of the trees.

"Did you see that?" We asked in unison.

"What was that?" I asked.

"A dog?" Shay mused. "But it disappeared."

"Or it went behind some trees."

"No," Shay corrected. "It was there and then it just… Let's get out of here." He glanced upward. "We don't need to be here after the sun sets."

We made our way back to the first stone Shay had uncovered, where our footprints were still visible in the soft earth. It took us a moment to orient ourselves, and I wished we'd had the foresight to leave a trail that we could easily follow back.

"Here," Shay said, spreading the low-lying branches of a tree.

"Are you sure?"

He hesitated. "I'm sure," he said with too much confidence. He held out his hand to me. I grasped it firmly, but our hands slipped apart as we struggled through the woods. He stopped just ahead of me more than once to shine his light on the ground. Recognizing a footprint, he continued onward.

I was wiping my forehead of perspiration that seemed to attract every mosquito within miles when a thunderous sound broke the silence. Shay stopped and turned his head toward me, his feet rooted to the ground.

"What was that?" he said.

I shook my head. It had been like no sound I'd ever heard before. It had been guttural, feral, and savage all at once.

"A bear?" he asked, though I could see his expression was doubtful.

I shook my head again, my lips too dry to move.

Shay reached for my hand again and curled my fingers around the back of his shirt. "Do not let go of me. Do you understand?"

"Yes," I managed to croak.

He shone his light on the footpath, found another print, and followed it. I stayed so close behind him that I thought I'd walk right over him if he hesitated. I was afraid to blink, concerned I would miss a key clue, and anxious that I could become lost. I found myself pondering how long it had taken us to reach the cemetery. I seemed to recall that Shay had said we'd walk for no more than fifteen or twenty minutes, but I couldn't remember whether we'd adhered to that plan. All I knew was that retracing our steps felt infinitely longer than finding the cemetery.

A few yards from where we stood, the trees rustled, and we froze in unison, both our attentions riveted on the swaying branches. While the trees around them remained immobile, the area we focused on undulated from top to bottom. Without a word, Shay stepped out again with a renewed purpose, and I struggled to keep up.

Another bird broke through the tops of the trees. I realized immediately that it was a turkey vulture. Its wingspan must have been five feet across, and as I stared upward, I saw the swath of distinctive light gray feathers splayed against the darker ones. Something caught my attention beneath the vulture, and a dark shadow emerged as I tore my eyes away from the bird. Whatever it was, it was semi-translucent. My feet became anchored to the soft, swampy soil as my brain struggled to make sense of what my eyes had registered.

"Hayley," Shay hissed. "Hayley!" I turned my head to him. My hand had lost its grip on his shirt, and he was reaching out for me. "Don't stop," he ordered. "Are you understanding me?"

I nodded. I grasped his shirt again and forced my leaden feet to move forward. As I stumbled along the uneven ground, I fought to remain focused on the footpath. My eyes, however, wanted to stray in an attempt to see the shadow again, as if I could avoid an attack by witnessing the strange apparition. I began to sense the presence of evil as a chill inched up my spine despite the warm and humid day. The hair along my forearms was erect and rigid, as if a static charge had prickled them. I swung my head in an attempt to see behind me, just as an exposed root tripped me up. I might have fallen had Shay not yanked me upward and forward. I heard ragged breathing mounting around me. Confused, I wondered whether it was my breath, Shay's, or a third and sinister presence.

When events occur out of the ordinary, it is as if the brain cannot register or process them. I tried to place the animalistic sound, the shadow, and the breathing into a neatly formed, identifiable box in my brain, but none of it would fit, like pieces of several mismatched puzzles. As we continued moving forward, I became increasingly disengaged from my body, moving ahead robotically, my feet disconnected from anything resembling my mind.

When we burst into the open and onto the familiar lane, Shay whirled me around. "What the hell was that?" he demanded. His eyes were wide and filled with so much alarm that it felt as though it was spreading to me. My heart pounded harder and louder, and I struggled against a shortness of breath.

"I don't know," I managed to respond haltingly.

"Was it a bear?" He grabbed my arm and moved me behind him as he stared into the woods. It was immersed in such thick shade that it was impossible to see where one tree ended and another began. I looked at the ground and was surprised to see the footpath we had taken; it was almost as though I expected it to close up behind us.

Shay didn't wait for my answer. Without another word, he grasped my hand and took great strides all the way back to the lighthouse.

27

Shay's voice was louder than I'd ever heard him. "I don't care," he was saying hotly. "This is not a safe place for you to be."

"We've been over and over this," I said tiredly as I paced the lantern room.

"Apparently not over it enough or you'd be packing, you would."

I sighed as I hesitated at the window overlooking the driveway. It all appeared so normal—the gate was closed and locked, my car was safely tucked between the gate and the lighthouse, and the swamps appeared as they had ever since I'd moved in, the reeds bowing with a deceptive serenity.

"You're going to your mother's tomorrow morning," he continued. "You'll pack what you can fit in your car, take me to the airport, and continue on to Midland Cove. Do you hear me?"

"I hear you," I said. The sun began to set, casting a rainbow of colors across the sky. I opened the window and closed my eyes. When I was anxious, I used to sit in nature, close my eyes, and ask myself what I heard, sensed, and felt. Now, I identified a symphony of crickets and frogs, the distinct aroma of marshes and mud, and the gentle, soothing breeze. It was difficult to reconcile this with the otherworldly experience we'd just had. Maybe it was the swamps themselves playing tricks on the mind. Perhaps it had been a bear. There were certainly bears in North Carolina. Weren't there? And we were in its habitat, not ours. That had to be it.

"You will be safe."

I turned in surprise to face Shay. "Here?" I asked.

He stared at me with a puzzled expression. "Here what?"

At the sound of his voice, I realized I had just heard a deeper voice with a more pronounced Scottish accent than Shay's melodic Irish one. "You didn't say anything just now?"

"Just this minute?"

I nodded.

He shook his head as though he didn't understand and turned to another window. "I'm just worried about you, darlin'. I'm deeply in love with you, and I feel helpless with what's happening here. It's quite frustrating."

"I know."

"I'm going downstairs for a glass of wine—or maybe the whole bottle. Care to join me?"

"I'll be down in a sec."

"Aye, then. I'll have it waiting for you."

I waited until I heard his footsteps across the bedroom landing and continued down the stairs to the ground floor. "It's you, isn't it, Jon?" I whispered. Nothing but the frogs and crickets answered. "Am I safe here with you?" After a moment, I closed the window, plunging the room into silence.

I made my way to the spiral staircase. I could hear Shay moving about the kitchen, closing cabinet doors and clinking glasses. As I stepped onto the top step, I heard a voice from behind me. "You are."

I whirled around, but of course, there was no one there. No one, I thought, but Jon. "Don't frighten me, Jon," I whispered, my voice barely audible. "Please don't frighten me."

A gust of wind whirled around the lighthouse, drawing my attention to the scene outside. Within a few more minutes, the sun would set, and darkness would close around us. It was my last evening with Shay before he left for the New York conference. And I knew I wouldn't be driving to my mother's house.

28

We were far more relaxed the next morning when I dropped off Shay at the Raleigh-Durham International Airport, having spent the night making up for our tense exchanges. Shay planned to be in New York for only one night, and when he returned, he would stay with me for another week before returning briefly to Ireland.

I also had a job to do. I had to get my head in the game and work on my latest historical book. I didn't have time to relocate, and I promised myself and Shay that I would not take off on any excursions through the woods. No problems there, as I didn't see a need to visit the cemetery again, though I briefly considered buying a drone.

I'd awakened a couple of hours before Shay's alarm went off, and I spent that time dutifully researching my ancestors' roles in the Revolutionary War. They all had fought on the patriots' side, and at some point, I intended to visit the land holdings they'd been granted in payment for their services. The lighthouse had remained blissfully silent in the darkness before dawn, and wrapped in a blanket, I was cozy as I worked. Shay had joined me for a leisurely breakfast on the patio before he brought down his luggage, and we left the lighthouse behind us.

An hour later, as I left the bustle of Raleigh traffic behind, I phoned my mother. She answered on the fifth ring.

"Hayley?"

"Hi, Mom. I'm calling to see how you're doing."

"You should have texted to see if I was available first. Why does everyone think older people have nothing else to do but answer their phones?"

"Are you busy, Mom?"

"Not at the moment. But one never knows."

"I'll keep that in mind. So, how's Midland Cove?"

"Fabulous. You really should come back and visit again. But ask me first if I'm available, because you never know…"

"Noted. So, are you meeting people?"

"Tons of people. They're not sitting around waiting for the phone to ring, either."

"Okay… How's the modeling business?"

"I've been holding auditions."

"Auditions?"

"Auditions. I'd explain them to you, but I don't have the time—"

"I know. You're busy. By the way, Mom, do you remember Harrison Cooper from New York?"

"Harrison Ellsworth Cooper?"

"Yeah. That's him." I turned off Interstate 95, heading east toward the lighthouse.

"Everyone in New York knew of him."

"Did you ever meet him?"

"I probably did. I meet so many people, you know."

"What was your impression of him?"

"Well, you never know with most real estate tycoons. Some will steal you blind and convince you that you like it."

"Was he like that?"

"Just the opposite."

"How so?"

"He was a philanthropist. His wife passed away— some form of cancer—and he donated huge sums for cancer research. He also founded a chain of hospice centers. He was a bit odd, though, in recent years."

"What happened? Did he have dementia?"

"You certainly have a lot of questions. You're just like your father, always researching something."

"Well, did he?"

"Did he what?"

"Have dementia."

There was a slight pause. "Well," she began, "I can't tell you firsthand. I wasn't in his social circle. I don't know if he had one after his wife died... He became increasingly isolated. Some said he hired various 'psychics'—quacks, if you ask me—in an attempt to communicate with his wife. He continued to fund important research in New York, still owning a substantial amount of real estate, but dropped out of sight. Why do you have so many questions about him?"

"Oh, no particular reason," I answered.

"Huh! I wasn't born yesterday. Give me some credit."

"Okay, Mom. I'm living in his home."

"You moved?"

"No. I'm still in the lighthouse." The speed limit slowed as I approached one of many tiny towns between the interstate and Dikshita.

"I don't understand."

"The lighthouse was his hunting lodge. I guess after his wife's death, he moved there. I thought I told you this already."

"Is that where the psychics were?"

"I don't know. This is the first I've heard of psychics."

"Well, don't get involved with them."

"I wasn't planning to."

"If you don't know what you're doing, you can open a portal, and all sorts of spirits can travel back and forth. Not all of them are Caspar Milquetoast, you know."

I thought of the evil presence in the woods and shivered. "I can imagine."

"Well," Mom continued, "I have come to the end of my free time. I have a gentleman friend who will be here any moment, and I need to check my lipstick."

"A gentleman friend?" I asked, amused.

"We don't dry up and ferment once we reach a certain age, you know."

"I didn't say that you did."

"Call me later. Text first, to see if I'm available."

"I know. Because you stay busy."

"Love you, dear," she said. She hung up without giving me the chance to respond.

"Love you, too, Mom," I said out loud to no one in particular. I slowed down considerably as I drove through a quaint town that the Irish would have referred to as a village. The only thing it lacked was the roundabout in the center of the main street. I thought of the traffic circle at Midland Cove, and my mind wandered to my mother finding a male interest so quickly after moving there. I doubt that she had half her boxes unpacked, but she had time to meet someone. I found myself smiling. It was so like her.

I came to a stoplight and dutifully came to a stop. While I waited for it to turn green—something I wouldn't have had to do in Ireland, because there would have been a roundabout—my eyes fell on a tiny building with "Dundonald Post Office" signage beside the door.

I recalled one of my visits to Scotland, when I toured Dundonald Castle. The castle had been built on a hillfort, a mound not unlike the one on which the lighthouse was built, but far larger and grander. The hillfort allowed the castle's inhabitants and defenders to see further and created a natural barrier to enemies who had to climb the hill to attack.

A car drove around me with its horn blaring as it passed me in the intersection, and I realized the light had turned green. I continued through the town and into the countryside, but my mind lingered on the town's name.

The first Dundonald Castle was built around 1136. It isn't clear what happened to it, but nothing remained of the original structure. The Stewart family built a second castle on the same hillfort in the 13th century. Although it was built of stone and quite impressive for its time, it only remained intact for a hundred years or so, when King Robert the Bruce of Scotland ordered it destroyed so that no one other than himself could lay claim to a castle.

The third castle—the one I toured—was built by a descendant, Robert Stewart, who became Robert III of Scotland. It was three stories tall and surrounded by other structures, including a tower, stables, a bakery, a brewery, and a barmkin wall.

Was it possible, I wondered, for a Stewart descendant to have left Scotland for America and replicate Dundonald in this new land? Of course, I reasoned, anything was possible. After all, the Stewarts sold the castle in the 17th century, as I recalled. It changed hands several times after that, so any number of owners might have sailed across the ocean to the New World.

I reached Dikshita before I realized I'd driven so far. I stopped at the empty intersection and stared at the general store. I wondered why this tiny spot on the road was no longer named after its Scottish founder. My mind raced with events that might have led to the name being stricken from the store and the abandoned granary.

I could think of only one reason. The inhabitants had fought on behalf of King George against the colonists. After they lost, they'd fled the region, abandoning their land holdings. The new owners had stricken the Scottish loyalists' names from the buildings—or, in Argo Dikshita's family, had renamed them after a non-Scottish relation.

I continued through the intersection and a few moments later, turned onto the rough drive to the lighthouse. I wondered how many times Jon had traveled this road on horseback. He'd mentioned his dear mare, Justine, and at least one other structure on the property. Perhaps there had been more.

I made mental notes to myself to look for photographs from Harry's earliest days here. I had a mounting urge to know if he had torn down everything on the mound, or if it had all degraded by that time into heaps of rubble. I was so engrossed in my thoughts that I nearly ran into a bicycle near the road's edge. I came up short and stared into the woods.

The bicycle undoubtedly belonged to Beckett. I'd seen it many times propped up against the side of the general store. It appeared he might have propped it against a nearby tree, but the strong winds could have blown it over. I saw the footpath just off the drive. It appeared innocuous, just as it had when Shay and I had first ventured down it.

I thought of Beckett making his way down the path to the cemetery. Perhaps he had been the one to break the glass in the mausoleum to toss bones inside for Lola. I wondered if he also stood on the trunk and talked to Harry.

I glanced at the sky. Clouds had formed, which appeared to be heading out to sea. Rain would no doubt flood the footpath quickly, wiping out any prints to lead Beckett back to the drive and perhaps creating a muddy swamp he'd have to navigate. I considered honking the horn or calling out to him to warn him of possible rain, but I realized he might have been a quarter of a mile or more into the thick woods and might not hear me.

Sitting in the car with the motor running, I squinted to see into the brush. I hoped Beckett would remain safe from the animal we heard the day before. I imagined alligators, bears, foxes, or even coyotes in the brush. But Beckett had seemed very familiar with the area, I thought. I imagined he'd been born nearby and spent his entire life here. Someday, he would inherit the properties from his father, and then, it would certainly be interesting to try to buy something from the store.

In the end, I shook my head as if to prevent Beckett from taking up residence there, and I continued my journey to the lighthouse. Before I made the final turn, I glanced into my rearview mirror. The bicycle was gone.

29

It was mid-afternoon when I finally pushed back from my laptop, stood, and stretched. I had been immersed in my ancestors' roles in the Revolutionary War for several hours. I'd settled in the lantern room, where I started a cross-breeze. The earlier clouds had never produced any rain, and as I studied the horizon now, I concluded that they'd broken up somewhere over the ocean. The skies had turned a gorgeous azure, becoming a picture-perfect day.

I stretched and made my way downstairs, brewed a cup of tea, and pulled a few scones from the cupboard. It was too quiet with Shay gone, but I had accomplished a great deal in the silence. My publisher should be appeased for a bit.

As I made myself comfortable in the chair by the window, my eyes settled on the journal. I placed my hand upon it, but then withdrew it. I still had a lot of work ahead of me. Then I placed my hand on it again. It was almost as though it was vibrating as if calling to me. I could surely read an entry or two for the short time I would spend with my tea.

I settled in and opened it to the next page.

"January 18, 1776

"I took the boat to Nova Dunglen for supplies yesterday morn. Win was nowhere to be seen. It wasn't unusual for him to be about chasing all manner of wildlife, but he had a sixth sense whenever I left the mound. I had an odd feeling as I left without him running alongside the bank, and I nearly turned around and came back straightaway, but for my dire need. Justine was grazing on some hay just outside the lighthouse. The water was calm and the temperature quite balmy for January, unlike the brash, wintry Scottish weather I was more accustomed to. I convinced myself that I was succumbing to superstition, and I needed to get on with it.

"I should have listened to that voice inside myself. My mother, no doubt, would have called it an omen, a portent of things to come. Had I listened, this day would no doubt have turned out far differently. As it is, I should not be writing this at all, and I would be far better served if I burned the entries I have already made. I can only blame my need to tell someone of my circumstances on my loneliness, even if it is naught but a page and quill I tell."

I thought I heard something, and I raised my head to listen. I glanced outside at a beautiful, calm day. It occurred to me that it might be the same type of warm and pleasant weather that Jon experienced that morning. I looked back at the book, my eyes falling on "my loneliness." My heart broke for him. This place must have felt far more isolated two hundred and fifty years ago than it did today. I felt the increasingly familiar frigidity, and I arranged the blanket around me.

I looked up to find the room exactly as it should have been, but I found myself peering into the shadows for signs of Jon's presence. Then I realized the sign was the rawness in the air as though the icy palm of death had touched my skin. It took me a long moment before I could return to the journal. A sense of dread and horror washed over me as I read.

> *"I arrived home several hours later. I saw the tall mast before I came into full view of her, but I knew to whom it must belong. As I paddled to shore and pulled my boat and supplies from the current, I experienced the most intense emotion I believe I have ever felt. My hand is shaking now as I write this.*
>
> *"Once I was content that the boat was secure, I went in search of Justine and Win. I found Justine lying in the pasture on the other side of the lighthouse. She was covered in blood, yet she was trying to raise her head. Her eyes conveyed an emotion that tore at my heart. She was pleading for me to help her, but the slice across her jugular prevented any sound.*
>
> *"Then he came into view as if he had been lying in wait for me. Captain Hugh Horton was smiling as he wiped his sword against his breeches. When he caught sight of me, any man with an inkling of decency would have run for Hell rather than be caught at his dastardly deed. But, no, he stopped and smiled more broadly as if he were proud of his evil doings."*

I clamped my hand over my mouth as I read the entry. A lone tear escaped, and I quickly wiped it from my cheek before it could roll onto the carefully scripted words and mar them. I could not read any more. I set the book across my lap and placed a hand on my chest, where I felt my heart thumping as wildly as if it were I, and not Jon, who stared into the face of the evil captain.

I wanted to clear my head of the image, to rise and stroll outside where the sun's warmth could remind me that I lived in a different time. However, something kept me frozen in my chair. I knew I was reading what Jon wanted me to read. I was seeing in my mind's eye what he must have lived with for the rest of his days and beyond—what he experienced even now.

And I knew I must continue.

I picked up the journal with trembling hands. Swallowing, I continued.

"We met halfway. By the time I was within arm's length of him, I saw the journal in his hand. This journal. My personal writings, my innermost thoughts. It had been hidden inside the lighthouse, which meant he had ransacked my home in my absence.

"With the heat rising dangerously in my head, causing it to throb, I accused him of as much and a murderer of innocent animals, too. The evil little weasel replied that he was merely searching for the logbook. He was a poor liar. Then he accused me of colluding with the enemy. He held up the book as proof, proclaimed it would be delivered to the Governor himself before the sun was down, and I would be in chains awaiting trial for treason.

"Had he merely wanted to arrest me, I might have been inclined to see out a fair trial or the gallows in the absence of one. But the sight of my beloved mare just beyond us sickened me to no end. He could kill me if he thought he could, but to

harm a helpless, loving animal... Well, I shan't share the details in this journal, because I do not recall them. In my rage, I was blinded. Let us only say that I assisted him in his earnest endeavor to reach Hell as expeditiously as possible.

"I used his own sword upon him, the same sword that was still streaked with the blood of my devoted Justine. He was of no physical match to me, especially as enraged as I had become. For me, it was Culloden all over again, but this louse was untested in battle and unworthy to remain standing. I most likely murdered him with the first powerful blow, but I was so incensed for my Justine that I continued stabbing and chopping him until the ground was saturated with his blood. Not even Satan would recognize his devoted disciple.

"Then, I realized my Justine, God bless her soul, was still attempting to rise despite her weakness and pain. I left him on the ground, the journal tossed out of his hand, and examined my dear friend. I could not stop the flow of blood, and I could not save her. I retrieved the pistol from Horton's holster and ended her agony, but not mine. I sank to my knees and cried like a woman as I prayed for God to receive her.

"I dragged Horton, no longer a captain, and nothing but a wretched spirit of Satan now, to his ship. Not knowing when another might be using the channel, I had to hide him and his vessel as quickly as possible. I loaded Horton's carcass, in pieces now from my onslaught, onto his ship for his final voyage. I tied my boat to his, hopped aboard the larger vessel, and piloted it a distance from the house, taking channels and tributaries none other knew, until I reached an area where the alligators bred. Had it been a cold winter, there might have been none about. But it was warm enough for the

sun to beckon them, and they were active as the evening descended.

"Let me say simply that they ate well that night.

"I don't know how I escaped that den of alligators, except that God was with me. I moored my smaller boat to a cypress knee and struggled to wedge Horton's ship between the dense swamp trees. I fired through the aged hull in a vain effort to sink it. As I left, the trees and brush seemed to close in around it, until even I would not have seen it there had I not known of the day's events.

"As I rowed through the swamps, the most ungodly noise rose up around me. In all the time I have lived in the lighthouse, I have never heard such an outcry. It was not of this world, but guttural, visceral, Satanic. I could not shake the sensation that I might have murdered the body, but the evil soul that had inhabited it was surrounding me, no longer confined by flesh and blood and the rules of human existence. Even after reaching the lighthouse and welcoming the sun's light cutting through the darkness, the air was heavy and menacing.

"God forgive me, but I must believe I have saved untold innocents from the evil clutches of Satan. I found my journal still lying in the grass, and it was only an act of God that kept another from venturing into the channel and finding it. The vultures have descended upon my poor Justine, and I cannot fight them all off."

The entry ended there. I sat, stunned, staring at the journal. The next page had been ripped from the book. I almost continued reading, but I could not. I felt an overwhelming need to make sense of what I had just read. I stared out the window without seeing. I recalled in my mind's eye how Shay and I had hurried back to the road from the cemetery. I could still hear the sounds of an otherworldly presence, see the shadow darting beyond the trees, and feel the terror I had experienced that day.

But now, I was alone in the lighthouse.

30

I couldn't sleep. I tried returning to my work in the dead of night, but I could not focus. My mind was filled with the sounds and images of Jon's horrific ordeal with Captain Horton. Earlier in the evening, I'd made a light dinner of seafood and salad and tried to fill my mind with positive thoughts, but I had been unable to eat. When I retired to the bedroom and turned out the light, my mind returned in relentless waves to that fateful day.

I watched the moonlight play across the bedroom floor. When I considered how quiet it was in my comfortable bed, it felt surreal that a man had been murdered just outside my windows. I struggled with whether Jon had been justified. While I didn't currently have a pet, Shay had a dog, and if anyone had attempted to harm her, I probably would have lost my mind. I imagined that was precisely what had happened with Jon, as he witnessed his beloved mare suffering from a purely evil act, driving him over the edge. Is that how a normal man snaps?

I sat up and turned on the light. I wanted a swath of daylight to envelop me, but the amber glow cast shadows and did little to illuminate the room. I realized that I hadn't encountered any remorse in his journal. On the contrary, he said he was obliged to help Horton to the other side as quickly as possible. My mind wandered to the dark spirit in the swamps. I wondered if Horton was the spirit that Jon could not tell us was harmless during the séance. I shivered involuntarily as I considered whether the ghost of Captain Horton had pursued Shay and me along the trail. Encountering Jon's ghost was one thing, and I'd made my peace with that somewhat, but Horton was another element altogether. Perhaps Shay's adamant insistence that I leave was rooted in a reality I hadn't seen coming.

I swung my legs over the side of the bed, slipped into my robe and slippers, and padded down the stairs to the ground floor. I curled up in the chair, rested my feet on the ottoman, and wrapped the blanket around me. Then, I picked up Jon's journal and continued to read. It occurred to me that it was just like watching a spooky movie; I had to get to the end to see that good triumphed over evil and all was set right in the world. Yet as I read, I could not shake the sensation that Jon's life had been forever altered.

"January 28, 1776

"Ten days have passed, and I have seen no sign of Win. I have scoured the area, and now I must believe the worst. If I could, I would punish the murderous, evil Horton all over again. Anyone who harms a helpless creature, whether human or animal, must have Satan himself coursing through their blood. My only solace is that Horton will now suffer through eternity while Win and Justine are in the care of loving angels.

"I have watched and waited each day for the British to arrive. It seemed ludicrous to me that no one had searched for Horton. I waited to be led away in chains, a quick trial, and a swifter hanging.

"I can't say that I did not think of fleeing. The route was well-known and well-worn to Canada or points west. I don't believe I seriously considered it

because anger had set in, that boiling, frothing
emotion that digs in my heels and squares my jaw.
And I knew what to do with that growing rage.

"When I spotted a small ship flying the
British flag, I retrieved my logbook and met them
along the shore. I recorded the names of four
redcoats as I'd been directed to do. They asked to
speak with me inside, as if there could be anyone
within hearing outside the lighthouse. I invited
them in and provided ale and bread."

I paused and studied the room. If Harry had rebuilt
the lighthouse on the exact spot of the former one, they
might have sat right here. My eyes stopped at the small
dining table, and I pictured Jon and the four British soldiers
squeezed around it. A cold chill passed through the room
as though a window had been opened. I had come to
associate the chill with Jon moving past me, somehow
soaking up the warmth as if warmth to a ghost was akin to
blood to a vampire. I thought of speaking, but thought
better of it. He spoke through his journal, and I had to
believe he meant for me to read it, page by page.

Shivering, I pulled the blanket more tightly around
me and continued reading.

"One man did all the talking. His name was
Captain Montgomery Fleming. I was tempted to
ask if he had replaced Horton, but I dared not
bring up the name. He spoke of Donald
MacDonald and Donald McLeod and their
continued efforts to raise a Scottish contingent of
10,000 men. They were to converge on Cross
Creek in the coming days, where they would receive
further orders.

"Captain Fleming confirmed my identity and asked questions regarding the lighthouse and its origins. I believe he was testing my knowledge of its construction, perhaps to verify that I was indeed its builder. Then he asked to visit the lantern room.

"It was on the gallery outside the lantern room that he stated his full purpose. He informed me that the HMS Blue Mountain Valley had been destroyed a few days earlier off the coast of New Jersey. It had been a clear colonial victory.

"Then, Fleming spoke of a skirmish in North Carolina. He could certainly see my interest, as the war had danced around me here. Now it was clearly moving in, having taken place at Fort Johnson, a mere day's ride from me—if I'd had a horse to get there. The HMS Scorpion had attacked the fort, firing 26 rounds before disengaging. Fleming was careful, I thought, not to have used the word 'retreat.' The HMS Cruizer, an 18-gun sloop launched initially in 1752, had attempted to join the battle but could not get close enough to the fort to fire.

"The following day, only yesterday, I realized as he spoke, the HMS Cruizer had orders to attack Brunswick Town along the Cape Fear River. They turned back when they discovered how well-fortified the breastworks were and how well-defended the town was.

"The British plan, Captain Fleming continued to tell me, was for British officers to join the Scottish troops amassing at Cross Creek. They would lead them from the Cross Creek region east to Wilmington, where they would be joined with additional forces from the sea. Once they established control over Wilmington, the British would dominate the waterways deep into North Carolina,

and the Crown forces would quickly suppress any further uprising.

"That is where my role was defined. I was not to report to Cross Creek. Instead, I was to remain at the lighthouse. I would be informed the night before the passing so that I would be at the ready. On the designated night, I would lead the officers westward along the channel I controlled with the lighthouse lantern. The channel route would shorten their journey by several hours.

"They surveyed the surrounding terrain from the height of the gallery. Afterward, we returned downstairs, and I prepared a meal of meat, bread, and ale for them. It was a paltry meal, but all I had.

"They resumed their journey by midafternoon. It has been torturous to wait until well after dark before I undertook my own. I travel tonight under the cloak of darkness to find Alasdair."

The entry ended there. I skimmed the following page but forced myself to stop. I had to process what had just occurred. Jon had been a man who had not wanted war, and who had traveled across an ocean to avoid it. When the winds of war had first begun, he had thought the colonists foolhardy for attempting to defeat one of the world's strongest armies, a well-disciplined and well-armed force. Yet, as I stared at this last paragraph in his stilted, precise writing, I realized that Jonathan Corbyn was now a spy.

31

I was surprised to awaken in my bed, cuddled under warm bedding while the sunlight streamed through the windows. I didn't remember going to bed. On the contrary, I had felt restless. My brain was filled with the Revolutionary War, from my ancestors to Jon and Alasdair. Knowing the broad history as I did, it had never occurred to me how dangerous and uncertain the times were. The British had been confident of victory, especially with one of the most highly trained militaries in the world. They had colonized one country after another on multiple continents. Yet, here was a less trained and organized militia that dared to believe they might topple one of the world's most significant powers.

Benjamin Franklin, America's first diplomat, was in France when Jon was writing in his journal. Franklin was using all his powers of persuasion to entice the French to come to the aid of the Americans. He was, perhaps, America's first celebrity. Frenchwomen wore wigs to match Franklin's fur cap as France applauded the New World Enlightenment. Yet, success was far from guaranteed, and traitors faced the gallows.

Jon admitted to murder in his journal. It would have been a matter for the court to decide whether he'd acted in defense of his property. However, a colonist killing a British officer—no matter how vile—would have stacked the deck against him. There was not even a guarantee he would receive a trial; he might have been summarily executed.

Yet, he did not run. He was alone now, without mention of a woman in his life and certainly no children. He might have navigated the waterways westward or northward and disappeared into another culture or a place far from the reach of the British soldiers.

I wondered why he didn't escape. I thought of the lighthouse, his lighthouse of lighter weight and wood, its lantern the only navigation nighttime travelers had as they came inland. He had loved his lighthouse. He had built it with his own hands, settled this small plot of land, and searched for peace far from the battlefield of Culloden. When the winds of war had found him here, it had sought him out despite his age and reluctance.

I thought of Shay's attempts to talk me into leaving. I certainly felt exposed here in a lighthouse with no window coverings, no close neighbors, a strange howling in the woods, and apparitions appearing or occasionally speaking to me. Yet, I resisted leaving it, and I didn't know why.

As I lay in bed and watched the sunlight grow and warm the room, I thought of the lantern shining its light without any known power. I felt a strange sensation travel up my spine as I realized that Jon had wanted me in the lantern room. He had been drawing me to it from the first night I was there. He had led me to tear apart that lantern stand to get at the source of the light—and in doing so, he'd made sure I found his journal.

Harry had lived here for decades, and I wondered if Jon had also attempted to communicate with him. I thought of all the times Jon had mentioned the cellar, a mysterious floor I had yet to discover. I felt a sudden, overwhelming desire to know whether this room still existed.

My cell phone rang, interrupting my thoughts. The chime sounded foreign to a mind wrapped in the 18th century. I grappled for it on the nightstand.

"Hayley?" Shay's voice sounded vibrant and fully awake.

When I spoke, my voice was gravelly. "Shay? How is everything in New York?"

"Did I wake you?"

I yawned. "I had a late night—working," I quickly added. No need for him to get concerned again. "But I was awake. Are you at the conference?"

"I am, and there's a wee bit of a change to my plans."

"Oh?"

"Well, I gave my keynote last evening as planned. I anticipated attending some talks this morning and flying back to North Carolina this afternoon..."

I sat up in bed as I listened.

"One of the other speakers has fallen ill," he continued, "and he won't be able to give his breakout sessions today. They've asked me to step in to take his place."

"Are you prepared to do that?"

"I am. The subject is the role that aristocrats, disconnected from the plight of most of their countrymen, played in inadvertently leading their countries into revolution. The organizers are printing out materials from my laptop now."

"Well, that sounds right up your alley."

He chuckled. "It is. But it means I'll be here through tomorrow. We don't know yet whether the original speaker has a twenty-four-hour bug or something more. Will you be okay with me gone?"

"Of course I will," I answered without hesitation. "This is a great opportunity for you. And it will give me more time to work on my book."

"How's that coming?"

"I'm making good progress. Writing is a slow endeavor, as you know, given all the research involved. But I'm remaining on schedule with my publisher."

"Good. No more howls or apparitions?"

I had a strange feeling that others were listening and eyes were intently upon me. I tried to shake it off. "None."

"I miss you, darlin'."

"I miss you, too, sweetheart. But you'll be back here before you know it. Have fun with the sessions."

He laughed. "If you could call revolution 'fun.' But I hope it will be enlightening for the attendees."

"Maybe I should have attended."

"Maybe you should have," he said warmly. "Then, there'd be no need for me to hurry back."

We chatted for another moment, and I wondered why I hadn't enrolled in the conference. Of course, there was the disconnect between my work on a revolution that had occurred two hundred and fifty years ago, and the conference's focus on modern-day red flags heralding seismic geopolitical shifts.

Or was it truly a disconnect after all?

~~~~~

I stared at the slate patio as I sipped a cup of tea that was rapidly cooling. Had I been Jon standing on this mound, I would have opted to build the lighthouse in the center of it. Without a measuring device and just my eyes to gauge the mound, I realized the present lighthouse was not in the center, but close enough to it. The patio was perfectly flat before the ground sloped away in all directions. I wondered if the chain-link fence had also served to hold the soil in and whether the mound had been much larger two hundred and fifty years ago. There had certainly been sufficient talk of coastal erosion, and the landscape had changed substantially with the channel diversion.

I wondered where the channel had been. There was no way of telling just by looking at it now, as the swamps had taken over the landscape in the same way that jungles might reclaim an ancient civilization. I studied the ground around me, almost expecting to find a pool of blood darkening the grass. I was saddened by the loss of Jon's innocent and helpless horse, and I didn't want to imagine what had happened to his faithful dog. Yet, I couldn't muster empathy for the man Jon murdered.

A strong coastal breeze passed by like a wave. The energy shift felt different from Jon's presence, and my mind wandered to whether Horton still existed here, a spirit in the swamps, destined to live out eternity stalking inhabitants of the lighthouse.

A seagull broke through a nearby canopy of trees, startling me. I faced the sudden urge to race back into the lighthouse and bolt the door. The naked windows had not bothered me in the least when I moved in, as no neighbors were close enough to glimpse the structure, let alone peer inside. Then, why did I feel increasingly exposed there?

I decided in the end to return to the lighthouse, though at a measured pace with my platter of tea and food. I set the platter on the kitchen counter and studied the floor. It might have been silly, as I could see the floor from my vantage point, but I decided to walk the circumference of the ground floor anyway. The hardwood was shiny and modern. Although it might have been considered vintage by Americans' standards, it was a far cry from an original 18th-century floor.

The planks were laid meticulously and solidly. I had watched enough renovation television to recognize they were tongue-in-groove and factory-precise. Not a single one creaked or moaned under my weight as I intentionally shifted in an attempt to discover a hollow room below. I even tilted the chairs, sofa, and area rugs to peer underneath. It made sense that a door to the cellar would be covered by the living room or dining rugs and anchored by heavy furniture lest a hapless renter—like me?—might fall into the opening. Yet, no clues or telltale hardwood areas pointed to a repair or concealment.

After nearly an hour of scouring a relatively small area, I felt foolish. I was wasting time.

I grabbed my laptop and headed upstairs to the lantern room.

~~~~~

My back had started to ache, so I pushed back from my laptop. Standing, I stretched my back while I gazed at the surrounding landscape. I had come to love the lantern room with its continuous windows and unobstructed view, despite sharing it with a ghost. Or maybe, I thought, because of him.

I thought of Beckett visiting Harry and wondered how much time they might have spent in this room. I sensed that Harry had been able to get more conversation out of Beckett than Shay and I had. My eyes wandered to the trail of trees in the vicinity of the cemetery, and I visualized Beckett standing on the tree trunk, talking to Harry and Lola through the broken mausoleum window. I wondered what he had to chat about. His world seemed small and isolated.

I realized as I stared in that direction that the trees were shifting in a way the surrounding ones were not. I thought of squirrels in the treetops or perhaps large birds, such as vultures. I followed the movement until it abruptly stopped.

I needed binoculars.

I wondered if such a thing had existed during Jon's time and whether he'd ever used one. I could sense him alone during countless nights, sitting in this quiet, torpid room, watching the hypnotic, rippling channel for an unexpected traveler. In peacetime, perhaps it wasn't very reasonable to traverse this swampland at night versus daytime. In times of war, it might have been essential.

I sat back down and stared at my laptop screen. I'd spent hours scouring genealogy and military records for information on my ancestors. I felt a yearning to utilize the same research functions to learn more about Jon.

I first went to an ancestry website and typed in his name. I suppose I shouldn't have been surprised when nothing came up. There had been no indication that he'd ever married or that he'd had children. I then searched North Carolina military records. There was no mention of him. Of course, there wouldn't be. Had he been registered in the colonial army, his name would have been amongst the others. I didn't know whether he was listed as a loyalist soldier or where those records might have been kept. Shay would know.

I leaned back in my chair. How sad for someone to have lived and died and be so forgotten.

I plugged my phone into my laptop and downloaded the tombstone pictures I'd taken with Shay. Then I switched to Photoshop and tried various options to clarify the writing. Eventually, I succeeded with some dating back to the early 19th century. None had Jon's name on them.

Wait, I thought suddenly. Jon had mentioned his brother in law, Alasdair, several times in his journal. He'd been married to Jon's sister, and perhaps they'd had children.

I switched back to the ancestry website. I didn't recall Alasdair's last name or whether Jon had ever mentioned his sister's name. I raced downstairs, retrieved the journal, and returned to the lantern room. I spent a good deal of time scanning through the pages. I knew Jon had mentioned her, but I could not find the passage.

I needed a family bible. Certainly, the family tree would have been recorded there.

I searched for the names of Scottish soldiers at Cross Creek during the Revolutionary War. I had almost given up when I came across a website containing a historical marker database. I tried Jon's first and last names, but neither returned a result. Frustrated, I discovered a location option in the menu. I clicked there, scrolled to North Carolina, and felt like I had struck gold when a list of battles dating back to the 1700s popped up.

He was there. It had to be him: Alasdair Glenn.

Nova Dunglen.

It was missing the last letter. I suppose my relationship with an Irish historian was paying off because I knew immediately that Glenn was a Scottish spelling while Glen was Irish. I pondered why he might have shortened the name of the village to represent the Irish. It was an intriguing question. Certainly, the Irish had a history of war with England dating back centuries, so it wouldn't have thrown off the British for very long if that was his intent.

And Dun was commonly found in Scotland. It meant a hillfort or a settlement. Nova represented something new, so the village was the new hillfort belonging to Glen—or Glenn.

My fixation on the village quickly dissipated when I discovered that Alasdair Glenn was buried in Pender County in 1776. A heaviness settled onto my chest in the same way it might have had I found out about the death of a friend or relative. With every colonist's death, the surviving family must have wondered if they'd been right to resist a powerful monarchy.

I opened another browser tab and searched for the cemetery. It was located in a rural area. Although the nearest city to the cemetery was Wilmington, it still looked to be a substantial distance away.

I felt Jon's familiar presence, like he was looking over my shoulder as the room took on a surreal glow. When I looked up, the sun had set, and only the thinnest of red lines remained on the horizon. I gathered up my laptop and the journal and made my way down the stairs. I couldn't quite put my finger on it, but the coziness of the living room chair beckoned. It was a far cry from the pristine lantern room with its hardback chairs.

After I arranged the laptop and journal on the end table, I took a break. I wasn't really hungry, though I knew I should be. I felt distracted as I brewed some tea and made a sandwich, my mind consumed with what I had learned. This often happened when I was writing, as I immersed myself in another world, and stepped into a character's shoes who was frequently vastly different from myself. Now I felt transported in time to the midst of the 1776 rebellion, with no way to know how the war would end. In hindsight, we know it was the beginning of a new democracy, but seeing events unfold through Jon's eyes, the stakes couldn't have been higher.

I wondered whether Jon had been with Alasdair when he had died. If my calculations were correct and Jon was in his 60s during the revolution, his brother-in-law may have been approximately the same age, as he'd mentioned in his journal that they'd been like brothers and best friends who crossed the Atlantic after Culloden.

I moved to the dining table where I could spread out with my dinner, the journal, and the laptop. I returned to the ancestry website and searched for more information on Alasdair Glenn. After several pages of false hope, I came upon his name—and his widow's.

Lili Corbyn Glenn.

I spoke the name aloud. My voice sounded reverent, as if I was reciting in the solemnness of a church sanctuary. The words hung in the stillness of the air as if the walls were the enraptured audience.

The quiet was abruptly interrupted by a bang from above, causing me to jump. I was hit by a draft as if the door to the gallery had been opened with force. I stared up the spiral staircase as though, if I stared long enough, I would be able to see all the way to the top. I was surprised that I wasn't frightened. Instead, I felt heaviness creep into my psyche, the burden of familial deaths and lives irrevocably altered. I pictured Jon pacing the gallery, staring across the landscape, perhaps seeing the channel as it had been. The revolution had changed everything.

After a long moment, I crossed to the front door, opened it, and stepped outside. It took a moment to register that the day had been balmy; that it was April in the twenty-first century and not January in the eighteenth. As my mind crossed into the present, the voices of frogs and crickets formed a symphony across the vastness of the swamps. I leaned against the lighthouse and closed my eyes while I listened.

I don't know how long I stood there, teetering between centuries. I felt like a guest in the lighthouse while the owner mourned his brother-in-law's death and his sister's fate.

I shook myself from my thoughts and returned inside to the dining table and the genealogical records. Lili died in 1798, twenty-two years after her husband's death. I felt as if Lili had been my sister, and I was suffering her loss. With my heart heavy and a deep sadness descending over me, it occurred to me that Jon might have been alive at the time of her death.

"Jon," I said, breaking the silence. The lamp on the end table flickered briefly. Somehow, I knew it was a signal that he was near. So much for spending money on an EMF detector. "Are you watching me now as I search for your family? Is this what you wanted from me?"

Though I cocked my head to listen, I heard nothing but the wind, the frogs, and the crickets, muffled now through the thick lighthouse walls. Eventually, even those sounds were quieted, and I was met with the heavy, forlorn silence of a tomb. The lamp's light was steady and dim, the soft, golden glow reminding me too much of a candle's light burning too long ago.

I sighed heavily and returned to the website to delve deeper into their family tree. Lili and Alasdair had three children and seven grandchildren. I clicked on each one, unsure of what I would find.

Then, as I clicked on the next-to-last grandchild, my heart skipped a beat. His name was Argos, and he had died at birth.

The last grandchild, Sarah, had married none other than Khalil Dikshita and given birth ten months later to Argo Dikshita. There, the trail went cold. It was obviously not the same man I knew at the general store, but if my rough calculations were correct, I might have met Sarah's grandson, perhaps six generations down the line.

32

The midnight hour found me restless and unable to sleep. After tossing and turning, unable to get comfortable, I gave up and returned to the ground floor. The chair by the window had become my favorite spot. I poured a small peach chardonnay, wrapped the familiar blanket around me, and opened Jon's journal. I sat for a long moment with my hand upon the page, feeling the energy of a man I had never known but wish I had. The stress and uncertainty of the revolution were taking their toll on him, and my heart ached with the loss of his precious animals.

When I began to read, it was almost as though a soft Scottish brogue recited the passage to me.

"February 15, 1776

"It is impossible to ignore the drumbeats of war. Many wish to carry on as they had in years past, hoping sane minds would prevail and both an agreement and peace could be reached. But the parties are too far apart; it is all or nothing for both. When compromise is removed from the table, it appears that there is nothing left but to pick up arms against one side or the other.

"I sit at my table more frequently now as British soldiers eat what little food and ale I have

while they advise me of my duties to the king. They speak to me as though I were their servant simply because I do not share their place of birth or lineage or speak in the same British accent as they. I have been told by others at Cross Creek that I am treated better because I talk with a Scottish tongue, and those with distinctly American accents fare far worse. I cannot imagine it being worse than my experiences.

"I have taken to feeding them alligator and watering down the ale with swamp water in the hopes they derive dysentery. I hide the decent food in the cellar, though the air has changed there since Horton's final visit. It is, perhaps, only my imagination or my nerves on edge, but I often think I hear whispering, though I know there is naught but myself about. It is not the murmurings of angels but of demons. I am always relieved once I leave its darkness and close and bolt the cellar door."

I hesitated as my thoughts once again returned to the shadowy figure in the swamps. I did not want to read in my isolation that a grown man capable of murder was apprehensive about living here. I wished I knew where the door was located, if only to ensure it was securely bolted. Then, I wondered how I—or Jon—could possibly think a manmade bolt could keep a spirit contained.

I almost set down the book and opted for something less sinister in my digital book collection, but the journal seemed to call out to me. After a long moment and a longer sip of wine, I continued.

"It is a depressing time for the colonists. On the 5ᵗʰ of February, the Hawke was captured by the HMS Syren off the North Carolina coastline.

Five days later, the USS America was captured on the Cape Fear River by the HMS Cruzer. I do not yet know the fates of the two ships—whether scuttled or held—or of their crews.

"Another conflict began yesterday somewhere up the coast, but I do not yet know of the victor.

"The British have seized on their victories and are determined to put down the North Carolina rebels in a decisive action. Alasdair has informed me that Scots are now massing at Cross Creek to march toward Wilmington at long last, where they plan to attack the fortified colonists. Meanwhile, the British have told me that the king's soldiers plan to meet the Scots to reinforce their ranks before they pass through colonial strongholds on their march to the sea.

"My role has not yet been fully explained. I only know I shall operate the lantern to speed the British forces. The British expect 10,000 Scots at Cross Creek before they march. Alasdair tells me the figure will be closer to 1,000. He is sending my dear sister and their children westward into the mountains where the British are fewer in number.

"Some of the other women are remaining to see their husbands off to fight for the king, including Flora MacDonald. I am told that Flora and her husband Allan are confident the king's men will put down this insurrection in short order. They have come a long way from their days fighting for Bonnie Prince Charles. They, like me, signed declarations of loyalty to the king in return for land ownership. They apparently intend to uphold their commitment. Perhaps they have more to lose than I."

I stared at the date of this latest entry for a long time. As Jon wrote these words and waited for his instructions, I knew the march had already begun from Cross Creek. On February 15, 1776, approximately 1,600 men, primarily Scots, departed Cross Creek en route to Wilmington. Flora MacDonald's husband would join them on February 20 as the loyalists picked up men along the way. What I did not yet know was the details of Jon's role in all of this.

I was soon to find out. Jon's precise and graceful handwriting appeared more rushed; the ink on the quill was smudged in several locations, and the letters were more difficult to decipher.

"February 20, 1776

"The entire colony is on the move.

"I have not heard further directly from Alasdair, though patriots have come through the channel with bits and pieces. I do not record them in my logbook; I treat them as apparitions, merely progressing on their way. I have been informed in clandestine engagements here that patriots march and sail from points north and south to engage the loyalists where they can. In the east, the patriots are fortifying their positions in anticipation of major assaults on Wilmington, the Cape Fear River, and various channels.

"Meanwhile, the British goal appears to be cutting off the supply lines to the patriots, capturing or killing as many men as possible, and securing North Carolina for the king. Now, my duty is beginning to be known to me.

"As the patriots march toward the Scottish and British regiments, the loyalists will use boats to navigate more quickly toward them. They aim

to cut off smaller groups of patriots before they can join together and amass greater numbers.

"Some loyalists will navigate Corbyn Channel. I have been instructed to place sackcloth at the junction at which my channel begins, for we are to assume that those who traverse it will have never encountered it before. It will cut off critical travel time, for the alternative is to continue up the Cape Fear River, which is heavily guarded by both sides at differing intervals. An encounter there could prevent them from completing their mission.

"They will pass by my lighthouse at a crucial time, and I have been ordered to keep the lantern burning to light their way through the darkness. I have been ordered to use a red cloth covering the lantern's light if I detect patriots in the vicinity. A solid white light signifies a clear path ahead. At no time am I to allow the light to go out.

"It is now that I swear my allegiance to God alone. It means I will renege on my sworn allegiance to the king, unlike MacDonald and those who march for Britain. I have instead readied to join Alasdair, Cuddy, and others as they fight against the crown. While Alasdair passes critical information on the loyalist movements to the patriots, I will use my unique position to thwart the loyalist forces from using these channels.

"I may only write one more entry in this journal before it becomes too risky. If the loyalists win this crucial campaign, I will be forced to flee or face the hangman's noose. No outcome is certain."

33

For such a small and unimpressive façade, the Dikshita General Store certainly did appear to have everything. I placed a pair of inexpensive, camouflage-painted binoculars in my cart alongside enough groceries to last for the next week. I found the binoculars in an aisle with deer hunting paraphernalia under a sign that stated, "Deer Processing—Pull Up Back," and another advertising a sale on Bogs Boots. I considered the boots a practical clothing accessory, living at the lighthouse. I left to get more groceries and returned to study them some more.

As I took my time, I couldn't help but notice Beckett's head sliding out from behind a stack of merchandise here or an endcap there. "Hello, Beckett," I called out. When there was no response, I added, "It's just me here today."

I held up a pair of boots. "Do you think these boots would work well around the lighthouse?" I called out.

A moment later, Beckett's head slid out from the next aisle over.

"Yes?" I asked.

His head disappeared.

I put the boots in my basket. I was killing time, and I knew it. I'd come not only to purchase binoculars and food, which I was pleasantly surprised to find, but also to speak with Argo. I checked my mailbox, looked through the circulars comprising my entire week's mail, and was just about to write down my list of items and prices when Argo came through the door.

"Hello!" Argo called out upon seeing me there. "Have you found everything you were looking for?"

"I have," I answered pleasantly as he slipped behind the counter. I placed the boots and binoculars on the counter. "I was even surprised to find these here."

"We have a lot of hunters come through here," he said as he rang them up. "Deer, duck, turkey… Even got some that enjoy rabbits and raccoons."

"Raccoons?"

"They taste just like chicken," he said with a smile.

I laughed. "Oh, really?"

"No," he answered, still smiling. "Not really. They're greasy little critters that taste more like lamb fat."

I made a face as I put my groceries on the counter. I grabbed an empty box, one of many stacked by the counter, and began to box up my groceries.

Argo nodded at the box. "Bring it back next time, and I'll give you a nickel off—even if you use it again."

"Well, thank you for telling me. You have an impressive selection here, you know."

He smiled proudly as he continued ringing up my purchases.

"How long has this store been here?" I asked casually.

"In its present incarnation?"

"How many incarnations has it had?" I laughed.

Argo chuckled. "This store you're standing in was built in 1920."

"Are you serious? It needs to be on the historic register. Or is it?"

He shook his head.

"You have such a great selection," I continued, "that I'm surprised you don't have more customers."

"We're away from the beaten path, as you've probably noticed." He finished ringing up the items as his smile faded.

I glanced at the total on the back of the register and pulled out my credit card. "Do you earn enough here?" I asked. "I mean, it's always so quiet…"

"There's more than meets the eye around here," he said as my card processed. His words had become curt.

"Yes," I agreed. "I'm sure there is. I mean, wiring electricity, running the post office for Dikshita… What are the silos for across the road?"

"Grain bins. For livestock," he added.

"Oh. Is there a lot of livestock in the area? I hadn't noticed."

He sighed, and for a moment, I didn't believe he would respond. When he did, I detected a bit of impatience in his voice. "What you see around here is farmland. Stay till the end of summer, and you won't be able to see beyond the road for the cornstalks. They're not grown for human consumption. It's for the chicken and hog farms."

"And do you own the land where the livestock and corn are?"

He laughed, but it sounded forced. "No. Never have."

"Did your ancestors?"

He narrowed his eyes. "Don't know if I recall." I felt a door shutting in my face.

"Oh," I said, placing the box in my cart to roll it out. "I was just curious… I'm doing research on the Revolutionary War. It's for my next book."

"I heard."

"You did?" I was startled at that, because I didn't recall saying much about my writing to anyone here, and it certainly wasn't news online. Writers can be immensely secretive about their next book. We often reach into the ether for our ideas and are paranoid that everyone else has done the same thing. "I guess Billie must have…"

"Anything else?" Argo's smile morphed into a smirk.

"Yes," I heard myself saying. I sounded surprisingly normal and oblivious to his changing demeanor. "Yes, there is. I came across some information about Alasdair and Lili Glenn. They lived in this area."

Argo abruptly closed the register drawer with a startling bang.

I had to have jumped at the sound, but I tried to recover quickly. I continued, "They lived in a village called Nova Dunglen, back during the Revolutionary War. Maybe you've heard of it?"

He turned toward the back office. "No. Can't help you."

As he started to disappear, I pressed, "Are you sure? I think they're your ancestors."

He stopped cold while I stared at his back. When he turned around, his face was dark. "Don't go poking around where you don't belong," he said tersely. "Beckett!" The boy's name was called out loudly and impatiently.

I was surprised to find Beckett appear at my elbow. He'd been so silent that I had no idea how long he might have stood there.

"Help Miss Hunter with her groceries," Argo growled as he moved out of sight.

"It's okay, I don't—" I started to protest, but Beckett had lifted the box out of the cart and was already halfway to the door.

I held the door open for him and popped the trunk of the car. "Beckett, I saw where Harry and Lola are buried," I said. My speech was rapid and a bit breathy. He had a habit of disappearing suddenly, and I found myself wanting to speak with him.

"Lola isn't there," he said as he situated the box and closed the trunk.

"Do you know where she is?" I asked.

"With Harry."

"But, you just said—" I stopped as he started back toward the store. I stepped forward, halfway blocking him, and tried a different approach. "Do you know about your ancestors, Beckett? Do you know who they were?"

He peered past me and kept walking. As I turned to watch him go, I caught sight of Argo standing at the window wearing a dark scowl.

"Thank you!" I called out cheerily, waving at Argo. He did not respond but continued to watch me. I felt an eerie sensation come over me, causing me to look over my shoulder. No one was in the parking lot except me. I didn't see another soul anywhere in sight, but the tops of the trees swayed slightly with a stealthy breeze. It seemed too quiet. Deathly quiet.

When I glanced back at the store, both Beckett and Argo had disappeared.

With my heart pounding, I slipped into my car, started it, and pulled out of the lot. As I headed toward the lighthouse, I began to feel its isolation more acutely than ever.

34

Rain had moved in. It wasn't a violent storm but a heavy, steady downpour that wouldn't let up. I was mesmerized by the landscape. It appeared to morph into something I no longer recognized. The swamps that had appeared distant on the other side of the chain link fencing now looked dangerously close, and as I stood in the lantern room and stared down the lane, I struggled to see whether the deep ditches on either side of the road were overflowing. I wondered what I would do if my escape route flooded. Then I realized there was nothing I could do. I tried telling myself that the lighthouse was the safest place to be, but it did nothing to banish my mounting trepidation.

I tried using my new binoculars on the swamps, but the torrential rain beat so heavily against the windowpanes that it was akin to peering through a watercolor painting. All I could see were mottled colors.

I was surprised when the phone rang; in my isolation, I'd seemed cut off from the rest of the world. It was Shay, and I was overjoyed at hearing his voice. I hadn't realized until that moment how much I yearned for him to be there with me. Somehow, even if we were marooned on the lighthouse mound, I knew everything would be alright if we were together.

"The conference went extremely well," he was saying. "The original workshop facilitator arrived this afternoon, and I've made arrangements to fly back to Raleigh on the first available flight. Unfortunately, it isn't until tomorrow morning."

"I'm just glad you're coming back."

"Is everything alright there, darling?"

"Oh, yeah. Yeah, everything's good." I heard the lilt in my voice as I tried to keep things light.

"You sound... different."

"It's the rain. I might be shouting to be heard."

"No more howling bears?"

"None." I chuckled. "I bought binoculars today."

"Oh? See anything of interest?"

"Nothing yet. The rain, you know."

"Ah. So, is it convenient for you to pick me up tomorrow? I'll text my itinerary."

My phone beeped almost immediately. "Seven in the morning?" I asked as I looked through it. I set the binoculars on the ledge and sat.

"Too early?" Shay asked. "I know it's a long drive for you—"

"Oh, no, no. I'm good."

"You sure? It isn't an issue for me to rent an auto—"

"I'm sure. There's nothing I'd rather do. In fact," I added, "since you're arriving so early, maybe we can pop in someplace and have breakfast before we head back home."

"Ah, 'home', you say?" His voice lightened as though he was smiling.

I forced a laugh. "Yeah. I guess it feels more like home to me now."

"And your ghost is okay with that?"

I tore my eyes away from the direction of the lane to glance around the lantern room. It felt snug, and it was thankfully dry. "Yeah. I think my ghost is okay with me being here." I caught a dark flutter just outside the window as if someone was pacing the gallery. My heart thumped so vigorously that I was certain Shay would hear it over the phone. As I stared, it faded from view like dissipating fog. I told myself that was precisely what I'd seen—ground clouds, I think they called it. My psyche wasn't convinced.

"Is that okay?" Shay's voice brought me back to the call.

"I'm sorry. The phone must have cut out on me," I fibbed. "Can you repeat that?"

"Don't bother parking and coming in if you don't want to. I'll look for you outside."

"I'll text you when I get there," I said. "I'll let you know where to find me."

"Sounds good, then."

We spoke for a few more minutes, mostly about his conference and my book, before he was dragged off to dinner with fellow attendees. When I clicked off, I felt suspended between isolation and—I don't know, something else. I slowly gathered up my laptop and some papers as I tried to put my finger on it. Anticipation, I realized.

But, oddly, it wasn't the anticipation of Shay's return, though I was certainly happy about that. No. It was something else entirely.

~~~~~

"February 26, 1776

"Perhaps I am a decent man, after all. Were I otherwise, I doubt I would have given Captain Horton another thought. But the truth of the matter is that I have dreamt of him every night since I tossed his body overboard.

"I thought him dead at the lighthouse. I could not detect a pulse, a breath, a heartbeat. His blood covered the grass. Yet, just before I reached the

alligator pits, he groaned. I knew he was coming to, and I could not risk another encounter on the boat, as it was too small to sustain a fight; we both risked going overboard. And that, I could not risk. It had to be him or me, and it certainly would not be me.

"So, as he groaned and attempted to speak to me, though thwarted by the blood rising in his throat and erupting from his lips, I heaved him onto the side of the boat. Though I tried not to look at his face, I caught a glimpse of his eyes. They were pleading and horrified simultaneously.

"I could not afford a thought other than how to get him overboard without him pulling me with him. I had to act quickly, and I did. He thrashed in the water with the strength of a man fighting against death. He tried repeatedly to grab onto the boat, but I beat his knuckles with the oar. Then I pushed off and away from him. Despite my desire to turn my back upon him, I could not seem to tear my eyes from him. I thought I saw through a sliver of moonlight as he grasped at a cypress knee, and for a moment, it appeared he might climb upon it like a marooned sailor. But all his flailing did was attract the alligators.

"They appeared in droves. The last I heard was an ungodly wail, unlike anything that had ever lain on my ears before or since. It was animalistic. It was not a howl, not a bark, and not a growl. It was all of them."

I set the journal on the table and stared out the window. It was dark now, the gloom so thick that I could only see the rain where the weak amber light from the room snaked outside. I pulled the throw blanket tighter about me. The room might have felt homely, pleasantly warm and dry, but staring into that puddle, the golden light undulated as if it was struggling against being extinguished, and no matter how much I tried to wrap myself in the warmth of the throw, a chill had permeated through to my bones.

My mind separated from my body, and I was back in the swamps with Shay, trying to get back to the road, struggling to escape the sound that echoed through the woods, fighting against the black shadow that flitted ominously through the trees. Then Shay was gone, and I was alone, and the shadow grew larger, and the howls filled my ears.

Animalistic. That's what he'd called it.

"You did what you had to do," I said aloud. The chill climbed up my legs as if he were running his hands up my legs. If the truth be told, I wasn't sure if it was what had to be done. It certainly appeared to Jon that it was the only way out. Who was I to judge whether he'd made the right choice?

I glanced across the room at the windows closest to the lane and ultimately the cemetery. I pondered whether Captain Horton's spirit could be out there still, trying to find his way out of the swamps and back to the lighthouse through an eternity. As cruel a man as he was, I wondered if he'd had someone who loved him: a mother, sister, lover, or wife. Maybe some men have no one. Perhaps that is why Horton remains here.

I stood quickly and turned off the light, plunging the room into an inky blackness that matched the gloom outside.

As my eyes adjusted, the landscape morphed into an uneasy focus. The trees bent low with the storm's wind. They weren't dodging and bowing as they might with a heavy squall. It was more like they were taking their time, the measured footsteps of a killer who knew his victim could not escape.

I darted to the door and checked the knob and deadbolt. They were locked tight, as I knew they would be. But I could not shake the sensation that I was as exposed as an unwitting mouse only inches from a snake. The windows that had let in such beautiful sunlight were now the harbingers of a murky gloom, a bleakness that was alive and encompassing. I backed against the wall by the kitchen, pressing myself tight against it.

I don't know how long I must have remained there, frozen as I stared outside. Yet, the minutes passed, and I grew impatient with myself. If my mother were here, she would curse like a sailor at my trepidation. In this case, I supposed she'd be right.

The journal's pages fluttered on the dining table like fingers rifling through them. I watched, mesmerized. Without thinking, I made my way back to the table. I picked up the journal once more. My fingers trembled with an energy that pulsed through the pages.

"It is now nearing the stroke of midnight. I have spent the last hours with Alasdair. I drew a map of the channels from memory, knowing which channels would end like a blind alley and which would circle in on themselves. I also knew which would lead away from the ship where I'd scuttled it.

"And we marked the channels, he and I. We marked them as if to lead the British past the lighthouse so they could reconnoiter with the others marching from Cross Creek. And, once a larger force, they intended to mount a surprise attack against the patriots to decimate their ranks. It would spell the end of the resistance in North Carolina, and the British would reign supreme.

"But the markings carefully dictated by the British in our meetings would not take them past

the lighthouse. I would not light the lantern's oil to lead the way through the darkness.

"The weather had been balmy this winter, unseasonably so; now, it had turned bitterly cold, and the frost and the freeze bit our fingers as we worked. But God did not freeze the channels, and when Alasdair and I parted ways, I watched his rowboat until it was out of sight, and the wake was gone as if it had never occurred and he had never been here. And I knew the same would happen to me as I quietly rowed back to the lighthouse under a waning moon.

"Any other man would have become lost in the swamps, but not I. I knew them intimately, and she carried me home to my lighthouse. I must admit that I searched for Win with my eyes, hoping beyond reasonable hope that he was out there still and would come running. Though crushed, I was not surprised when he did not appear.

"I spent the remainder of the night between the lantern room and the gallery in the shadows of the night. I heard nothing more than the hoot of the owls and howls of coyotes. I saw no one approaching the channel to lead them where they needed to go. And I knew Alasdair was not rejoining the Scottish troops marching from Cross Creek. I knew, instead, he was rowing under the cover of darkness to find the patriots as they moved west for their own surprise attack."

35

I awakened in the night in an icy sweat. It was a strange sensation akin to fighting the flu, realizing the air was warm, yet my flesh was chilled to the bone. Yet, I knew I was not physically ill. I sensed something else permeated my senses, and the unrelenting blackness did nothing to reassure me.

I rose from the bed and wrapped my robe around me as I stepped to the window. The rain descended in torrents, and the cloud cover was so heavy that any light from the waning moon and stars was effectively obstructed. As I peered toward the horizon, shades of gray and black undulated like hovering spirits. I realized as I stared at the phenomenon that I was watching the crowns of the trees shifting with the wind, their branches struggling against the growing storm. A whistle began in the distance. At first, I thought it must be a distant train, and I couldn't figure out where the tracks were. As the sound grew, I realized it was not a train at all, but the wind making its way through the swamps to wrap its tentacles around the lighthouse.

I backed away from the window, grabbed my phone as though it were a lifeline, and headed downstairs. I settled on the sofa, which was furthest from the windows, and attempted to check the weather report. My mobile service was spotty, and the Wi-Fi appeared to be affected by the storm. Unable to discover what danger I might face, I prepared for the worst.

I returned to the bedroom and dressed for the day
ahead. Instead of my usual shoes, I donned my new boots
built for the bogs, though I felt a bit silly doing so. I
reminded myself that this lighthouse had stood for
decades. During that time, there had been major hurricanes
and a plethora of tornadoes that rolled in from the sea on
their quest inland. The lighthouse had withstood them all,
and it would certainly weather this bit of rain as well.

Returning to the living room, I made myself
comfortable on the sofa, pulled the blanket around me, and
reached like an addict for Jon's journal. There was only one
more entry left to read before the final pages had been
ripped out.

"February 27, 1776,

*"Dawn had not yet arrived in full when I
observed a lone rowboat making its way along the
channel. As it drew near, I noticed with relief that
the boatman was dressed in dark clothing and not
a British uniform. Still, I remained in the lantern
room and watched as he rowed his boat to shore
and stepped onto the lighthouse grounds.*

*"I waited until I heard the door open on the
lower level. I crept down the stairs and listened as
the man called for me by name.*

*"I continued to make my way to the ground
floor. I did not recognize him, but he had a note for
me from Alasdair, sealed with wax. He handed it
to me and began to take his leave. I asked if he
needed food, water, or ale, but he declined,
indicating he must get on with his missives. In
parting, he suggested I prepare to leave with little
warning.*

"I waited until he left before opening the note. I will tuck it into this journal for safekeeping, and the journal itself will be hidden after this entry in the cellar below. I can't say why I have endangered myself and others by writing my thoughts, but I do not feel compelled to destroy them now.

"Alasdair wrote from the Widow Moore's Creek Bridge. He stated that approximately fifteen hundred regulators and Scots had begun a march from Cross Creek, but the ranks had dwindled with a high number of deserters, including himself. He had successfully located patriots led by Alexander Lillington and Richard Caswell, entrenched until the day prior on the creek's east banks. Donald MacDonald had arrived the day before with loyalist troops. Seeing his route blocked, he attempted to evade the patriots by marching several miles to a separate crossing near the Widow Moore's Creek Bridge. A forced march ensued on both sides, with the patriots arriving first. Now the patriots were in place, awaiting MacDonald's arrival. They anticipated the battle to begin at any moment. Alasdair feared the patriots were outnumbered even with the loyalist desertions, and victory was anything but certain.

"His last words were for my safety, advising me to flee the lighthouse before the light of dawn.

"I must heed his words. If God is willing, I shall return in a matter of hours or days. If He is not, I will continue westward to meet Lili and ensure her safety. I will now pack provisions and set out post haste."

I held the journal in my lap. The note from Alasdair that should have been placed within the pages was not there, and I wondered where it was and why the last pages had been torn from the journal. Though I gazed across the room, I was focused on another lighthouse, a wooden one erected on this mound more than two hundred years ago, and a lantern that might have led loyalists to join MacDonald's forces had Jon made a different choice.

But I did not read ideology. Jon never pontificated about a monarchy versus a democracy past his initial entry. He never envisioned his future either way. He'd simply wanted to live in peace with his animals in his isolated lighthouse.

His decision was personal. Had Horton not shown cruelty, had he been generous or compassionate to Jon's animals, Jon might have chosen a different path. I would never know. My mind wandered to all the others: Alasdair, Lili, Cuddy, the Scots, and each American. Perhaps this was what the revolution had boiled down to: a series of personal decisions that had no bearing on the greater ideological picture. The ideology had been born by a handful of men in clandestine quarters. Perhaps the majority who fought had chosen one side or the other based on the opportunities and livelihood each presented.

My fingers moved over the worn leather. It felt alive beneath my fingers. The mere fact that I held it meant it had been found in its hiding place in the cellar. I envisioned Harry overseeing the destruction of the old lighthouse and the erection of the new and discovering it hidden within the walls. I pictured a removable brick or slab, perhaps, behind which was a hollow piece of the wall, dry and protected for decades.

My thoughts were interrupted by my phone's alarm, and my heart raced with the abrupt noise. Modern life, with all its devices, felt so foreign to me in this instance.

As I shut off the alarm, I knew it was time for me to prepare to leave to pick up Shay at the airport. I peered outside. It was not yet dawn. The skies remained dark and foreboding, the inky blackness replaced by an equally murky gray that interfered with visibility. I rose, went to the window, and attempted to see the lane, but I could not even glimpse the gate in the gloom. I knew from my drives and walks that the ground sloped away from the mound upon which the lighthouse stood, and I hoped I would not encounter a flooded part of the road. If I did, I doubted I could turn the vehicle around and head back.

I was already dressed, so I entered the kitchen and started my electric teapot. I had just enough time to have a cup of tea and a breakfast treat before I had to leave.

I grabbed a teacup and saucer from an open shelf and set them on the counter. I had the strangest sensation as I pulled a spoon from the drawer. It must have been my new boots, as it suddenly felt as though my steps were more complicated than they needed to be. The wind howled just outside the door, sounding eerily similar to the animalistic sounds Shay and I had experienced in the woods. I swallowed and tried to tamp down the image of malevolent spirits circling the lighthouse, but I could not rid myself of the thought that I was prey.

I considered texting Shay to let him know of the storm and a possible delay, but something caught my attention out of the corner of my eye, and I slipped my phone into my pocket as I looked down.

Water was seeping from underneath the pantry door.

Instinctively, I opened the door, and water gushed onto the floor, flooding the kitchen hardwood. For a moment, I was overcome with confusion, as there were no windows in the pantry. It was a simple, built-in storage area that couldn't have been more than two feet square. There should have been no way for the water to come in.

I realized as I stared downward that a small area rug rested on the pantry floor, its muted colors almost invisible through the water. I knelt and pulled the mat onto the kitchen floor. The water gurgled along the edges of the pantry, and I bent further to run my hand along the joints.

My fingertips located a seam that ran in an equal distance around the perimeter of the pantry, broken in places by what might have been hasps. I pulled my phone from my pocket and shone it into the water. It appeared as though the seams had been sealed at some point, but they had been tampered with. Two hasps were lying back, the topmost piece resting against the inner wall, causing the hatch door to bubble upward with the rising water.

My mind shouted for me to leave. I was already dressed, and Shay would expect me at the airport. I should telephone Billie, let her know of the problem, and pick up Shay. As I wondered what I might do to stop the water from rushing in until Billie arrived and Shay and I could return, I heard the sound of a voice.

I froze. It had to have been the wind playing tricks on my senses. I could not see the windows from my spot on the floor, but certainly the rain and winds had picked up enough to encircle the lighthouse. I grabbed the rug, intending to place it back where it had been, as if by hiding the entry point, I could somehow contain it, when I heard it again.

This time, the words were plain: "Help me!"

"Beckett?" I called out. It had been his voice—hadn't it?

"Help me!"

It came from under the door. It was unmistakable that I was staring at the cellar opening. There had to be another entry point, and Beckett had found it, but became stranded in the rising water. I yanked the rug out of the way and pulled the lowest shelf with all its contents away to maneuver over the door. Then I lifted it, expecting to see Beckett on the stairs below.

Instead, I found myself staring into a black abyss. Once more, I heard my mind shouting at me. It sounded far away and disconnected from my body as it begged me to leave now. "Beckett?" I shouted.

"Help! Help me, please!"

I navigated the small opening, sticking one leg into the water to grope for the stairs. The water was surprisingly frigid. My foot found a narrow piece of wood. As I ran my foot across it, I realized it was a ladder. I hoped it wasn't an 18th-century piece that would collapse under my weight. I brought my other foot below that one and then shone my phone's flashlight into the swampy water. "Beckett? Where are you?"

I heard a gurgle. It was unmistakable now. It was just ahead of me, inches from my flashlight beam. "I'm coming to get you, Beckett. Hang tight. Are you hurt?"

The gurgling continued along with words I couldn't decipher. I climbed several more steps into the cellar. As I held onto the ladder with one hand, I fumbled with the other in a futile attempt to find something else of substance—storage shelves or the outer wall. As I descended, my hand grasped at soil. My confusion mounted as I ran my hand across it. It seemed like a dirt ledge, and it was dry.

I continued moving into the pool, my clothing now soaked and the icy water seeping into my bog boots, all the time calling for Beckett. My teeth began to chatter. Yet, I continued hearing his voice, garbled and distant, as if he were moving away from me.

Then, as my head was about to clear the cellar door, the heavy wood swung downward with a vicious blow. What little vision I had in the depths swam before me like my eyeballs had become disengaged from my head. I felt myself slip from the ladder.

As I plummeted downward, I saw my cell phone, the light still shining as it lay on the ledge while I drifted away from it. Floating toward me was the torso of a man wearing a red uniform, his head blending into the murky depths. The last thing I saw was a Native American sitting on another ledge deeper into the abyss, his face adorned with stark white war paint and feathers woven into his long, black hair.

I involuntarily gasped at the iciness as my body hit the water in full force. My head throbbed, and as I sank lower, I realized I was bleeding. I tried to keep my eyes open, but it was as if they were forced shut. Then the flow pulled me down further until I was powerless to resist the water's call.

36

I was angered at the insistent shaking of my shoulders. I longed to remain in the bliss of oblivion, floating in a colorless sea, my thoughts disengaged from my body.

"Hayley!" The shaking began again. "Are ya hearing me?"

When I opened my eyes, searing sunlight sliced through the nearby window. I groaned as I quickly closed them, my hand instinctively moving to protect the thin skin over my eyes from the onslaught.

"Wake up, dammit!"

My eyes flew open. Shay was hovering over me, his brows knit and his face dark. As my eyes sought to focus on him, his face softened.

"I've been trying to wake you," he said. "Did you take a sleeping pill?"

"I—" I tried to sit up, but my head was throbbing. I leaned back, sheltered my eyes from the daylight, and tried to get my bearings. I was lying on the sofa on the ground floor, and my clothes were dry. I moved my hand to my hair. I expected to find it wet, matted, and slimy from the dirty water, but to my surprise, it was none of those. It was dry and even silky. I groaned as I attempted to sit again. "What time is it?"

"Nearly noon," Shay answered. As he ran his hand through his hair, I realized it was shaking.

"What are you doing here?" I managed to croak. "Did I—?"

"I couldn't reach you," he said. He moved my legs so he could sit on the sofa and then arranged my legs on his lap. "You weren't at the airport—I couldn't reach you on your mobile—and I thought—I thought—"

I forced myself to lean toward him, though my head was splitting. I'd always wondered what that meant when someone said their head was splitting. Now I knew. It quite literally felt as though a giant was standing above me with a nail in my head, determined to hammer it in until my skull split in two. "I'm so sorry," I said.

"Did you take a sleeping pill? You've been unresponsive. You frightened me half out of my wits."

My shoes were on. I don't know why I became fixated on my shoes, but I did. They were dry. Perfectly dry. As my eyes moved slowly up my body, I registered socks, long pants, and a cozy t-shirt. "I must have taken one by mistake," I said. "I woke up early. The last I remembered, I was getting dressed to meet you at the airport." My eyes painfully glided toward the kitchen. The pantry door was shut, as it always was. The floor was dry. "I'm so sorry."

He sighed deeply. "No matter. I'm just relieved you're alright. I didn't know what I'd find."

"I can't believe I left you waiting at the airport."

"It wasn't like you. That's what caused me to panic, especially when I couldn't reach you." He looked beyond me to the table by the chair. "Did you leave your mobile upstairs?"

I saw my phone in my mind's eye as I floated away from it, the flashlight beaming through the darkness as it rested on a dry dirt ledge. "I don't know," I heard myself saying. "I must have."

Shay sighed again. He leaned against the back of the sofa and closed his eyes. After a moment, they opened slightly. "Are you alright then?"

"Yes," I said. "I'm fine. I'm so sorry, Shay. Really, I am."

"You can stop saying that now. You just gave me an awful fright. Were you okay here then?"

"Yes. I was okay here. I just—I'm so sorry."

He rubbed his eyes. "Darling, I want to lie down. Just a short nap, if you don't mind."

"Of course, I don't mind."

"It's just that I was up before dawn. It was a cramped flight—"

"—and then, I wasn't there to meet you."

"And you're sorry. I know." He smiled tiredly. "Just give me a few minutes. Then I'll make us some lunch. And I'll need a drink."

"Of course." I slipped my legs off him so he could rise. "I'll take a quick shower and have lunch ready for us when you wake up."

"You've got a deal, you do." He moved toward the stairs. "I'll get my bags after I wake up."

"I can—"

"No, darling. Do me a favor and stay inside, 'ey?"

Before I could respond, he disappeared up the spiraling staircase. I remained on the sofa for a long moment. I was stunned. Had I imagined everything? I placed my hand against my forehead. It was hot and dry.

When I was finally able to summon the energy to get off the sofa, I stepped toward the kitchen. The floor was perfectly dry. I moved to the pantry. I could hear Shay moving around upstairs and the creak of the bedsprings as he lay down.

I opened the pantry door, expecting to see the rug crumpled and wet. Instead, I was stunned to find it perfectly in place with assorted heavy items on top of it. I knelt. The vinegar bottle had dust on it as though it had remained undisturbed for some time. As I ran my fingers along the outer edges of the rug, I discovered it was fastened in place. I pictured a workman with tack strips and a carpet chisel, efficiently tucking in the edges beneath the baseboard.

I don't know how long I remained there, staring at the bottom of the pantry. Shay was right. It wasn't like me at all not to show up at the airport. I was more likely to be there an hour early than a minute late. To leave him stranded there was unthinkable. Yet, here I was, and there he was upstairs, and he must have rented a car and driven himself here.

I crossed the room to the stairs. I could hear Shay's heavy breathing as I approached the bedroom. Before stepping into the room, I could see my phone and its charger on the nightstand. I felt as though I had stepped into an alternate universe. It must be my head. It was pounding, the skull ready to split wide open at any moment.

I made my way past the bed and into the bathroom, where I closed the door behind me. I turned on the shower as I undressed and reveled in the warmth of the water as I stepped under it. I leaned against the front wall with one hand and closed my eyes as the water streamed over my head and coursed over my body. I could have stood there forever as I relished its healing power. It poured downward more quickly than it could drain out, and after a moment, I felt it rising around my feet. Unlike the cellar, it was welcoming, soothing, and restorative.

When I opened my eyes, I found myself staring at the floor of the clawfoot tub as the water continued cascading over my shoulders. I was surprised that the water was murky. As I continued staring, I realized it was turning an odd shade of red.

My hand went instinctively to the back of my head. As my fingers found the huge lump that had formed on the back of my skull, I winced and nearly cried out at the relentless pain. As I continued watching the blood trickle into the water, a refrain began in my mind.

It was real. It had all been real.

37

I hugged the towel around my body as the cool air chilled my skin. I stepped toward the bed, but Shay was deep in slumber. His brow was still furrowed, his lips downturned. He'd lain across the bed with his clothes and shoes still on. I couldn't awaken him.

I moved past the bed, quietly grabbing fresh clothes. Before I left the room, I turned back to unplug my phone from its charger. I pressed it against my naked skin. It was perfectly clean and dry and fully charged.

Once I felt like I could breathe without waking Shay, I made my way down the stairs and dressed in the living room. I ran my hand through my hair, combing it out with my fingers. The bleeding had stopped, but I still winced when I touched the expanding lump.

I couldn't tell Shay what had happened. The truth was, I didn't know what happened myself. I was as stunned and dumbfounded as I had ever been.

As crazy as it sounded, I wanted to talk to Jon and ask him if he'd saved me. As the images flooded my mind, I knew Beckett hadn't called me in the cellar. It was someone else, someone not of this world. As the thought occurred, goosebumps popped along my arms, and I trembled as I hugged myself. My body began to shake, and I sat down in an attempt to calm myself.

I didn't remember anything past the wood hitting the back of my head. Yet, somehow, I was pulled from the cellar, moved onto the sofa—and, hadn't I been wearing something else? Certainly, it was impossible for a ghost to have changed my clothing.

I felt suddenly vulnerable and naked, unable to defend myself because I didn't know what I was protecting myself against. I couldn't fight unseen spirits. I couldn't— but Jon could.

Struggling to make my mind work properly, I remained on the sofa for an hour or more. I felt like I was moving through two different realms, even though I knew it was realistically impossible. When I heard Shay stirring and the water running in the upstairs bath, it jolted me into the present. I made my way into the kitchen, looked for the ingredients for a proper lunch, and began preparations. As I cooked, I glanced out the window. A second car sat beside mine. It was undoubtedly a rental car, and a pang of guilt swept over me as I thought of Shay trying to reach me before driving to the lighthouse, not knowing what he would find here.

38

After dropping off Shay's rental car, we turned toward the tiny hamlet of Currie, North Carolina, in rural Pender County. Best known in popular culture as Uncle Phil's hometown in the hit sitcom *The Fresh Prince of Bel-Air*, I was about to discover another, perhaps more sinister, claim to fame, as we followed Shay's phone's navigation to Moore's Creek Battlefield.

As Shay drove, I perused the internet in search of information. "It says here," I said as I scrolled, "that the Moore's Creek Bridge battle was the first Revolutionary War battle in North Carolina. The widow, Elizabeth Moore, owned property nearby."

He turned onto a well-maintained rural road devoid of traffic. After glancing right and left, he mused, "It's difficult for me to imagine the Scots and the British troops converging by water." He waved his hand. "Do you see a river?"

"You have a good point." We were silent for a bit as I stared out the window. All I could see for miles was gently rolling terrain with scattered crops and occasional houses. They looked idyllic in the sunshine of a clear, spring day, much like the brilliance and serenity of the 18th-century era. I tried to imagine the tranquility disrupted by the chaos and turmoil of gunfire, cannon, and men's screams as they were cut down. "Jon mentioned in his journal that his channel was a shortcut along the Cape Fear River, leading me to

believe that the river snaked not far from the lighthouse."
I looked back at my phone to get our bearings.

"Ah," I said after a moment. "The Cape Fear empties
into the Atlantic near Wilmington, and it meanders for
nearly two hundred miles north-northwest. Cross Creek—
now Fayetteville—looks to be about halfway."

The navigation system steered us onto another rural
and vacant road. "So," Shay said thoughtfully, "we have
the Scots navigating the Cape Fear from Cross Creek and
the British on the same river coming up from
Wilmington."

"That's right. About ten miles northwest of
Wilmington, the Black River comes in, which looks to be
closer to Moore's Creek Bridge." I was interrupted by the
navigation system directing us onto yet another rural road.
As Shay dutifully made the turn, I marveled, "How can
anyone possibly find this battlefield way out here?"

Shay chuckled. "It isn't as though the organizers of
the battle thought of future visitors."

The road became narrower and darker as thickets of
trees and underbrush grew alongside, often blocking out
the blue skies with deep green foliage that attempted to
reach above our heads to the other side.

"Are you sure we didn't take a wrong turn?" I asked
nervously.

He shook his head, but he glanced at the navigation
screen nonetheless. "We're on the right road."

The road abruptly ended at the Elwood Ferry
Crossing. We stole glances at one another in puzzlement.
As we waited at the stop sign, we caught a glimpse of
someone running from a nearby vehicle. We watched as he
entered a tiny building, apparently pushing a button to raise
a railroad-style crossing guard.

As Shay pulled through, he rolled down his window
and shouted loud enough for the man to hear him. He
wore a Park Service ballcap, a pair of shorts, and a neon

safety jacket. "Are we in the right spot? We're trying to reach the Moore's Creek Bridge Battlefield."

The man grinned and strolled to our car. "Scottish?"

"Irish."

"Welcome to North Carolina."

"Thank you." Shay reached out to shake the man's hand.

"This will be a special treat for you," he said as he pumped Shay's hand. "The ferry takes about five minutes. When you get to the other side, you'll be very close to the battlefield. You'll see signs. You can't miss it."

"Thank you. How much do I owe you?"

"Nothing." His grin got larger. "Consider it a gift from the Carolinas."

With that, he directed us onto a single-wide platform. Shay slowly pulled the car onto it, pulling to a stop at a cable stretched across the far end. I was infinitely relieved that he was behind the wheel. Just driving onto something so small threatened to engulf me in a panic attack, and I envisioned myself driving straight off the other side into the water.

As if reading my mind, Shay asked, "Does anybody ever drive off?"

"You wouldn't believe how many times," the man answered.

"Oh, yes, I would," I said under my breath.

"Turn off your ignition and keep your car in park." As Shay complied, the man walked around to my side. Directly beside me, as if an afterthought, was a building similar to a toll booth that appeared from my angle to levitate over the water.

As he walked into the booth, Shay turned to me and grinned. "Want to get out?"

"Oh, hell, no," I answered.

I didn't hear the roar of an engine, but as the platform began to move, I found myself grabbing the overhead handle like a white-knuckle passenger. The water was blue-gray, the skies were cloudless, and pure azure in color. Thick trees lined either side of the water as a curve appeared not far from where we sat.

As I stared at the trees, I became aware of thick, roiling clouds moving swiftly over us. Within seconds, it was as if the clouds had descended like hands reaching for the water, enveloping us in a fog so thick that I could no longer see in front of us. Even the man who had stood just a foot from my car window had disappeared.

The seconds inched forward as though we might become frozen in time, and I found myself panicking as I willed the far shore to materialize. When I was met with nothing but dense, seething fog, I turned to look at Shay. "Are you—?"

The words froze. As I stared past Shay, I saw a flotilla of boats floating toward us. There were so many that it almost appeared as if a person could walk from one shore to the other simply by stepping into each boat in turn. As we continued to float in place, the boats became larger, and it was evident that they would crash right into us. We could not move, and the boats were clearly not going to stop.

I tried to scream out, to alert the crossing captain of our predicament, but my throat felt frozen as the fog engulfed us. I was paralyzed, and yet, I was acutely aware that my limbs were as frigid as if I had stepped outside naked on a wintry night.

Then the boats drove through us.

In one moment, they were solid and so vivid that I could see the men's faces. In the next, they had become vapor.

A noise startled us both as the ferry reached the shore. Our faces jolted forward as the captain stepped off the ferry to lower the ramp and cable. He motioned us forward, and Shay dutifully started the car. As the vehicle rolled forward, I glanced at Shay. His eyes were riveted on the single lane ahead of us, but his skin had turned ashen.

I dared not speak as we watched the captain raise the crossing guard.

Shortly after Shay passed through, the crossing guard came down behind us, and he pulled off to the side of the road. He stepped outside, and I hurriedly joined him, apprehensive about getting separated.

We stood side-by-side as the captain began the return journey to the other side. The skies were cloudless and a gorgeous azure that only the Carolinas can produce. As we watched the ferry chug across, there wasn't one hint of fog.

39

We didn't speak again until Shay pulled the vehicle into the Moore's Creek Battlefield Park parking lot. We sat in stunned silence after he turned off the ignition, each of us staring straight ahead. Somewhere in the back of my mind, my psyche registered the sound of tourists chatting as they walked to and from their vehicles. As I came back to the present, I was surprised to see the sun shining brightly and the surrounding woods filled with people.

"Did you see them?" I asked. My throat was dry and constricted, and my voice sounded strained.

"I don't want to talk about it," Shay answered curtly.

After a moment, I reached for the door handle. "Okay..."

"They were ghosts," he said abruptly.

I released my hold on the door and turned toward him. "You did see them." When he didn't respond, I continued, "Did you see the boats? Do you think they saw us there?"

"I don't want to talk about it."

I continued staring at his profile, but my mind was back on the water.

"They didn't see us," he said. "They went right through us as if we weren't there."

"How is that possible?"

"I don't want to talk about it." Shay opened his door and stepped out. After a moment, I did the same. I was amazed at the warmth of the sun. Perhaps I felt as though the apparitions had siphoned every bit of warmth out of my blood when they passed through me. I hadn't expected to be thrust back into the world of the living so abruptly. I'd been grateful that Shay was driving and not me, as I didn't recall the rest of our drive. However, as I looked at his face now, I realized he had been on autopilot, too.

"Let's walk," I said.

We found the entrance to a trail that wound its way from the visitor's center across a bridge and through the woods. We found ourselves surrounded by a variety of birds. With spring upon us, their songs filled the air. Some may have been trying to find mates while others were busily building nests. As we stopped at the first sign about an eighth of a mile from where we started, a bright red cardinal flew past us and alighted in a nearby tree. We watched as he called out to a mate, their back-and-forth trills like a gleeful conversation. When its mate joined him carrying a small twig, they flew off, disappearing into the tops of the trees.

Shay was observing our surroundings. "They would have converged through those woods," he said solemnly. "Though some traveled by boat, others would have marched from Cross Creek, gathering soldiers as they went."

"Says the historian that said he didn't know much about American history," I chided in an effort to lighten the energy.

"I had some time to research it while I was in New York," he answered with a sly smile. He grasped my hand and we took off down a well-maintained trail. "Of course, the entire area would have been wooded, so I imagine the soldiers on foot had quite a challenge marching through swamps and around trees."

My mind returned to our trek through the swamps to reach the lighthouse cemetery, and I understood perhaps all too well what the soldiers might have experienced. As we strolled, the bright sun gave way to muted skies as we entered the woods with their heavy canopies. Crickets and frogs joined in the chorus, causing the area around us to become saturated with the sounds of nature. If I listened closely enough, I could almost hear the sounds of men's voices as they marched through the black swamps and around treacherous cypress knees, ready to trip them up at any moment. "Jon had written that February had been a warmer month than usual," I said.

"Malaria would have been an issue in these parts later in the year," Shay offered. "Perhaps not so much in February, even if it was warm." He pointed toward a ribbon of water a short distance from us. "The patriots arrived before the loyalists. They would have encamped in this area, building earthworks from the mud and debris in which to conceal themselves and offer protection from gunfire."

"I've been doing some research, also," I said, smiling. "There's a possibility that at least one of my ancestors was here on the patriots' side. Moore's Creek was said to have ranged from about thirty feet wide to as much as fifty feet. The loyalists would have had to cross that water with the patriots firing upon them."

"Ah," he said. "And if I might add, Richard Caswell arrived before the Scots. The loyalists expected to find the patriots closer to the town of Currie. As the patriots reached this general area, they encamped on the western side, where some of the Scots were expected to arrive after a forced march, while others came by boat."

"And those coming by boat," I added, my excitement growing, "would not only have come from Cross Creek to the west, but the English expected to meet them as they came up from Wilmington. They planned to cut miles off their trip by taking the Corbyn Channel, but Jon and his brother-in-law, Alasdair, intentionally drove them off course, away from the lighthouse and into dead ends." I filled Shay in on the journal entries I'd read in his absence.

"The loyalists would still have outnumbered the patriots," Shay said thoughtfully when I finished. "Had the reinforcements arrived from the east, they might have sandwiched the patriots between them at this point on which we stand."

We paused for a moment to breathe in the air. I could imagine the smell of tobacco, mud, campfires, and men's bodies sweating in the North Carolina swamps.

"They set up camp," Shay continued as if reading my mind, "pitching tents, setting campfires. It might have appeared like they intended to remain for several nights."

"Why?" I said, peering through the dense forest.

"It was all a ruse. The loyalists sent spies ahead of the troops who would have counted the number of tents in an effort to calculate their enemy's force. But the patriots had their own spies." As we continued down the winding trail, he continued. His voice grew deep and quiet as though he did not wish to disturb the spirits that might have remained there.

"MacDonald could have attacked as the patriots were setting up camp. Had he done so, the tide might have turned in favor of the British. And had the British won here—"

"—The whole war might have been lost."

Shay nodded. "The patriots weren't doing so well against the well-trained British forces. They needed a win. And Caswell's spies had discovered MacDonald had become ill on the march, which slowed the loyalists' progress."

"Alasdair," I exclaimed suddenly.

Shay stopped and cocked his head. "Alasdair?"

"Jon's brother-in-law. He'd been with the Scots from Cross Creek. He must have come by boat, and he knew the channels as well as Jon. He knew what was happening with MacDonald. He had to have known."

Shay began walking again, but more slowly. He rubbed his chin thoughtfully.

"He'd been with MacDonald and McLeod all along," I continued, my enthusiasm growing.

"MacDonald had fought at Culloden," Shay interjected. "He would have known Alasdair and Jon. He would have trusted them explicitly."

"Could Alasdair have offered to go ahead as a spy, or perhaps to help Jon mark the channels for the reinforcements?"

"If so, MacDonald would have had confidence in him."

"No one would have known the channels and swamps better than Alasdair—except Jon."

We stopped at a bridge overlooking Moore's Creek. A nearby sign stated it had been recently built; the original bridge that had been there in 1776 was probably long gone, like Jon's original lighthouse. Shay leaned his elbows on the bridge rail and peered below us. "MacDonald, as I recall, was born around 1712." He grinned. "Scottish history now. He was already in his mid-30s during Culloden and considered past his prime. By the Revolutionary War, he would have been in his 60s."

"Around the same age as Alasdair and Jon."

Shay nodded.

"He could have contracted all manner of disease as he made his way from Cross Creek,' I continued. "Malaria, like we talked about earlier—"

"—Dysentery, the flu. Even exhaustion. In any event, Donald McLeod was his nephew by marriage and a younger man, though not by much. He would have been in his 40s, I believe. MacDonald turned over the men to the command of his nephew, and they determined to strike at dawn."

"That left an entire night for the patriots to prepare. If Alasdair had arrived that evening, he might have told Caswell of MacDonald's illness and the plan of attack."

"It gave Caswell an entire night to order his troops from the encampment and over the bridge. When the loyalists attacked the next morning, the campfires were still smoking and the tents still up, as though the patriots were asleep and unaware."

"In reality," I continued excitedly, "the patriots were already on the east side of the bridge." We continued to a replica of the Moore's Creek Bridge that had been taken apart. "The patriots removed the planks and smeared lard on the runners so the loyalists wouldn't have been able to balance on them single-file."

"I love it when both of us have done our research," Shay chuckled. "This is a bit like traveling with a fellow scholar! So," he continued, "when the loyalists routed the camp the next morning, the patriots were lying in wait for them on the other side. I pity the first men on those runners. They would have been picked off like sitting ducks."

"Alasdair would have been with them," I said, my voice reverent. "He spent part of the night helping Jon reroute the enforcements, and then he left to join the patriots. Alasdair and Jon might have turned the tide to the revolutionary forces."

"Are you understanding what that means?" Shay's voice was equally in awe. "Both are heroes."

"But—" I hesitated. "Why haven't we heard of them?"

40

The museum was like a candy store for two historians such as Shay and me. I might have wandered through with a memory for dates and places, but this experience was different. It felt personal. When we encountered the display with one patriot killed and another wounded, I stared at their names just as I might have had I lived in 1776 and had a loved one in the battle. Neither one bore Alasdair Glenn's name, which caused my heart to drop. I wanted to call out that it was wrong; he was there and had given his life for the birth of the American democracy.

And when we encountered the numbers for the loyalists, I found myself holding onto Shay's arm. The numbers were approximate: 30 killed, 40 wounded, and 850 captured by the patriot forces. The names did not appear there, and my eyes remained riveted to the word "approximate," as though that would cover Alasdair. But my mind cried out that he couldn't be included in those numbers, because he had not fought for the loyalists.

I imagined the Scots, many of whom had fought in the Jacobite Rebellion against the same country. Some might have fled to America after the grisly Battle of Culloden. I wondered what it might have been like to desert those forces as they left Cross Creek, only to face off against them here. War was closer back then and personal; there were no drones, tanks, or planes. There was the command to fire when they saw the whites of their eyes. Loading a musket was complicated and time-consuming when the loader might have been another's target.

I imagined Alasdair on one side of the bridge as McLeod, who Alasdair had reported to only hours before, commanded, "King George and broadswords!" as the Scots charged. These were men he might have lived among, attending church and social functions with their families, and conducting business. He might have lived alongside some of them for years.

And now, he was on the other side, aiming to cut them down.

By the time we finished perusing the museum and watching the short film, I was as emotionally spent as though I'd sent Alasdair off to war myself. I could not begin to imagine the anxiety Jon experienced as he waited for word on the battle and his brother-in-law's fate. If the loyalists had won, he could have been hanged for treason. Instead, he might have received the news that Donald McLeod had died instantly as more than 20 bullets tore his body apart. He might have learned that Donald MacDonald had been captured in camp, still reeling from sickness, as his troops retreated from the slaughter. I did not know what Jon was told or when, because his journal had ended before all the results of the battle might have been known. He'd hidden it with a note from Alasdair, whose final act was to warn his brother-in-law mere hours before his own life ended on the ground on which I now stood.

"Are you alright then?" Shay's voice awakened me from my gloomy thoughts. He peered at me with wide, curious eyes. "Would you care to join me in the gift shop? They may have some good books for your research." He attempted to muster a smile, but I could tell that he, too, had been affected.

"Yes," I said, grateful for his suggestion. "I would."

We left behind the pristine displays, the minute-by-minute accounts of the battle, and the gruesome statistics for the well-lit, well-maintained gift shop and the broad smile of the park service ranger behind the counter. In the modern shop, I brushed off the melancholia that had enveloped me as I focused on the reference books. I found myself touching a particularly poignant cover depicting the swamps before my fingers moved to the book next to it.

"That is the one." The voice was husky and heavily-accented.

"This one?" I asked, picking up the thin paperback. It had a plain white cover and the title "Those Who Fought" in a simple font. Thumbing through it, I realized it contained the names of all the participants who had participated in the Battle of Moore's Creek Bridge. I felt excitement well up inside me as I flipped to the index. I located two ancestors easily and read the short descriptions of their involvement in the battle. This book was a keeper; it would find its home beside my own book when it was eventually published, and I may even have future need for it as I continued my genealogical research.

I held it against my chest for a moment as I continued to browse before abruptly looking at it again. Hurriedly, I returned to the index to find where Jonathan Corbyn was listed. He had two page numbers referenced, and I began to hurriedly read them before I forced myself to slow down and properly digest the information.

He was listed as a loyalist. On the first referenced page, the book provided an overview of his duties on that fateful campaign, confirming his journal entries with the lighthouse. However, the book claimed that the English reinforcements did not arrive until May, long after the battle had ended in a decisive defeat for the crown. Thirty-four British ships arrived near Fort Johnston, four miles from the mouth of the Cape Fear River. The Scots from Cross Creek and other loyalists in the area were ordered to

join them for an assault on the patriots, but too few arrived
to mount an attack.

I turned to the second reference in a section outlining
what happened to key figures after the battle. Beside Jon's
name was one word: missing.

I stood for a long moment with the book in my hand.
Tears stung the corners of my eyes, and my heart felt as
though it might break. The room faded around me. I felt
like a member of his family, standing near the swamps and
fields searching for closure.

When I felt composed enough to continue, I turned
back to the index and found Alasdair Glenn. He, too, was
listed as a loyalist. I first turned to the second reference,
since I'd just left that section, and found his name followed
by the words "Killed in Action."

Then I turned to the first reference. It stated that he
had breached the patriot lines on the east side of the bridge
and got as far as the unit firing toward the loyalists when
one patriot stopped his advance with a single bullet to the
head. The patriot—the hero—was Cuddy Dikshita.

"But you know the truth."

I whirled around, expecting to find Shay reading over
my shoulder, but no one was there. The park ranger who
had greeted us was gone. Shay was gone. A glance around
the corner told me the entire gift shop was empty. An ice-
cold chill permeated my entire body, leaving me shaking. I
wanted to rush from the building into the sunshine, but my
feet felt planted on the floor like I was frozen in a bad
dream.

"Ah! She's found it already."

The voice caused me to jump, and I whirled around
to find Shay and the park ranger returning from the
museum.

The ranger continued, "She'll find everyone listed in
that book as well as their roles, if they're known. The
authors did extensive research. A lot of it is based on

diaries and first-hand accounts, including newspaper articles of the time."

I didn't hear the rest. I don't remember paying for the book or walking to the car with Shay. I barely heard Shay say that the ranger had suggested an alternative route to avoid the ferry. When the chill finally began to dissipate, I was still holding the book pressed to my chest, a spirit's words ringing in my ears.

"Are you okay?" Shay was saying. When I didn't respond, he added, "You don't seem okay."

I opened my mouth, but the words would not form.

"Come," he said, taking the book from me and tossing it into the seat. "I want another stroll before we hit the road again."

41

We stood in front of the Grady Monument on the grounds of the Moore's Creek Battlefield. If I turned around, the visitor's center would have been in view, but I suppose that by turning my back on it, I was somehow communicating to whatever spirit lurked within that I was not in the mood for a chat. Instead, I focused on the obelisk towering above us. It had been erected 81 years after the Moore's Creek Bridge battle had taken place here, imported from Philadelphia to honor the only patriot that history recorded as having died here, Private John Grady from Duplin County. The ironies did not escape me. Not only did I now know that another patriot was killed here—by a fellow soldier, no less, and a friend—but within just four years of the monument's installation, North Carolina would secede from the country they both had fought to establish.

"It couldn't have been Jon," Shay said quietly after he'd listened intently to what happened to me in his absence. I was grateful that Shay had insisted we take another walk through the battlefield. I suspect he was unwilling to get behind the wheel of a car as we both ventured increasingly between realms, imagined or otherwise. I certainly was not going to drive the car onto that ferry.

"The gift shop was empty." My voice sounded distant and monotone.

"I have no doubt. The door was within my view the entire time; I'd only stepped away with the park ranger to ask a question about a display."

"Then, you know no one came in or out."

"I do know that. Yes." Shay took a deep breath. "The thing is, it's unusual for a spirit to leave a particular area." He pointed to the obelisk. "Take Private Grady here. He was reinterred here. Who knows if the reinternment caused his spirit to visit from time to time? If for no other reason than to look back on what he did to help create this country?"

"I don't want to talk about Private Grady's ghost."

"My point being, we are not going to get in our car and find he's come along for the ride. We won't be walking into the lighthouse and calling out, 'Oh, Jon, look at the friend we brought to visit you.' Now, will we?"

"Stop it."

Shay placed his hands on my shoulders and turned me toward him. "My point is, Jon was not in that car with us. He's back at the lighthouse where he's been for the past 250 years."

I nodded. We stood silently for a moment before I blurted, "Was it Alasdair?"

"Jon's brother-in-law?"

"He died here. If ghosts remain in a place that has meaning, couldn't he have stayed at the place of his death?"

"Well, certainly. It happens all the time."

"He wanted me to see that book. He wanted me to know that Cuddy Dikshita—undoubtedly Argo and Beckett's ancestor—murdered him in cold blood. Right here." My voice became pleading and tortured. "Cuddy was their friend, Shay. I read about him in Jon's journal. They met him on the voyage from Europe. He had joined the turncoats. He was one of them. And he knew that Alasdair was one of them, too. He'd known it from the start. He'd even helped to recruit Jon."

A vulture circled overhead, its distinctive cawing splitting through the air above us.

"It could have been an accident," Shay debated. We made our way to a nearby bench and sat. A few visitors roamed the battlefield, but I felt as if we were utterly alone with a ghost. Shay continued, "It happens all the time, even in modern battles. Friendly fire is what they call it. In the heat of a battle with gun smoke and chaos all around you, there are only split seconds in which to make a decision. It has occurred throughout all of history."

I shook my head. "I know, but..." My voice trailed off, my words hanging in the air.

"Alasdair might have come through the smoke and fog, and Cuddy Dikshita had a split second to make a decision. Perhaps he was still clothed in a loyalist uniform—"

"No," I answered firmly. "He wouldn't have been. He worked undercover with Jon to reroute the loyalists away from the Corbyn Channel. He then set out across the countryside to find a patriot unit. He wouldn't have taken the chance of wearing a loyalist uniform as he marched into a patriot camp. He could have been captured or killed by a patriot."

"Like what might have happened here?" Shay's voice was soft.

"It doesn't feel right. Not here, in my gut. If it was an accident, why would it have been important for me to find this book? We already knew Alasdair died here. It's part of the historical record."

"But the historical record has it wrong. He died not as a loyalist but as a patriot. He fought for independence, just like Private Grady over there. Maybe that's the message."

I sighed. "I suppose we can never know, can we? I mean, Cuddy Dikshita and Alasdair Glenn are both gone, aren't they?"

"Unless—"

"Oh, no. Not doing another séance. And invite the two of them over? They might not leave afterward." I shivered. "I don't like the thought of Cuddy taking up residence in the lighthouse. It wouldn't be fair to Jon." My words hung in the air, my unwillingness to harm Jon's spirit not lost on either of us.

We sat in silence for a few moments. I couldn't say how long it might have been, because time seemed to stand still. I was in the present and somehow in February 1776, and I'd just wandered the countryside all night before meeting my death at dawn by a friend and fellow patriot. I couldn't shake the feeling.

"Hayley," Shay said, his deep voice pulling me from my thoughts. "How did you say that Harry died?"

"Harry? From the lighthouse? Lighthouse Harry?"

"Yes, that Harry, unless you know of another."

I cocked my head. "His niece, Billie, never said. But," I added, "she did say that he'd become obsessed with finding the cellar."

"I don't understand," Shay said, frowning. "Didn't Harry have the original lighthouse torn down and the new one erected? Wasn't he the one who found Jon's journal hidden in the cellar?"

"I've only assumed…" My voice faded as I contemplated the conflicting evidence.

"Assumed what?"

I took a deep breath. "I assumed the cellar was still intact when the lighthouse was torn down and the other was built. But what if it had caved in or the swamps had taken it over?"

"A cave-in would have plenty of precedence," Shay said, thoughtfully running his hand over his beard. "Plenty of archeological sites like the pyramids and—"

"And I don't know if Harry found the journal in the cellar," I interjected. I did not wish to begin a conversation about cave-ins half a world away when we might have one under our noses. "I only assumed that he had because that's where Jon said he planned to hide it. I found it," I added, "in the lantern stand."

"Then why would Harry have become obsessed with finding the cellar?"

"I don't know. Maybe Harry discovered the truth that Cuddy Dikshita killed Alasdair, just as we have. Maybe he found more clues that the cellar hid evidence." I winced as I reached my hand to my head and felt the lump there. The headache was beginning to rear its ugly head again.

"Let me have a look at that," Shay said, turning me about. He parted my hair. "How the hell did that happen? And why am I only finding out about it now?"

42

Shay clicked off his call and handed his mobile to me. "Billie's in her office," he said. "She's with a client now and will be available shortly after. She's expecting us."

I exhaled a sigh of relief. "Maybe now we can get answers." I'd filled Shay in on my adventure into a cellar that didn't have a door and may not even exist. Upon closer inspection of my head, his first inclination was to get us back to the lighthouse, packed, and on the road to my mother's house. Funny how her sudden close proximity made her home the default rallying point. Somehow, I didn't think she'd appreciate that, so I managed to stall the inevitable by suggesting that we speak with Billie. With Argo unwilling to discuss the village history with me and Beckett a bit unreliable, to say the least, Billie was our best chance.

The minutes passed as we drove along one dusty country road after another. We were able to avoid the ferry by taking an alternate route, and we weren't far from Billie's office near Wilmington. When we came to a pleasant yellow service station with a wide, welcoming porch complete with rockers, I was ready for a break. I needed to connect with living, breathing human beings.

Shay pulled next to a tank. He'd barely stopped the car before I opened my door. "Want anything?" I asked.

"Something salty," he answered. "And something with ice."

"Got it." While he prepared to fill the gas tank, I made my way onto the broad porch. A sign beside the door announced the building's name as the Maco Depot. Inside was brightly lit and leap years from the Dikshita General Store. I filled up two large soda cups with ice and lemonade and grabbed something salty for Shay and something sweet for myself.

I was on my way to the register when a row of books stopped me. I was pulled in by a dozen titles on North Carolina history, and I shuffled the food and drinks in my arms to grab a book on the Revolutionary War.

"That one's our most popular." I felt a shiver fly up my spine and was relieved when I turned to find a young man stocking shelves nearby.

"Which one?" I asked.

"This one." He reached a bit past me to pull the book off the shelves. "Ghost stories of the area."

"Ghost stories? Why would you think I'd be interested in that?"

He shrugged. "It's okay with me if you're not. You just look like you're not from around here, is all, and most tourists like reading about the ghosts." He started to put the book back on the shelf, but I intercepted it.

"Any story in particular?" I asked as I balanced the book in my hand.

"The Maco ghost light."

"Maco—like this store?"

"It didn't happen here, but close by." He returned to stocking the shelves but continued talking amicably. "There was a train conductor by the name of Joe Baldwin. He was coming down the Wilmington and Manchester Railroad. The rail began in Wilmington and ended at Manchester, a town that ain't there no more.

"Story goes that when he came through Maco— that's this here place—the caboose came loose. Well, there was another train a'coming shortly after his, and he knew he had to get that caboose hooked back up to his train, only he didn't have the time. And of course, being a caboose, it was too heavy to haul off the tracks." He hesitated with several boxes in his hands as his eyes took on a faraway look. "It was the middle of the night and dark as Hades, and he knew the next conductor weren't gonna see that train. So, he got his lantern and stood on the tracks in front of the caboose and waited for the next train. The story goes, he swung that lantern back and forth, just frantically trying to get the conductor to see him and stop." He returned to stocking the shelves.

"Well?" I said after a long pause. "What happened?"

"The conductor never saw him."

"So, the train derailed?"

"It was a big mess, as you can imagine."

"And, Joe Baldwin?"

"Oh, he was kilt right off. They couldn't find him in the dark on account of it being, well, dark. But they found his body the next morning, near 'bout the break of dawn. They found his body," he continued, stopping to peer at me, "but his head was gone. Sheared clear off."

I had the vague sense that Shay had joined me, but I dared not take my eyes off the young man.

"That happened way back around the time of the Civil War. And ever since, people still see Joe Baldwin swinging his lantern back and forth in the dead o' night, trying to stop that train. The tracks have long since been pulled up, but he's out there still. Some folks say he won't rest 'til he finds his missing head."

I backed up and into Shay. "I've gotta get out of here," I said, cramming everything into his arms. I barely heard him answer as I made my way through the store and into the sunlight. I had the car running and waiting when Shay exited the store.

He slipped into the passenger seat beside me. "You okay to drive?" he asked.

"What is it with ghosts and this place?" I demanded.

"Kind of like Ireland, is it not?"

"That's different."

"Different how?"

I pulled through the parking lot and onto the main road. "Just different."

"Maybe it's the accents," Shay answered as he dug into his bag of chips.

43

I hadn't calmed down by the time we arrived at Billie's office. In fact, I was pretty wound up. Shay spent the last five minutes trying to convince me to pull over and let him drive, but I was determined to get there without another stop. I would have bounded out of the car and rushed into the building like a madwoman—or maybe just someone who'd just seen a ghost—but he gently pulled me back into my seat. He shoved the candy bar in one hand and my drink in another and managed to persuade me into taking a few deep breaths.

When we entered the building, we were greeted by a pleasant young woman with a wide smile that became even wider when Shay asked for Billie. "Scottish?" she asked coquettishly.

"Irish," he answered.

As the receptionist called Billie on the interoffice phone, I said to Shay, "Can she not see me standing here?"

"Don't you think you're a bit twitchy?"

I made a sound that was something between a cough and a chuckle, and even I was embarrassed at it. Fortunately, Billie appeared at the door and beckoned us into a nearby conference room. She was impeccably dressed in a tailored suit that my mother would have been compelled to comment on. She moved gracefully into the room on stilettos. I couldn't help but imagine myself in them, taking one step in front of a client I'd been hired to impress, and falling flat on my face, perhaps glancing up to see if anyone noticed I'd knocked out my two front teeth. Shay was right. I was twitchy.

"I don't believe we've met," Billie said, offering her hand.

"Only on the phone just now," Shay answered smoothly. "Shay MacGregor."

"Scotland?"

"Ireland."

"He's a professor and historian with the University of Galway," I offered in an attempt to move things along.

"Whatever are you doing in North Carolina?" Billie purred.

"I could ask the same of you, now couldn't I?" Shay extracted his hand.

Billie giggled before glancing at me. "Hayley, it's good to see you again. Please, do sit down." As we sat, she carried a tray of sweets from a sideboard to the table. "Do have something," she coaxed. "They're from a fabulous shop in Wilmington. They bake them fresh every morning." As we both declined, a slight frown formed between her brows. "Is something wrong with the lighthouse?"

"Well, we—" I began.

"It isn't the electricity, is it? The solar has never gone out. WiFi?"

"The lighthouse is fine," I said as Billie sat across from us.

"You've not decided to leave, have you?"

"Why would you ask that?" Shay asked.

She waved her arms at the table. "You're here, aren't you? A simple phone call would have resolved a lot of things. You've driven quite a distance to meet with me in person. Normally, that only happens when a tenant wants to return a key."

"Have you had other tenants at the lighthouse?" I asked. My mind raced back to the real estate listing and Billie's comments when we'd first met. "I thought Harry only passed away a short time ago."

"Oh," Billie said, averting her eyes, "I don't mean the lighthouse, per se. Just in general."

"It was rented before, wasn't it?" Shay asked. "And they told you it was haunted."

"No," Billie said firmly. "You—rather, Hayley—is the first to rent it since Harry passed. I'd shown it to others, but..." She brushed an imaginary speck of dust on her sleeve.

"But they sensed something there," Shay finished.

"It's an isolated place. It isn't for just anybody. It looks romantic online, but when you drive out there, you really get a sense of how rural it is."

"Yes," I said. "You do. But the lighthouse is just fine for me. I wanted peace and quiet while I work, and it gives me that."

"Then, why are you here?" Billie asked, puzzled.

I took a deep breath and stole a sideways glance at Shay. He nodded as if to let me know that he had no intention of stealing my thunder. Suddenly, just blurting out a question about Harry seemed irreverent. "Well, there has been some unexplained activity there."

"It's easy to imagine things in that place."

I could sense Shay leaning forward to study Billie's face. "Yes. Well, we were wondering if Harry ever mentioned anything to you."

"Like what?"

"The atmosphere. The lighthouse lantern comes on by itself, even though it isn't plugged in. Windows are opening and closing on their own. Things are getting moved around."

"I'm sure there's a logical explanation," Billie said. She reached for the tray and placed a Danish on the napkin in front of her. She stared at it for a moment but didn't take a bite of it.

"Like what?"

She waved her hand as if to dismiss the question. "The wind there can be relentless. There's nothing to stop it as it comes off the ocean. It could easily force windows open or closed or appear to move things…"

"And what about the cellar?" I asked quietly.

"The cellar?" She nearly shrieked as her eyes widened. "You haven't been in there!"

"No," Shay and I said in unison. I continued, "Is the cellar still under the lighthouse?"

"Why?"

"You mentioned it, but I've never seen a door to it."

"Oh, for goodness' sake," she said with more than a hint of frustration, "I should never have told you about it."

"Did Harry have an accident in the cellar?" Shay asked.

Billie looked from Shay to me and back again. "Harry died of natural causes. He had a heart condition. The doctors warned him to slow down, but he didn't listen."

"The lighthouse seems like the perfect place to slow down," I said quietly. "What was he doing that took so much effort?"

Billie stared at her Danish. After a moment, Shay asked, "Did it have something to do with the cellar?"

"Oh!" Billie pushed herself away from the table and abruptly stood. She marched to the window and peered onto a busy parking lot. The building and the lot were a world away from the secluded lighthouse, and I found myself wishing that we hadn't come here. Just as I'd decided our little chat was over, Billie spoke again. "Harry was obsessed with that cellar," she spit out. She turned around and braced her hands on the windowsill behind her.

"Why?" Shay asked. "What was he looking for?"

"I don't know. He became increasingly irrational."

"How so?" I asked.

"He was convinced he heard things. The wind can sound like voices sometimes, especially whipping around that circular building." She moved her fingers in a frenetic circle.

"Was Harry aware the cellar existed, or was he trying to find it?"

"Oh, he knew it was there. The original lighthouse had collapsed in on it when he bought the property."

"Then—"

"He had the original lighthouse torn down—or what was left of it," Billie continued. "Most of the wood was rotted. It had been condemned."

"But the cellar?"

"The cellar was dug out of the soil. There were no walls shoring it up. It was smaller than the circumference of the lighthouse, from what Harry said about it. And, if you learn anything about homes in this area, you know we don't usually have cellars. The ground shifts here, and basements flood." Her words hung in the air.

Shay asked, "Is that what happened?"

Billie nodded. "The cellar had caved in long before Harry found the property."

"So," I said slowly, "When Harry rebuilt the lighthouse, he didn't know if he was building on top of the original cellar?"

Billie shook her head. "It was a complicated process. I don't know much about it—so much happened before I was even born. After Harry's death, I obtained the licenses and permits from the county courthouse. He'd hired professionals. And they assured Harry that the mound would support a building constructed from concrete bricks. The inspector signed off on it. The cellar must have collapsed decades earlier—"

"Or centuries earlier?" My eyes met Shay's.

Billie shrugged. "Perhaps. Who knows? When Harry bought the property, it was caved in, like I said. Apparently, the soil had compacted to such an extent that there was no problem building on it. The builder might even have added more soil."

The three of us stared at one another for a long moment. I had so many unanswered questions that I didn't know where to start. As it turned out, I didn't have to. After a long pause, Billie continued as she sat back down across from us.

"Harry was convinced that he needed to find the cellar," she said in a resigned, flat voice. "As he got older, he got less rational. He became obsessed with finding it. Just before his death..." Her voice wavered. She swallowed hard and then continued, "Harry dug up the entire first floor."

"The living room?" Shay asked incredulously.

"The living, dining, kitchen..."

"Did Argo Dikshita do it?" I asked.

"No," she said forcefully. "Absolutely not. Harry wanted to do this himself. He was very secretive about it. I only knew about it because I visited him."

Shay and I exchanged glances. Beckett had been a frequent visitor also, but I couldn't bring myself to say it aloud.

"Maybe," Billie was saying, "he knew that others—more rational others—would talk him out of it. He pulled up each plank one by one until there was concrete, and then he drilled into the concrete."

"Concrete?" Shay asked.

"The foundation for the new lighthouse."

"He was trying to remove the foundation?"

"He wasn't in his right mind. Anyone could have told him that tearing out the foundation would cause the whole thing to collapse."

I suddenly felt physically vulnerable in the lighthouse. "But, you rented it to me—"

"No worries," Billie said, waving her hand as if to dismiss my objection. "When I inherited the property, I had the concrete repaired and the floor replaced. It passed all inspections. It's more solid than most of the houses I sell."

Shay steepled his hands. "So, when you say that Harry died..."

"He'd dug down into the dirt beneath the concrete rubble. The exertion was too much for him. He tried to climb out, but he had a massive heart attack and died."

"Who found him?" I asked quietly.

"Beckett."

"Beckett Dikshita?"

Billie nodded. "He was the only one Harry trusted with what he was doing."

"Why?" Shay breathed.

"Well, you've met Beckett," Billie said with a frown.

"And, Beckett—"

"He got back to the general store, told Argo, and Argo phoned me. When I arrived, the sheriff was already there."

Shay stood. "We didn't mean to make you relive that awful event." He gave me a sideways glance.

"Absolutely not," I agreed as I came to my feet.

"Is there anything else?" Billie remained seated, her voice small. Her entire body seemed to have shrunk during our conversation.

"No," I said. "Thank you for your time."

"So, you're staying?"

"Yes," I said. "For now. I don't know what my publisher will want from me next, and I travel..." My voice faded as I studied her. I felt sorry for her and ashamed that I'd felt so catty when we first arrived. Billie was still seated, her shoulders slumped, when Shay and I reached the door.

"We're sorry to have troubled you," Shay said as he held the door open for me.

Billie didn't respond.

I started through the door and then turned around abruptly. "Oh, there is one more thing," I said, despite Shay's exasperated glance, "was the hole Harry dug underneath the pantry?"

Billie looked up, puzzled. "No," she said. "It was under the chair in the living area, the one between the sofa and the window."

44

The lighthouse windows glowed red from the setting sun as we approached. It was strange how a simple color change could alter the mood of a place. No longer welcoming, the windows felt instead like so many flaring eyes watching us arrive.

My heart quickened as Shay turned off the ignition. Though we both exited the vehicle simultaneously, he stepped out with a purpose, quickly clearing the terrain between the car and the lighthouse. In contrast, I hung back, my eyes traveling not to the lighthouse but beyond it. The reeds danced in a rhythmic sway like so many shamans dancing under the sun's waning light. An occasional vulture broke free from the cypress canopy, causing the treetops to pirouette. Vultures had never bothered me much before, but they did tonight. They seemed ominous somehow, an omen that I couldn't seem to shake.

Shay had left the door cracked open, and I moved inside, carefully turning to lock the door behind me. I heard him in the bedroom upstairs, but by the time I'd reached that floor, he was already in the gallery atop the lighthouse. I found him pulling two chairs toward the center of the room nearest the lantern.

"Are you sure this is the right thing to do?" I asked. The air had become chilled. It was a familiar feeling by now of goosebumps popping along my arms, the atmosphere charged like someone's frigid breath upon us.

"I have to. If you don't want to, you can—"

"I'm staying."

He paused to look into my eyes. "Good."

I took my seat and waited for him to take his. He set the phone to record and placed it in the same spot as our last séance. "Jon," he said. He took a deep breath. "We need to communicate with you."

My phone buzzed with an incoming call. Shay gave me a sideways glance, and I silenced it. "It's just Mom. I'll call her back."

Shay settled into his chair beside me and placed the EMF detector on the lantern stand.

My phone buzzed again. I hesitated and then shut off my phone. "She'll leave a message. I don't want anything to interrupt us."

After a moment, Shay spoke again. His voice was deep-throated as if he felt tense, and I reached out to take his hand in mine. "Jon," he said, "Jonathan Corbyn. I know you can see Hayley and me sitting here. I've set my phone to record. We might not be able to hear your voice, but the phone will pick it up. And this device, beside the lantern, will help us get some 'yes' or 'no' answers from you. Just like before, if the answer is 'no,' don't do anything. If it is 'yes,' come close to the device and it will light up."

A strong breeze swirled around us, and I found myself searching the windows to determine whether any were open. I suppose I wanted one to be open, so I could calm my nerves with a physical, mortal reason for the vortex forming.

Shay and I opened our mouths at the same time. He motioned for me to speak.

"Jon," I said, my voice trembling, "Shay and I just returned from the Moore's Creek Bridge." I hesitated. "Do you recall the Widow Moore's Creek Bridge?"

Five lights on the EMF device lit up.

"Thank you," I said nervously. "There is a museum there to honor the patriots who fought there and to tell the story of the battle. The patriots won, Jon. Did you know that?"

Again, the device lit up with all five bars.

I swallowed hard. After the lights went out, I struggled with the next question. Sweat popped out across my forehead despite the frigid air.

Shay squeezed my hand. "Jon," he said, "we know Alasdair was killed during the battle. You know that, too, don't you?"

All five lights lit up.

"Do you know who killed him?"

The lights lit up so quickly that I gasped. I could feel a state of rage swelling up inside me, and I knew the furious emotion was not coming from me but originating from Jon's spirit. I glanced at Shay to see if he felt it, too. His eyes were downcast, watching the lights.

"We are here to help you," Shay said. He squeezed my hand again as if to reassure me. "We want to know what happened, and we want to help you."

The lights finally went dark.

After a moment, I asked, "Do you know Cuddy Dikshita?"

All the lights came on simultaneously, and several windows flew open. I wanted to throw the EMF device out the window and dive out after it. It was only Shay's hand upon mine, somehow willing me silently to remain calm, that stifled the urge to flee. I don't know why I ever thought that a séance was a good idea.

"Please don't frighten us," I said when I found my voice. "Like Shay said, we're here to help you. Help us understand."

There was no response. After a moment, Shay asked, "Was Cuddy a friend of the family? A friend to you or Alasdair?"

The room remained so quiet that I wondered if Jon had left.

"Had he been a friend at one time?"

The device remained dark. "You wrote about him in your journal," I offered. After a moment, five bars flashed briefly.

"Thank you," Shay said. "Please help me to understand. Cuddy had been someone you knew, even a friend, but he betrayed you, didn't he?"

All five lights began flashing. It was a frenetic energy we had not yet experienced.

Shay swallowed hard as our eyes met. "Okay, thank you, Jon." After a moment, the device went dark. "Was Cuddy a patriot?"

The device remained dark.

"He was with the patriot troops," I whispered to Shay. I felt the atmosphere turn dark, and I feared an evil we could not see. A sensation began in the pit of my stomach. As it moved upward, panic set in. I wanted to rush down the stairs, but I felt frozen in my seat. By the time the tingling reached my throat, I wanted to scream, but the sound was suspended at my lips as though hanging in midair.

I could tell that Shay was having difficulty forming his next words. When he spoke, his voice was barely a croak. "Was Cuddy a British spy?"

All the windows flew open at once, the wind so charged that they banged like the room was filled with men shaking them in frustration. All the lights on the device remained solidly lit. I tried to stand, but my knees would not straighten, and my body felt as though all the bones had disintegrated. I fell back into my seat.

"Are you alright?" Shay managed to say, his voice barely above a whisper.

I could not nod or shake my head. I simply stared at him, but the words I attempted to convey were lost on me as if my mind had gone completely blank.

"Jon," Shay said, "are you aware that Cuddy fired the shot that killed Alasdair?"

The device's lights flashed furiously as the air swirled around us. The sound of the wind grew in intensity until it howled. When Shay spoke again, he had to shout to be heard. "Do you believe Cuddy killed Alasdair on purpose because he knew he was helping the patriots?"

The howling morphed into a scream. I jumped up, my sudden movement startling both Shay and me. The air was so charged that I thought the EMF device would fly off the stand at any moment. "Who is in the cellar?" I shouted.

All the windows slammed shut, and the wind stopped abruptly, plunging us into stunned silence.

After a moment, Shay asked, "Jon? Are you still with us?"

The device remained dark. Slowly, the temperature in the room began to rise, and I stopped trembling. I could see the color returning to Shay's cheeks, and I knew he felt it, too.

"Jon?" he asked. "Do you want us to know who or what is in the cellar? Is there something you want us to find there?"

After a very long pause, I spoke. "I'm sorry, Shay. I lost him."

It took a moment for Shay to answer. "He's still here. He's just done… for tonight."

I felt a wave of exhaustion sweep over me. Shay rose and strode to the window. He looked not to the west, where the final ribbon of sunset had faded over the horizon, but to the east, to the undulating reeds and black swamps.

I stood for a moment and watched him. His shoulders seemed a bit more rounded, his head cocked in puzzlement. I joined him at the window and wrapped my arms around him from behind. His hand touched mine as they joined in front of him. "Are you okay?" I asked quietly.

He didn't respond at first, and I wondered if he'd heard me. Then he nodded silently.

"I don't know why," I said, "but I feel so drained." When he didn't answer, I said, "I need to lie down."

"Can you get downstairs on your own?" he asked, squeezing my hands.

"Yes. I just feel very tired and very sleepy." I dropped my arms from around him and took a few steps toward the stairs. When I turned back around, he was still staring toward the sea. "Are you coming?"

After a pause, he said, "You go ahead. I'll be there shortly."

I hesitated for a moment. When he did not turn toward me, I continued toward the staircase. As I descended, I glanced back to find he'd shifted and was now staring outside at a rising full blood moon.

45

I awakened sometime later to the sound of rain driving sideways against the window glass. I felt suspended between sleep and wakefulness, not quite a part of either. I rolled over to face Shay's side of the bed, my eyes still closed, my mind filled with fog. A bright light cut through my closed eyelids, and my first thought was that Shay had awakened and was surfing the web on his phone. I pulled the bedding closer to my face and placed a hand over my eyes, but my actions did nothing to reduce the glare.

I opened my eyes expecting to see Shay propped against the headboard, but he was not there. The pillow was exactly as I'd placed it when I'd gone to bed a few hours earlier.

The thought cut through the fog that if Shay wasn't there, neither was his phone. The light was painful, like tiny razor blades cutting the nerves. I blinked several times before I was able to keep my eyes open.

Outside my window, a series of flashes pierced the night sky. Lightning, I thought, before rolling back onto my other side. I felt myself drifting back to sleep, unable to fight the fatigue that rolled over me like anesthesia.

The light abruptly turned to darkness. In my confusion and grogginess, I felt relief that Shay had stopped playing with the lantern. Maybe now, he would come to bed.

As it started flashing again and my mind struggled against shutting down, I knew it wasn't Shay. It was Jon. And I didn't know where Shay was.

~~~~~

I awoke again to a heavy mist that clung to the windows, transforming the normally blue skies into something sallow and dreary. I rolled over to find that Shay was not beside me, but the pillow and bedding were rumpled, an indentation of his body still visible in the sheet. I turned back around to grab my phone off the nightstand and check the time. The screen was blank, and I groaned, my first thought being that I had forgotten to recharge it and the battery had died. Then I remembered turning it off the night before during the séance, and I rebooted it.

A series of messages came in from my mother, consisting of texts, missed calls, and automated transcripts of phone messages. The last ones came in the middle of the night, begging me to call her back.

I sat up and threw my legs over the side of the bed. It wasn't like Mom to hound me like this. Something must have happened. I would have to phone her, but I needed coffee in me first so I could comprehend and process our conversation. My head felt as foggy as the mists outside my window.

I made my way downstairs and started the coffee machine. As it began to hum, I glanced outside. Shay was standing just outside the window beside the chair I always sat in. I walked outside, hugging myself against the impenetrable humidity that threatened to drench my hair and clothing.

"What are you doing?" I asked.

"Morning," he answered.

"Morning. What are you doing?"

He kissed me lightly and then pointed to the window. "Just inside that window is the chair, presumably where Harry died trying to get into the cellar."

"Thanks for reminding me. It used to be my favorite spot."

He pointed to an area of the lighthouse about ten feet away. "And that's the location of the pantry where you— well, I don't rightly know what happened to you there."

"Neither do I." I shivered with the chill in the air.

"I believe Harry was led to that area, and you were led to that one." He seemed oblivious of the air's harshness as he walked between the two points. On his return, he stopped in the middle. "And this is the center point."

I waited for him to continue, but he stood there grinning at me like he was waiting for me to catch the joke. Finally, I said, "Okay, I give."

"I know you do, darling."

"Stop it!" I made a move to bat him, but he ducked. "I'm getting soaked out here, and so are you. I'm going back inside."

As I started toward the door, he wrapped his arm around my waist, halting my progress. Pulling my back against his chest, he pointed downward. "That's the spot, sweetheart."

I peered at the ground. "The spot?"

"That's where we're going to dig."

"You're what?"

"Not inside. That was Harry's mistake. It took too long and was too much effort to dig through the foundation, especially the concrete. No. We're going to dig outside."

"The cellar isn't outside!"

"Do you know that for sure?" He turned me around to face him. "Do you know for certain that Harry built the new lighthouse directly atop the old? Or do you think, perhaps, the original was just a bit further in this direction?"

"Why would it be?"

"It's the center. If I bought a mound of dirt like this and was to build a home atop it, wouldn't I place it in the center?"

I hesitated. "Not to rain on your parade, but not necessarily."

He made a loud groaning sound and released me. "You're as bad as the weather."

"Besides," I said, "we don't even have a shovel."

"Ha!" He placed his hands on his hips. "Another folly. Too slow and too much work."

"So, what do you propose? We order a few hundred moles?"

"Ha, ha. Very funny. A backhoe."

"A what?"

"A backhoe. One of those commercial excavators that moves a ton of dirt without elbow grease."

"I know what it is, but—"

"Then, why did you ask me?"

"You can't be serious."

"I can't, can't I?"

"Where would you even get one? We're out in the middle of nowhere."

Shay held up a finger. "Ah. The Dikshita General Store has had everything else."

"You're kidding me."

"I kid you not."

"You're going to the descendant of Cuddy Dikshita to ask for a backhoe?"

"Argo and Beckett do not know what we know."

"Why will you say you want it?"

"A garden, if they ask. But they won't ask."

I made a noise that came out like an awkward raspberry.

"You don't have to come with me."

"You'll just tow it behind the car when you get it?"

He shrugged. "I'll figure it out." He made a move toward the car.

"Okay, wait." As Shay stopped and half-turned toward me, I continued, "Exactly what do you expect to find there?"

He shrugged. "To be quite honest about it, I haven't the foggiest. I just have this strong, very strong, urge to get to that cellar."

"Like Harry did?" I placed a hand on my hip.

"It isn't like that."

"It isn't, is it? Aren't you becoming obsessed with finding it just as Harry was?"

"No. It is not an obsession." He turned back toward the car.

I audibly groaned. There were a thousand reasons why this was a bad idea. I didn't own this property, and I could be held liable for any damage I caused to it. A mishap this close to the lighthouse could bring the whole structure down or wreck the foundation's integrity. I couldn't afford negative publicity when my next book was scheduled for release this year. "You're not going anywhere without me," I said. "Give me ten minutes to change clothes and get my coffee." As I opened the lighthouse door, I heard my phone ringing from the upstairs room and sighed. A wave of guilt swept over me. I'd have to call my mother on the drive.

46

I'd heard weather forecasters warn of zero visibility, but I always thought it was possible to see something. It might be the stripes in the roadway, the taillights of the vehicle ahead of you, or the windshield wipers. But as Shay inched our way from the lighthouse, I could see nothing through our windows except something resembling gray cotton candy.

"Are you sure that you're okay?" I asked, my hoarse voice betraying my anxiety.

He didn't answer promptly as his eyes remained riveted on the windshield and presumably what was beyond it. "We're fine."

I wasn't convinced. I jumped when my phone vibrated in my pocket and then rang with my mother's personalized tune, a few chords from Madonna's Vogue. "You gonna be okay if I'm talking?" I asked Shay nervously.

He nodded, and I answered the phone.

"Where the hell are you?" My mother's tone brought back all the times as a teenager when I thought I was fine until Mom told me I wasn't.

"The lighthouse. What's up?"

"I've been calling, texting, emailing—why haven't you responded?"

"My phone battery died," I lied.

"And your laptop wasn't working? Your tablet? You have redundancies for these situations."

I stole a sideways glance at Shay. His eyes were riveted on the drive. "I wasn't aware I was in a 'situation,' Mom. Anyway, what's going on? You sound..." I struggled for the right word. Moms can be tricky. "...stressed."

"I'm heading to your place. I'll be out the door in minutes."

"Why? I told you I'm fine. My battery's charged now." When she didn't respond, I continued, "Anyway, why were you trying to reach me? Has something happened?" My stomach began to feel woozy. The last time my mother had phoned like this, my dad was dying. My mind surged through the list of known relatives.

"I have a feeling," she stated flatly.

"That's why you were calling and texting? Because you 'have a feeling'?"

"A mother experiences these things."

"What kind of feeling?" I asked. The car began to tilt in my direction, and I grappled for the grab bar as we started to roll off the drive into the parallel ditch. I stifled a cry as Shay expertly steered it back onto the road.

"What's going on?" Mom asked.

I ignored her question. "Is anybody with you?"

"What? No."

"Maybe we should be driving to you. You don't sound so good. Do you know where you are?"

"Oh, for crying out loud," she said. I heard car keys jingling in the background and envisioned her locking her door as she exited her house. "I'm at my home in Midland Cove," she confirmed. "You want the address?"

"Who's the president?"

"Fuckwad."

She was herself, alright. "Mom, why are you coming here? We're kind of in the middle of something. Can't you break the news to me over the phone?"

"I just have a bad feeling. Are you alone?"

"Shay is with me. And we're fine. We're just heading to the general store."

"Turn around. Go back home and wait for me."

I looked at Shay. He slowed the car, though we had been going at a snail's pace, and our eyes met. Then he silently turned his attention back to the road.

"We're just picking something up," I said. Distress was taking over me. It came in the form of a lump in my stomach that roiled and tumbled like clothes in a dryer. As it grew into a state of alarm, I added, "We're going straight back to the lighthouse. Don't worry, Mom. We're fine." As I said the final words, I wondered whether I was attempting to convince her or myself. Then I realized I was kidding myself. We weren't fine.

"You're not fine," Mom said as if reading my mind. "This is mother's intuition."

"Okay, suit yourself. Just be careful. There's really heavy fog here. Maybe it will burn off before you get here." There was no response. "Mom?" I glanced at my phone. Either she'd hung up or we'd been disconnected.

"We're here," Shay said. I could hear the relief in his voice.

I returned the phone to my pocket. There was a strange mist here, but we could see the store and the parking lot, which was a huge improvement. Shay parked the car, and we both got out. I hadn't realized how tense we were until I tried to stretch my legs. I must have been bunched up like a coiled spring.

"Aren't you going to call her back?" Shay asked, motioning toward my pocket.

I shook my head. "She'll be here in a couple of hours."

"Are you sure she's alright?"

I hesitated. "I think she would have told me if she wasn't. You heard her. Something about a mother's intuition."

"I believe in those things, you know."

"Of course you do." I waved toward the empty lot. "Argo isn't here."

When I turned back around, Shay was already halfway to the door. He held it open for me, and we both strode in. I felt a bit like a cowhand who'd ridden his horse hard and was now walking into an unfamiliar saloon.

I was relieved to see Beckett behind the counter. He must have been engrossed in paperwork because he didn't see us in time to disappear.

"Good to see you again, Beckett," Shay said as we approached the counter. His voice sounded surprisingly light and friendly.

Beckett looked from Shay to me and back again. His head barely nodded. Though his eyes were wide and unblinking, it was impossible to read him. I realized with a start that I'd recently read an article about that stare and how common it was among a generation that grew up texting one another instead of talking. Maybe that was why he always hid from me. I wondered who he texted. I couldn't imagine a school in these parts, and he always seemed to be at the store.

Shay placed his palms on the counter, and as my mind returned to a bad western, I imagined him ordering two whiskeys. Instead, he said casually, "I need a backhoe. You know everybody, Beckett. Where can I find one?"

He shook his head and took a step backward.

"Farm equipment," I said. I stepped forward to keep him from placing distance between us and tried to make my voice soothing. "Or construction equipment. We just want to do a little digging."

"Digging." Beckett said the word as if he were trying to make sense of it. He shook his head again. As he took another step backward, I knew his next move was to flee to the back office.

"Beckett, please don't run away," I pleaded. "You liked Harry, didn't you?"

"Harry." His eyes lit with recognition, but his expression was one of puzzlement.

"Harry tried to find the cellar, didn't he?" I could feel Shay's eyes on me. I knew I was laying all our cards on the table, but I gambled that Beckett would never repeat anything. There had been nothing to indicate a close relationship with his father, and I assumed he hid from everybody else. For a fleeting moment, I pictured him texting a class filled with students and everybody within fifty miles converging on our little lighthouse to watch us dig for a cellar that might not exist. I shook my head in an effort to expel the image.

"Harry," Beckett repeated.

"Harry was trying to find the cellar. You know that, don't you?" I locked my eyes with his. I had forgotten how doe-like his eyes were. They were large and gentle. Another image popped into my mind of Beckett standing on a trunk talking to two crypts as though their spirits could hear him. Just as quickly, I realized they probably could.

He nodded silently. His eyes did not waver from mine.

"We know where the cellar is," I continued. "But a shovel would take too long. We need something bigger. We have to find what Harry was searching for."

Beckett abruptly left the counter, moving so quickly that it startled Shay and me. He was at the door before we could react. My heart sank. I knew he would be out the door and riding his bicycle into the fog in another heartbeat, and we'd be back at square one.

But he stopped at the door. Holding it open, he gestured for us to follow him.

~~~~~

The grain silos appeared far larger as we walked around them than they had from the nearby road. The fog and mist had lifted to a hover at least thirty feet from the ground, obscuring the full height of the hulking structures. Once silver in color, they were mottled with corrosion, and rusted stains crawled down the sides.

We made our way around the one I'd always seen from the road. I was surprised to discover there were more behind it, and as we strode deeper onto the property with Beckett ahead of us, beckoning us forward, an uneasy feeling crept over me. I began to feel like we were walking into a trap and wondered if the mild-mannered young man could be a secret serial killer. Shay was just ahead of me, glancing back periodically to ensure I kept up, but he was clearly focused on staying with Beckett.

My mother's words echoed in my mind, and I couldn't recall another instance in which she warned me of impending doom. As I kept my eyes on Shay's broad back, I realized that a man could never understand the trepidation a woman could feel. It was born from a lifetime of believing we could easily be overcome and physically subdued.

Just when I was ready to turn and run or phone for help, we came to the outskirts of an overgrown field. Perhaps at one time, it might have grown tobacco, cotton, or corn, but it was now a hodgepodge of tall weeds, crippled saplings, and debris. About a hundred feet in were several pieces of farm equipment nearly obscured by nature's onslaught.

The three of us stopped at the edge of the field while Beckett pointed. It took us a moment to peer past the broken-down tractors, rusted balers, and harvesters to a boom and bucket.

"Do you own these?" Shay asked. When Beckett did not reply, he rephrased his question. "Are these yours?"

"They don't mind," Beckett said. He was smiling broadly. I realized it was the first time I'd seen any semblance of pleasure in his expression.

"Stay here," Shay said to me. "There might be snakes."

"You think?" I quipped.

He didn't respond but took off through the knee-high underbrush, as I waited at the edge of the field, shifting anxiously from one foot to the other. Several vultures appeared against the turmoil of the gray skies, plunging through the overhanging mist for a better view of the ground below. I heard a piercing sound in the distance that I did not recognize; it was not a bird, but an animal, and no animal I'd ever heard before. Before Shay reached the Bobcat, I was striding through the weeds in an attempt to remain in the narrow path their bodies had cut.

By the time I'd reached them, my heart had plunged. It was doubtful any of this equipment had been moved in years. Shay pulled himself into the tiny cab and looked for a key, but I could tell from his fallen expression that he was as disappointed as I was.

As Shay climbed back down to the ground, Beckett said, "Lithium batteries. They last."

"They might last," Shay said diplomatically, "but I can't use it without a key."

Beckett's smile grew wider, and his eyes gleamed. "Here. Here." He dashed back along the underbrush toward silos. Shay and I exchanged a doubtful glance before following him.

"We've come this far," Shay said. "But I'm beginning to form Plan B."

"I'm glad you are," I said.

When we caught up with Beckett, he was standing behind a shack that appeared about the size of an outhouse. In fact, had I been able to spot it from the road, that is exactly what I would have thought it was. I had a fleeting image of Shay venturing inside, Beckett locking him in from the outside, and then kidnapping me. The thought was quickly replaced with the realization that a strong wind or a swift kick could probably topple the whole thing.

Shay's thoughts must have been along the same lines, as he held his hand up for me to wait where I was. While he went inside, I glanced down at my jeans to find them covered in burrs and sticky weeds. Brushing my pants with my bare hands did nothing to expel them, and I realized how likely it had been that we'd walked through poisonous plants. I brushed my hands off on my shirt, which had been too high for the weeds to catch, hoping my palms didn't harbor spores and hitchhikers. The thought led me to ticks and fleas, and I was suddenly ready to get the heck out of there.

Shay emerged from the shed grinning with his hand held high. As he drew closer, I caught a glimpse of a key ring dangling from his hand. As I did, my eyes landed on a security camera affixed to the eaves of the shed.

"How much do I owe—?" Shay began, but Beckett was already halfway around a silo in full flight mode, presumably heading back to the general store.

"What's the plan?" I asked.

"Get this thing started," Shay said. "Then you'll follow me back to the lighthouse. That way, if I break down along the way, you'll be there to help out."

He made his way back to the boom and bucket, and almost immediately, I heard a whir. I backed away from the field as he lurched and bobbed the equipment over uneven soil. I had a sudden impulse to shout, "Hold my beer and watch this!" but I refrained, which took tremendous willpower. As I hurried back to the parking lot to get the car, I wondered if I had ever done something this ill-advised before. I quickly determined that I had not.

47

If I thought the going was slow on the way to Dikshita, following Shay on the Bobcat back to the lighthouse was excruciating. As I watched him bob up and down in the cab as he lurched along the dirt and gravel road, I came to the conclusion that my mother could reach this road before we would get much further. I glanced into the rearview mirror, half expecting her sedan to pull up behind us. I imagined the sight from above, a traffic jam on a one-lane dirt road. I stifled a laugh at Shay's head bobbing. This had to be the most insane thing I'd ever done.

The fog had appeared as if it might dissipate when we were in Dikshita, but as we left the crossroads behind us, it returned with a vengeance. Though I could still observe Shay's head like a piston in the bright yellow equipment, the heavy, humid air formed a cloud around us, often feeling as though it was swirling. As trepidation rose inside me, I told myself it was only the wind that made the fog appear to be moving. I tried not to counter with the logic that the treetops remained as still as death before realizing that death might not be so still.

As we drew closer to the lighthouse, I was grateful for the lights left on within, though I didn't remember having used them that morning. They cast a golden glow that extended beyond the structure, pooling on the ground beneath it. I nervously glanced at my watch. It was barely past midmorning, but it looked like evening. I tried to scan the skies to spot an incoming storm, but the lowering fog blocked my line of sight.

Shay pulled alongside the lighthouse but didn't shut down the engine. As I got out of my car, the air felt damp. It clung to my clothing and hair as resolutely as if I were standing in the rain.

Then the air stood still.

The change was so abrupt that I found my feet frozen to the ground, much as they had during past nightmares. My eyes seemed to be the only part of me capable of movement, and as I peered upward, the fog appeared to be frozen as well; the water droplets comprising the grayish matter looked to be suspended. The birds, cicadas, crickets, and frogs that I'd become so accustomed to hearing were silent, their morning songs replaced by a vast nothingness that wrapped itself around me like a tightening vise.

I hadn't realized how many sounds surrounded me on a typical day until they all disappeared at once. The reeds stood still as though in a watercolor painting. The skies remained blocked as if we were no longer of its world.

Then Shay lowered the bucket to the ground and removed the first thin slice of earth before rotating the boom to place it in the furthest spot from the house. It was so wafer-thin that I almost scoffed before I realized that, being a noted historian, Shay would also have some knowledge of archeology. He wouldn't dare remove a bucketful at once. As he leaned forward to view the ground below, I heard the first sounds since we'd arrived: the steady scrape of metal against earth. It would be a long day.

~~~~~

Beckett arrived within the hour. He rode his bicycle, carefully propping it against the gate I'd left open. By that time, I had managed to gather my wits about me and was sitting on the stoop with a jacket around me, despite the warmth of summer. I had a chill that I could not shake, and I wrapped my arms around myself.

"Beckett," Shay called from the cab as casually as if he'd done this type of thing on a regular basis. "Let me know if you see anything."

Beckett nodded wordlessly and took up a position beside the long, narrow hole that had begun to take on the appearance of a giant's grave. He appeared engrossed in the activity, his body occasionally trembling with excitement. I found myself peering down the drive for his classmates before realizing how ridiculous that was. Still, this undertaking was probably the most excitement he'd seen in these parts in quite a while, if ever.

The lantern flashed on so abruptly that we all looked upward at once, our eyes wide and unblinking. The solid glow illuminated the ground below like a floodlight expertly trained on a specific area. It cut through the gray fog but did not eliminate it so that it felt like we were all in a parallel dimension. As I shielded my eyes from the glare, I thought I made out the outline of a man standing in the window, staring down upon us. As I squinted to see more clearly, the image disappeared. I was imagining things.

"Jonathan," Beckett exclaimed with a broad smile.

I looked toward Shay. His eyes met mine, but he must not have seen the apparition in the window. He wiped his forehead with his forearm and lowered the bucket again. Pencil-thin scrapes followed one after another, a growing mound forming in the murky gloom beyond the lighthouse.

The hours crept by. I brought glasses of water to Shay throughout the day, but he did not want to break for lunch. His shirt was drenched from the humidity and perspiration; a hand towel I brought him did nothing to keep the sweat from his forehead. He looked miserable, but there was a fire in his eyes that concerned me. I imagined the same obsession in Harry's eyes as he tried to tear up the flooring and concrete foundation.

When I brought yet another glass of water to Shay, I hoisted myself up to stand alongside the cab while he idled. "Why don't you let me take over for a bit?" I asked as he slugged down the water.

"You don't know how to run the machinery," he said curtly.

"You're doing it. How hard can it be?"

He gave me a withering look.

"Please, sweetheart," I pleaded. "You need a break."

Before he could respond, we heard the sound of tires crunching on the road, before we saw the car emerge. I thought it was Mom and expected to see her polished sedan slice through the haze, and I tried to lean around the cab to flag her down lest she whip precipitously close to the widening and deepening hole. But it was not my mother.

As the car materialized, I caught sight of flashing blue lights atop a black and white sedan, causing us both to attempt to shield our eyes from the onslaught as it neared us. I sensed Beckett moving near me, but my eyes were riveted on the man who jumped from the passenger side before the vehicle had come to a complete stop just beyond the trench.

"I've called your daddy!" The man bellowed, pointing his finger. Confused, I thought he was pointing at me until I turned to see Beckett hiding on the far side of the Bobcat. Only his head slid outward as it had the first time that I'd seen him at the general store.

"Now, Travis." A woman slipped out of the driver's side, leaving the car running and the headlights illuminating the bucket.

Between the lighthouse lantern, the flashing lights, and the headlights, I began to feel as though I was starring in a disco stage show, and I didn't feel like dancing.

"Let's just calm down," she continued. "Take a breath." She was stocky with broad shoulders, her figure bolstered by a thick bulletproof vest whose square edges protruded slightly beneath the brown uniform. A shock of white hair was visible across her forehead before disappearing under a crisp hat.

"I've called your daddy!" Travis thundered again. "He's on his way! He's on his way!"

I felt sorry for Beckett as he ducked behind the equipment. He acted as though he could disappear if he willed strongly enough.

"Sir," the deputy said, motioning at Shay. "Sir, I'm going to have to ask you to shut off that equipment. Ma'am," she added, pointing to me, "come down off that equipment."

Shay motioned toward his ear as if he was straining to hear her. I don't know why I didn't immediately comply with her orders; I felt frozen in place like an appendage of both Shay and the Bobcat.

"Sir," she said more loudly as she neared him, "turn off the—"

She was interrupted by the sound of tires whirling through the gravel. Argo's truck burst off the road and nearly became airborne as it bounced through the gate and onto the mound. Directly behind him was my mother's sedan, her once-shining car now covered in road dust.

Shay shut off the Bobcat, plunging us into silence.

The deputy turned her attention to Argo, who leaped from the truck cab, his face crimson with anger. I feared for Beckett, but as I followed Argo's line of sight, his eyes were trained on Shay, who had begun to stand but was now motionless as he stared back.

Argo began shouting, and in my bewilderment, I didn't understand his rage or his words. As he marched closer to us, his words became clearer. "You have no right!

You have no right!" Travis was also shouting, his words drowned out by Argo's.

My feet felt rooted to the cab step, blocking Shay's exit. To our left was Travis, whose attention had turned from Shay to Argo. The deputy also pivoted from us to Argo, her elbow bending as her hand extracted the pistol on her belt; her body lowered, and both arms reached out to clasp the weapon between them. Her shouts added to the cacophony, the three voices overlapping one another so that all their words were lost in the charged air.

As I followed her sightline, I watched as my mother, all five feet of her, burst from her car, both arms raised in the air like a miniature volleyball player. Between them was Argo. My voice burst from my lips, shouting "No!" as Mom lunged toward Argo at the exact moment that he raised a rifle and aimed it at Shay and me.

The lantern was abruptly extinguished, plunging us into a surreal, heavy fog that felt as if it was deliberately seeking to separate us. The headlights and flashing blue lights bounced back through the haze in an unnatural and dreamlike swirl.

I grabbed Shay's upper arm, pulling him out and down with me as a series of shots seemed to come from every direction at once. The glass enclosing the cab was shattered, the shards bursting around us. As I tumbled onto the muddy ground, the sound of gunfire still erupting around us, Shay threw his body atop mine. He jerked in tandem with the gunshots. I caught a glimpse of Beckett's face as he watched us, his head popping up instinctively as though he planned to rush to our aid, his mouth open. It was as though he was shouting "No!" as I had only a split second ago, but I could no longer hear the voices as the bombardment continued.

48

There was a moment of total silence. My ears reverberated with a whooshing sound as if a massive white noise sought to drown out the rest of the din. In an instant, the heavy fog that had dogged us all morning evaporated like a massive ghost disappearing back into the ether.

"I can't breathe," I managed to croak as I sought to move Shay off me. "Are you okay?"

Shay rolled off me slowly. "Are *you* okay?" His eyes were wide and tortured as he stared at me.

I was shaking violently as I crawled onto my knees. My clothing was covered in blood, and my ankle had twisted in the fall. "I don't know," I answered. Both of us began to pat me down, searching for the source of the blood, before I saw a growing stain emerging on Shay's shoulder. "You're shot!" I shouted, but my words were drowned out by everyone bellowing at once.

I was consumed by a rage unlike anything I had ever experienced before. My trembling ceased in an instant, and a calm, murderous madness possessed me. As I lifted myself off the ground, each limb seemed to stretch out as if to lengthen my body. My mind focused on taking the few steps between us and Argo in great, purposeful strides, wrenching the rifle from his hands with superhuman strength, deftly turning it around, and shooting him dead on the spot. I had a vague sense that Shay was also coming to his feet, albeit more slowly, pain now emanating from both his shoulder and his thigh. He was shouting at me as he motioned for me to get back behind the bulky equipment.

As I rounded the back of the Bobcat, my eyes were riveted on Argo. He was on the ground, grappling the rifle with unsteady hands, while a madwoman in a powder blue Giorgio Armani seemed to have six arms flailing all at once above him. He screamed in a high-pitched voice more suited to a teenage girl as he lost his grip on the rifle. As I closed in on them, he attempted to double over but was thwarted by sharp, multiple jabs from two objects that looked suspiciously like red-soled stilettos.

The deputy's voice rose above the fray, ordering Argo to release the rifle even though it now lay on the ground beside them. I stopped in my tracks, the rage vanishing as quickly as it had arisen, the emotion replaced with awe that my mother was beating the muck out of a man with a rifle.

I turned to look behind me as Shay joined me with a profound limp. I wrapped an arm around him, but I don't know if I was managing to steady him or if it was the other way around.

When I looked back in Argo's direction, I discovered the deputy tossing the weapon away from Argo, who was doubled over and grabbing his crotch. At the deputy's direction, my mother stepped off Argo and reached for her shoes.

"Ma'am, I'm afraid you're going to have to leave those right where they are," the deputy said, peering at her.

"Why?" Mom's eyes met mine across the mound as Argo groaned.

"They've been," the deputy started to answer as she fought back laughter, "used in the commission of a crime."

"You can't be serious!" Mom shouted.

"They're weapons," the deputy insisted.

"Do you intend to charge me?"

"Not right now, ma'am." While she wrestled Argo onto his stomach and handcuffed him behind his back, she shouted to Shay, "Sir! Sir, are you alright?"

I hung onto Shay as he started to falter. With Argo secured and the rifle out of his reach, the deputy joined me as he collapsed onto the ground.

The deputy pushed a button on her shoulder mike and requested an ambulance at Harry's lighthouse. Through the trance-like state my mind grappled with, I realized she didn't need to give an address.

"How long?" I asked as I knelt over Shay. His face was ashen and his eyes were closed.

"About twenty minutes for the ambulance. But a volunteer paramedic lives about five minutes away."

Shay opened his eyes and reached for my hand. "Don't worry about me, love. I'm just a bit woozy, is all." He said something else, but his voice faded, and I leaned forward in a futile attempt to catch the words.

Travis had backed away from the unfolding scene, his expression a jumble of confusion and fear, his palms open and outstretched as though to say that he didn't want any part of this. My mother moved forward to join us at Shay's side, her outfit covered in grass and mud.

As the deputy left to pop open her trunk for her first aid kit, Beckett's voice rang out.

All eyes seemed to move at once. Beckett stood at the far edge of the hole. His clothing was muddied, and a toothy smile spread across his face as he raised his arm in the air. "Look!" he shouted. He raised a grimy bone around eighteen inches long above his head. "It's Jonathan!"

49

One month later

Though I stood on the mound only a few yards from the lighthouse, it felt a world away. It was no longer my home and hadn't been since the day we discovered the bones. The moment that Beckett held up the femur, it became a crime scene.

I discovered how quickly word could travel in a small community and how many would step forward to assist. Shay and I were given only an hour to evacuate under the watchful eye of sheriff's deputies. At the time, we didn't know if we would be allowed to return within a day or two, or if it might be slightly longer. However, within two days, the State Police, who had arrived to process the crime scene, called in an unexpected partner: the North Carolina Office of State Archaeology. With their ground sonar technology, they discovered there wasn't just one body buried in the mound, but possibly as many as two dozen.

The mound, as it turned out, was a Native American burial mound. It was larger than most in eastern North Carolina; while the average rose only three feet tall and up to forty feet in diameter, the Corbyn Mound, as the archaeologists were calling it, was more than twice that height and almost sixty feet in circumference. It would take months, if not longer, for the experts to piece together what lay beneath the surface.

Unlike Shay and the boom and bucket, these archaeologists approached the mound's secrets in a completely different manner. They would not physically dig up the remains beyond the body we exposed. Rather, they sought to preserve and protect the others where they lay. Their sonar technology would be used by experts to reconstruct the burials of the men, women, and children contained within, so they could provide historians and the public with the knowledge everyone seemed suddenly to crave.

The bones we exposed were likely those of Jonathan Corbyn. They'd been able to determine that he'd been shot through the head, the bullet penetrating one side of the skull and exiting on the other side. I hoped his death was instantaneous and that he didn't suffer. Remnants of his clothing were still attached to the bones, including an ivory broadcloth shirt with ballooning sleeves, woolen gray breeches that might have reached just past his knees, and sturdy leather boots. The position of the body led the researchers to determine that he had likely been tossed into the cellar after he was murdered, as he was face-down at an angle, his legs spread further apart and further up what might have once been a ladder. There were no defensive wounds.

His hair had apparently been pulled back in a ponytail, as they discovered a thin ribbon still attached to an intact strand. Unlike the flesh, which likely began to decompose as soon as he was left in the cellar, hair lasted much longer. His hair had turned a deep shade of red.

The archaeologists sent hair samples to Raleigh for DNA analysis. Although Jon had never married and had no known descendants, his sister would have carried the same markers. Ironically, the individual who agreed to be tested was none other than Beckett Dikshita. The results were not due back for some time, but one wouldn't know it by watching Beckett, who was elated that he could be related to the ghost he'd befriended as a small child on his visits with Harry.

His father, however, had suffered a different fate. Argo was sitting in a jail cell awaiting trial on a multitude of charges stemming from that fateful day. He admitted to investigators that he had known all along of Cuddy's allegiance to the British and that he had murdered both Alasdair and Jonathan. He'd spent his life, as his ancestors before him, protecting the Dikshita name and obliterating any Corbyn and Glenn legacy. Shay and I might have taken the magnanimous approach and not pressed charges against Argo, but neither of us was accustomed to someone shooting at us. We were still shaken by the realization of what might have happened, particularly with Shay's wounds.

The attempt to erase history was why we were here today, standing a respectable distance from ropes that cordoned off parts of the mound in neat grids. Two ropes were strung from the gate to the front door, creating a path. A podium had been set up a few feet from the door, and I watched now as Billie and community leaders gathered to make statements.

Harry's Lighthouse would officially become known as the Corbyn Lighthouse Museum, and the swamps surrounding it as the Corbyn Channel. I would never move back into it, and neither would anyone else, as today would mark it as a monument to a man who gave his life for the birth of a new nation. As they spoke, I dabbed at my eyes. Jon's life weighed heavily upon me, from his birth in the Scottish Highlands, his passionate belief in the Jacobite cause, his participation in the Battle of Culloden, his journey to America, the land grant and subsequent pledge of loyalty to a crown he'd fought against in his native Scotland, to the erection of the original lighthouse and his role in thwarting the British from reinforcing loyalist troops. It would all be there in the Corbyn Lighthouse

Museum, no doubt further enhanced as more information was provided.

The portrait had been moved from the lantern room to the ground floor, where visitors would see it as soon as they entered. Jon apparently approved, because it had not been returned upstairs. However, the centerpiece of the museum was Jon's journal. Billie had commissioned a Wilmington printer to reproduce every page on poster boards, which were covered in plexiglass and mounted on the lighthouse walls. The ground floor began with his first entries, and by the time that visitors reached the lantern room, they would be able to look out across the swamps while they read of Jon's and Alasdair's frantic attempts to prevent the British from reinforcing the Scottish loyalists. The North Carolina government was officially acknowledging Jon's and his brother-in-law's sacrifices, which meant they would no longer be known as Scots loyal to King George but patriots.

With Argo in jail, the Dikshita General Store was under Beckett's management. To nearly everyone's surprise, he had risen quite admirably to the occasion. Everyone's surprise, that is, except mine. I'd revised my opinion of him since that first awkward meeting, and I knew now that the little crossroads was in good and honest hands.

I squeezed Shay's hand as we stood on the mound among members of the community, press, and even my mother and a few of her friends.

As the voices rumbled on, my mind continued to wander to the events that had transpired after we discovered Jon's body. After we vacated the lighthouse, we followed my mother back to Midland Cove, but we stopped short of staying with her. We moved into the bed and breakfast instead, where we'd spent the past month and planned to remain through the summer. When Shay was obligated to return to Ireland for the university's latest school year, I would relocate to the Netherlands, where I would begin my next historical book set against the backdrop of World War II. It felt much closer to Shay simply because it was in Europe, though it was a seven-hour flight from Galway. By next summer, I should be permitted to return to Ireland, having fulfilled the requirement of leaving it for twelve months.

My eyes met Billie's across the mound as she finished speaking and sat down beside the podium. In a place of honor, a few feet from where she sat, was a new portrait of Jon on a sturdy easel. It appeared exactly as he had in the original portrait in the lantern room, but with one distinct difference: he now wore the clothing of an American patriot. This would be placed beside the original painting, accompanied by a plaque that described the error in the historical records, an error that the Corbyn Lighthouse Museum would seek to correct.

To Billie's credit, she hadn't wished to press charges against us for defiling the mound, though she could easily have done so. The archaeologists recommended keeping the crude trench unfilled and surrounding it with a fence where visitors could see into the remnants of the cellar and where Jon's body had been found, the ground carefully preserved with plexiglass to keep out the elements.

Travis had also declined to press charges after Beckett insisted that he gave us permission to use the Bobcat, which was corroborated by the video evidence. I suppose Travis could have pressed charges against Beckett, but no one wanted to put him through an arrest and court case, and Shay paid Travis a generous rental fee for the use of the equipment.

When the formal speeches ended, we were all invited into the lighthouse. The press was eager to file in with their cameras and notepads, but I hung back. It was public knowledge now that I had rented the lighthouse, and I wanted to avoid interviews. I was not going to betray Jon by speaking of his ghost, our séances, and the mysterious lantern flashing at will. It was enough that they knew I'd found the journal, and a hunch led us to attempt an excavation of the grounds. I had nothing more to add.

"You're not coming?" Mom demanded more than questioned.

I shook my head. "We're heading back."

"It's a long way to drive to sit in a lawn chair for half an hour."

I glanced at Shay. "Yeah, well, we might stop for lunch and tour the countryside."

"No more screaming at the sight of a lynched ghost," Mom admonished.

"What?"

"You heard me." She turned toward the lighthouse. "I'll be back late. I'm serving as a tour guide for my friends."

"Wait," I called out. As she hesitated and half-turned toward me, I joined her. "How did you know I saw—?"

"We all see them in this family. We just don't talk about it." She waggled a finger. "Remember, they're not all—"

"Caspar Milquetoast," we said in unison.

She smiled, called out to her friends, who had already reached the door, and took off after them without even a cursory goodbye.

I hesitated as I stared at the lighthouse. Billie had already gone inside with the others, so after my mother disappeared inside the door, only Shay, Beckett, and I remained.

"Do you need a ride back?" Shay asked Beckett, rousing me from my thoughts.

He shook his head shyly. "I have my bike."

My eyes followed him as he marched to the fence where he'd propped his bicycle. No doubt, he was old enough to obtain his driver's license, and with Argo in jail, he would need to run errands in the family truck. It was difficult to imagine him managing it all, but I knew that somehow, he'd rise to the occasion.

A flash of white caught my eye, but before I could react, Shay gasped and Beckett's head jerked toward the object emerging from the reeds. I thought we were all witnessing a ghost in some sort of shared hallucination, but as the animal came into full view, Beckett tossed his bicycle to the ground and raced for her. "Lola!" he shouted.

We joined them near the open gate as two more dogs emerged behind her. They were nearly as large as she, but they acted like puppies. As we knelt on the ground, they sniffed us and played with one another without fear.

"This is Lola?" Shay asked. "Harry's dog?"

Tears rolled down Beckett's cheeks as he held her. "Yes," he said through his cries. "This is Harry's dog."

"And who are you?" I asked one of the others as I stroked it under its chin. They were all much thinner than any dog I'd known, and their fur was matted and sparse. While Lola was a solid white German Shepherd, these two were predominantly silver, with distinct masks on their faces that began over the eyes and extended along the muzzles. The fur on their legs also tapered from silver to white.

"I don't know," Beckett acknowledged as Lola licked his face.

As the others joined Lola in licking Beckett, Shay pointed at her. "She's still nursing," he said.

"How did she manage to keep them alive in the wild?" I breathed.

Shay spoke a bit louder so Beckett could hear him. "Beckett, she needs care. She needs food and probably medical attention, and so do her pups."

"Yes," he agreed. "I have plenty of food and water at the store. Whatever she wants." He nodded toward the others. "Whatever they want."

"And a vet?" I ventured.

"I'll call Doc Lyon. He makes house calls."

"And he's a vet?"

Beckett nodded. "Mostly livestock."

Shay stared at the two pups. "These might be wolf hybrids," he said.

"They wouldn't be the first in these parts," Beckett said.

"Do you—or they—need a ride?" Shay offered.

Beckett shook his head. "Lola will follow me." With that, he made his way back to his bicycle, whistled, and began to ride down the mound onto the drive. Lola dutifully followed while her pups bounded along behind them. We watched as they disappeared beneath the shadows of the trees.

"Those are the most words I've ever heard from him," I mused.

Shay nodded silently.

"Somehow, I feel better knowing that he won't be all alone." As I finished speaking, I noticed a man with a camera starting to exit the lighthouse. "Let's get out of here," I said as I made my way quickly to the car.

50

Shay pulled the car to the edge of the drive as we stared down the path to the cemetery. It was now much broader, having been widened to accommodate the archeological equipment required for the second site. The mound upon which the cemetery had been built was another Native American burial mound. Like the first, this would remain intact—but without Shay's crude excavation—and would be analyzed with ground-penetrating radar.

We stepped outside and leaned against the car. We gazed at a "No Trespassing" sign on one side of the path that had been erected by the state government.

"Want to—?" Shay started.

"No."

"Me, neither."

"I'm sure whatever we heard is gone now. Don't you agree?"

"Undoubtedly. There's too much going on now with people and equipment. It would drive off any wild animals." Despite his strong words, his tone didn't convince me.

"Would it also scare off any ghosts?" I ventured.

He hesitated. "I think it's more likely that the ghosts would scare off the people."

"Maybe the sounds we heard were Lola and her pups." As soon as the words escaped my lips, I knew they were untrue. It had not been a white dog I'd seen through the woods, but a much larger, darker shadow. The sounds had been otherworldly.

"Sure," Shay answered, still staring into the darkened woods. "That's got to be it."

"You think?"

"No."

"Let's get the heck out of here."

"Best idea you've had all morning."

As I turned to get into the car, my phone rang. It was my editor, who had a habit of phoning at exactly the wrong time. I answered as Shay went around to the driver's side and started the car.

"Got your book," Lindsay said by way of a greeting. "I love it."

"Oh?"

"I particularly like the way you addressed your ancestors having fought for King James in Northern Ireland before turning on England when they came to America."

I chuckled wryly. "I had a little bit of inspiration."

"Well, you should thank your influencer. It added a rich layer to the history."

I glanced over my shoulder at the lighthouse rising above the trees. "I owe him a lot."

"Just wanted you to know that the first round of edits will be coming your way. You know how that goes."

"I do," I answered, picturing weeks of deciphering notes in the margins and squiggles all over the pages.

"By the way," Lindsay continued, "how's your mam?"

"My—" I smiled. "She's doing great. Thanks for asking. How is yours?"

"Still hanging in there."

"Thanks for asking."

"See ya." Before I could respond, the call clicked off.

I held the phone for a long moment before returning it to my pocket as Shay asked, "Everything okay?"

"Just dandy. She loves the book. Editing comes next."

"I know how you enjoy that." He smiled sarcastically.

"Well, I won't receive the changes today," I said as we drove toward Dikshita. "Maybe we can catch that new band at the pub in Midland Cove."

"The Wonkers?"

"Close enough."

We reached the intersection and paused for a long moment. The parking lot was empty except for Argo's truck at one corner and Beckett's bicycle propped next to the door.

"You think the dogs followed him all the way back?" Shay asked.

"Almost certain of it," I answered. "He's got food."

Shay started to turn the wheel in the opposite direction and hesitated.

"What is it?"

He pointed to a sign at the intersection. It read:

Former Village of
Nova Dunglen
Humans: 10
Spirits: Unknown

"Well, I'll be," I breathed. "I know Argo didn't put that there."

"I'd say that's a safe assumption." He turned the wheel, and a moment later, the sign, Nova Dunglen, and the Dikshita General Store were behind us.

I settled into my seat and sighed contentedly. Time to start my next adventure.

Notes from the Author

Although this is a work of fiction, I often draw inspiration from true stories. Here are some of the places and events that influenced this book:

It is common for lighthouses to be built in inland waterways, only to have the channel dry up or be diverted later, rendering the lighthouse inaccessible or useless. One example is the Ocracoke Light Station, located at the southern end of Cape Hatteras National Seashore in North Carolina. It was built in 1794-1798 to guide mariners along the Ocracoke Inlet toward Elizabeth City, New Bern, and Edenton. However, the channel shifted only twenty years later, rendering the lighthouse unusable. The original was struck by lightning, which destroyed both the lighthouse and the keeper's home. A second lighthouse of the same name was built at the southern end of Ocracoke Island in 1824. This is a shorter lighthouse than average because it was considered secondary to taller ones nearby. Both the short stature and the original structure's limited useful existence inspired the lighthouse in this book.

The intersection of Dikshita was inspired by Dundarrach, Hoke County, North Carolina, located on NC Highway 20 between Lumber Bridge and Raeford. According to the US Census Bureau, Dundarrach covers an area of 1.3 square miles. The population numbered around 41 as of 2020. It was officially established in the early 20th century by Scottish immigrant farmers. The agricultural community was often referred to as "God-blessed Macks" and consisted of the McKenzies, McGougans, McMillans, McInnises, and others. The original Dundarach was located in the Scottish Highlands. The name is spelled differently.

The mounds upon which the lighthouse and Harry's cemetery sit were inspired by various mounds in eastern North Carolina. According to the Native Heritage Project, various discovered locations have been identified in the following counties: Cumberland, Duplin, Robeson, Sampson, and Wake. The eastern mounds are approximately three feet tall and range in diameter from 15 to 40 feet. They were used as burial sites. The bodies of the deceased were laid on top of the ground, and soil was used to cover the bodies, eventually resulting in the mound height and circumference. These differ in use and size from mounds identified in western North Carolina.

The terrain surrounding the lighthouse was inspired by the low swamplands prevalent in parts of North Carolina, including along the Neuse River, the Cedar Point Tideland Trail, and the Croatan National Forest.

With regard to the runaway slave Jonathan Corbyn helped to escape, the North Carolina Runaway Slave Notices Project provides an online list of notices posted between 1751 and 1865. According to the African American Registry, it was common for various Native American tribes to accept runaway slaves into their communities, even though tribes could lose their status, land, treaties, and trade to do so. Two known safe havens for runaway slaves were with the Tuscarora and Lumbee tribes of North Carolina.

Midland Cove is a fictitious retirement community located between Lumber Bridge and Raeford on NC Highway 20 in the vicinity of Dundarrach. The area had been agricultural until recent residential construction.

The dates in Jonathan Corbyn's journal regarding Revolutionary War skirmishes and battles are all historically accurate, as is the background information concerning the gathering of Scottish troops at Cross Creek and their subsequent march eastward to engage the patriots. British troops did not bolster the number of loyalists in North Carolina as expected, which historians believe contributed to turning the tide in the patriots' favor.

Jonathan Corbyn and Alasdair Glenn are fictional characters, and their roles in diverting the loyalists from the channel shortcut are also fictionalized. They represent scores of Scottish survivors of the Jacobite ideology and subsequent rebellion, including the Battle of Culloden, who immigrated to America. To settle land and earn a livelihood, they were often required to pledge allegiance to the English monarchy. Some honored those pledges when the Revolutionary War broke out, while others fought alongside the colonists.

The Widow Moore's Creek Bridge is located between Lumberton and Wilmington, North Carolina, near Currie. Today, it is the site of the Moore's Creek National Battlefield. I attempted to remain true to the events surrounding the patriot and loyalist positions, maneuvers, and engagements. The patriots reportedly captured around 850 loyalists during and in the aftermath of the battle, along with 1,500 muskets, 300 rifles, and approximately $15,000 in Spanish gold, worth more than $1.8 million today. According to the National Park Service, there were approximately 1,000 patriots against 1,600 loyalists at Moore's Creek. One patriot, John Grady of Duplin County, perished, while more than 30 loyalists were killed.

The story of the ghost in Maco near present-day Leland, North Carolina, is a local legend.

The ferry depicted in this book is real. Located in Bladen County, it is the only inland ferry in North Carolina. It currently operates around 12 hours a day, or during daylight hours, and does not charge a toll for the five-minute trip across the Cape Fear River.

Some of the place names used in 1776 are as follows: New France refers to present-day Canada, Virginia was originally the Colony and Dominion of Virginia, South Carolina was known as the Carteret County Colony, and North Carolina was referred to as the Albemarle Settlements or the Province of North Carolina.

There are numerous tales of ghosts at the site of the Moore's Creek battle as well as throughout eastern North Carolina. The orbs in certain scenes are based on personal experience; however, I have not participated in a séance as of the time of this writing.

About the Author

My full name is Patricia McClelland Terrell, and I have been writing under the pen name p.m.terrell ever since a publisher presented me with my first fiction book cover. The graphic designer had also entered my name in lower-case letters; my editor hated it, and I loved it. It's been p.m.terrell ever since.

I began writing when I was nine years old, inspired by a schoolteacher and elementary school principal. Scott-Foresman published my first book, a computer instructional for universities, in 1984. Scott-Foresman, Dow-Jones (Richard D. Irwin branch), Palari Publishing, Paralee Press, and Drake Valley Press have published 26 books to date.

Before embarking on a full-time writing career, I founded McClelland Enterprises, Inc. in the Washington, D.C. area in 1984, specializing in computer instruction for employees in the workplace. I opened another business, Continental Software Development Corporation, in 1994, which focused on custom application development, programming, website design and development, and computer crime. I held two Top Secret security clearances with the United States Secret Service and the CIA. My favorite assignment was detecting Medicare fraud and abuse for Health & Human Services, which helped recover millions of dollars.

I was honored to be the first female President of the Chesterfield County/Colonial Heights Crime Solvers. I also served as the Treasurer for the Virginia Crime Stoppers Association. Since moving to North Carolina, I served on the Robeson County Friends of the Library and Robeson County Arts Council.

I launched The Book 'Em Foundation with Waynesboro, Virginia Police Officer Mark Kearney, and assisted in Virginia, New Hampshire, and South Carolina events before establishing the Annual Book 'Em North Carolina Writers Conference and Book Fair, chairing it for several years before turning it over to Robeson Community College in Lumberton, NC.

Other Books

Dani's Decision
A Struggle for Independence
April in the Back of Beyond
The Adventures of Blade and Rye
Checkmate: Clans and Castles
A Thin Slice of Heaven
The Banker's Greed
Ricochet
The China Conspiracy
Kickback

Black Swamp Mystery Series (in order):
Exit 22
Vicki's Key
Secrets of a Dangerous Woman
Dylan's Song
The Pendulum Files
Cloak and Mirrors

Ryan O'Clery Mysteries (in order):
The Tempest Murders
The White Devil of Dublin

Mary Neely Historical (in order):
River Passage
Songbirds are Free

Non-Fiction:
Take the Mystery Out of Promoting Your Book
The Dynamics of Reflex
The Dynamics of WordPerfect
Memento WordPerfect, Progiciel de traitment de texte
Creating the Perfect Database